W9-CMB-808

The Foster Girls

Jo - Deborah
Another mountain girl
and a writer-friend —

May 2009

Lin Stepp

WEST GEORGIA REGIONAL LIBRARY SYSTEM
Neva Lomason Memorial Library

The
Foster Girls

A Novel in The
Smoky Mountain Series

LIN STEPP

Parkway Publishers, Inc.
www.parkwaypublishers.com
Boone, North Carolina

Parkway Publishers, Inc.

P.O. Box 3678
Boone, North Carolina
www.parkwaypublishers.com

Copyright © 2009 by Lin Stepp
All rights reserved.

AUTHORS NOTE:

This is a work of fiction. Although there are numerous elements of historical and geographic accuracy in this and other novels in the Smoky Mountain series, specific environs, place names, and incidents are entirely the product of the author's imagination. In addition, all characters are fictitious and any resemblance to actual persons, living or dead, is entirely coincidental.

Book design by Ann Thompson Nemcosky

Library of Congress Cataloging-in-Publication Data

Stepp, Lin.
    Foster girls : a Smoky Mountain novel / by Lin Stepp.
        p. cm.
    Summary: "A gentle, inspirational, regional romance set in the Smoky Mountains of East Tennessee. Vivian Delaney arrives in the quiet Wear's Valley, on the backside of the Smoky Mountains, carrying a heavy load of hidden problems - and eager to find a quiet place to escape the recent troubles of her past"--Provided by publisher.
    ISBN 978-1-933251-66-0
    1. Great Smoky Mountains Region (N.C. and Tenn.)--Fiction. 2. Tennessee--Fiction. I. Title.
    PS3619.T47695F67 2009
    813'.6--dc22

                                    2009006745

July 2009

Cover Art

The beautiful work of art, featured on the front cover of this book, was painted by the well-known regional artist Jim Gray. It is entitled *I Look To The Hills*.

Jim Gray is a nationally recognized artist who has been painting Smoky Mountain scenes and southern landscapes for over thirty years. In 1966, Gray and his family moved to East Tennessee so that Jim could explore and paint the beauty of the countryside surrounding the Smoky Mountains. Today, Jim Gray has three galleries in East Tennessee and one in Alabama. He has sold over 2000 paintings and 125,000 prints to collectors in the United States and abroad. Jim is listed in *Who's Who in American Art* and has been featured in many publications, including *National Geographic* and *Southern Living*.

Prints of *I Look To The Hills*, or other fine works of art, can be purchased in Jim Gray galleries or ordered through Jim Gray's website at: http://www.jimgraygallery.com

Jim Gray's business address is:

GREENBRIAR INCORPORATED
P. O. Box 735, Gatlinburg, TN 37738
Business Phone: (865) 573-0579

Acknowledgments

*W*arm thanks and gratitude go to those who helped to make this book a reality ...

... To Patsy Daniel, who thought I was a great writer with promise and introduced me to another fine area writer, Christy Tillery French;

... To Christy French, who became my writer friend, loved the concept of my stories, and suggested I submit my book series to a regional publisher in North Carolina;

... To Parkway Publishers in Boone, North Carolina, who did like my books and decided to publish them;

... To the wonderful staff at Parkway who have now become my publishing family: Vice President of Marketing, Wendy Dingwall; Founder and President, Rao Aluri; manuscript editor and friend, Sandy Horton; graphic artist and text designer, Ann Thompson Nemcosky, and fellow author and mentor in North Carolina, Rose Senehi;

... And to the Lord, who, undoubtedly, orchestrated it all.

Dedication

This book is dedicated to my husband, J.L. Stepp – my best friend – and my greatest support in pursuing all my gifts and dreams.

Map for *The Foster Girls*

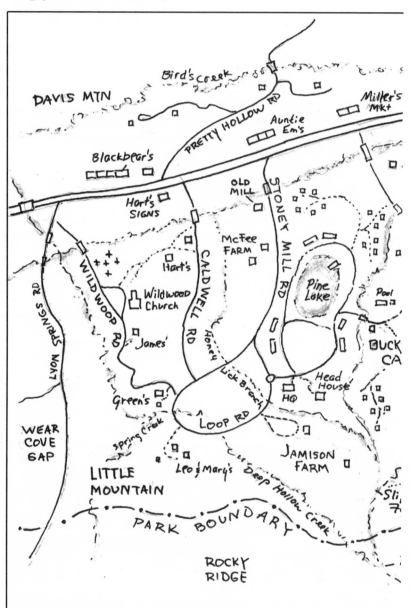

DAVIS MTN

Bird's creek

Miller's Mkt

PRETTY HOLLOW RD

Auntie Em's

Blackbear's

OLD MILL

STONEY MILL RD

Hart's SIGNS

McFee FARM

Pine Lake

Pool

Hart's

Wildwood Church

CALDWELL RD

Honey Lick Branch

BUCK CA

WILDWOOD RD

James'

Head House

HQ

LYON SPRINGS RD

Green's

Spring Creek

LOOP RD

JAMISON FARM

WEAR COVE GAP

LITTLE MOUNTAIN

Leo & Mary's

Deep Hollow Creek

Sli 7

PARK BOUNDARY

ROCKY RIDGE

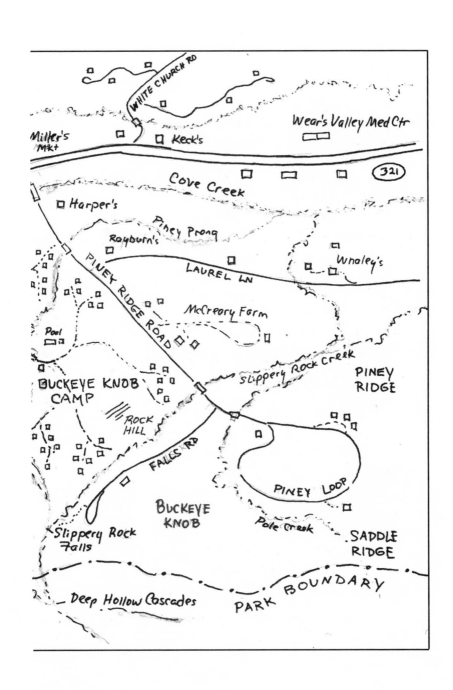

Chapter 1

Vivian checked the highway sign again to make sure she was on the right road. A thread of anxiety needled through the back of her mind. Her hands felt clammy on the steering wheel, her head fuzzy. The niggling edge of a panic attack was trying to creep over her.

"You're almost there now, Vivian," she told herself firmly. "You're okay; you're just feeling tired. After all, you've been on the road for days now. Anyone would be tired and a little shaky at the end of a long trip."

She took a few calming, deep breaths and purposefully began studying the scenery outside the car window to refocus her thoughts away from herself. Fumbling in her purse, she found an apple to snack on for an energy boost. All of this seemed to help, and she began to feel a lot steadier as she drove on.

Vivian checked the time on the car's dashboard, mentally adjusting the earlier 3:45 Pacific time to 6:45 pm Eastern time in her mind. It had been over a week now since she'd started her journey from the west to the east coast. She'd left Arcata, in Northern California, on Friday, spent two nights in nearby Redding with her foster parents, and then set out for Tennessee. Even with stopovers, the long week of travel over thousands of miles of interstate highways had been utterly exhausting. Vivian had been almost giddy with relief to see her final exit announcing the Smoky Mountains. Now, after passing through what seemed like endless miles of tourist sites and backed-up traffic in the busy resort areas of Sevierville and Pigeon Forge, Vivian was winding her way out a rural highway through the Wear's Valley.

Her cell phone rang, startling her. She dug it out of her bag to answer it, relieved to hear a familiar voice on the other end of the line.

Vivian smiled. "It's good to hear your voice, Betsy," she answered, feeling her anxiety lift even more now.

"I'm sorry to call you on the road, Vivian, but you'll be pleased to know I'm calling you as a friend and not as your editor at Picardi Press." Betsy chuckled.

"Seriously, I've been thinking about you and wanted to check up on you."

"No need to apologize, Betsy. I'm glad you called. Plus I can't tell you how glad I am it's you on the phone this time and not Tad again."

A note of irritation touched Vivian's voice. "Honestly, Betsy. Tad has called me constantly all the way from California to Tennessee. Worrying about me traveling alone. Worrying about whether I got to all the stops he planned for me. Worrying about whether I've made the right decision to come here. He's been worse than an overprotective mother, and he's started to make me nervous, too. I was actually about to kick into a panic attack coming down the highway just now.

"Plus, get this," she added. "Tad programmed the kids' song 'It's A Small World' on my cell phone as one of his little jokes before I left. I've had to listen to that play every time this phone has rung. I can't wait to change it when I have the time."

Betsy's laughter floated over the phone and helped to further elevate Vivian's spirits. Betsy had always had such a great laugh.

"Vivian, we've both worked with Tad Wainwright a long time, and we both know he can be a little overly solicitous."

"Well, that's a diplomatic way to put it." Vivian paused. "Still, you know I'm grateful for all the work Tad did making my travel arrangements."

"Are you almost at the rental house now?" Betsy asked.

"Yes, I think so." Vivian looked out the car window. "I'm on this little rural highway winding out into the Wear's Valley now, and my turn to the house shouldn't be too far down the road. It is lovely here, just like you said, Betsy. It's incredibly green, and the mountain ranges are much softer and gentler than the ones in California. When I was driving down the freeway and first saw the mountains, I could see six or eight layers of overlapping ranges spanning across the horizon. They were all in hazy layers of blues and purples, each layer growing mistier and softer as they faded off into the distance."

Betsy chuckled. "That's why they're called the Smoky Mountains, Vivian."

"Well, it takes my breath away, even when I'm tired from traveling."

"I wish I was there with you, Vivian. My family has spent a holiday or two in that area of the country, and I hope you'll enjoy your time there as much as I did. Do all the tourist things, but just don't stay away too long. We'll miss you."

Vivian sighed. "Listen, Betsy, I want to thank you again for working all this out for me. I don't know what I would have done without you and Tad through this difficult time."

"No thanks are necessary. And everything is going to work out wonderfully, Vivian. You'll see."

Vivian had heard this spiel before and very much wanted to believe it.

"You just keep writing there in Tennessee, Vivian, and we'll see that you stay hidden away. And for goodness sakes, call Tad when you get to the rental house and tell him you've arrived safe and sound. Since you've quit answering his phone calls on your cell, he's started calling me."

They both laughed over this.

Betsy shared some needed messages with Vivian, and on a more serious note before saying goodbye, she asked, "Are you really doing all right, Vivian?"

"Yes, I'm fine. I'm tired, of course. Even with the stopovers, I've been traveling for a week, you know. But I'm wired to finally be here." She paused to look at a passing road sign.

"You know, Betsy, I probably need to pull off the road and look at my map. I don't want to get lost back here on these rural roads after dark."

They said final goodbyes and hung up. Vivian pulled over on the side of the road and studied the hand-drawn map her realtor had sent her. She felt a prickle of conscience as she tried to figure out how much further she had to go to find her turn at Stoney Mill Road. She knew she should have called the real estate agent as soon as she arrived in town. The woman had promised to bring her out to the house, so she wouldn't get lost back in the country. But Vivian was a week early and she hated to call anyone on a Friday night at suppertime. Working people were so glad to get off and head for home to relax on Friday - so eager for the break of the weekend. Vivian remembered how that felt with a little wince of discomfort. That kind of nine-to-five working day no longer existed for her.

With a sense of resolve and independence, she pulled back on the highway. She had a good map. She had found her way all the way across the United States alone. Surely, she could find her way to the rental house where she would be staying for the next year. By then she would know more what she wanted to do - whether she wanted to stay here, move somewhere else, or go back to California again.

She had a lot of options, a gift she had not had for much of her life. Vivian was thankful for options. Life had surely taught her to count her blessings. But, right now, she just wanted a change. To be more truthful, she critically needed a change, and she needed a place where no one knew her.

As the day lengthened and the sun began to set behind the mountain, Vivian felt a new apprehension prickling up her spine. Those darkening clouds on the horizon definitely meant a storm was moving in. Had she missed her turn already? She didn't want to get lost in this valley out in the middle of nowhere at night, especially in the rain. Seeing a little market up ahead, Vivian pulled over, glad to see two older men in overalls sitting on a bench in front of the store.

"Excuse me," she asked. "Can you tell me how to get to Stoney Mill Road?"

One of the older men nodded at her and smiled. "Well, I think that's down the road about where the Hart Sign Store is, Missy.

Hart's place looks like an old barn, so you'll recognize it when you come to it. In fact, it used to be an old barn about twenty years or so back. You know, Charles Hart can make ye a real fine sign there for yer garage sale or fer a little business iffen you have one."

He looked over to his friend. "Isn't that where Stoney Mill Road is, Zeke, just past Charles Hart's place?"

"Naw, Bill, that's Lyon Springs, the road over to Metcalf Bottoms. Stoney Mill Road's more up this way, just after Blackbear Restaurant."

"Naw. I think you're wrong, Zeke." He scratched his chin and looked down the road thoughtfully. "That's Piney Ridge Road that's just after Blackbear's. It's the road that runs back in the valley past Drew Miller's place and then all the way up to the base of Cove Mountain."

Vivian listened patiently while the old men argued back and forth.

"Well, it must not be much further." She made an effort to sound pleasant but her patience was wearing thin. "At least I haven't passed it yet from what you're telling me."

"Naw, it's just on up a ways on yer left. You haven't passed it yet, Missy. You'll see the old Millhouse right by the creek at the turn to Stoney Mill. The McFees still make cornmeal in that mill sometimes during tourist season. There's nothing like real cornmeal ground in an old millhouse."

As they started talking about the merits of cornmeal, Vivian jumped on the opportunity to wave and escape. It amazed her how locals could live right near a place and not be able to tell you how to get there with any clarity at all.

Ten minutes later, she easily found her left turn at Stoney Mill, crossed a broad creek over an old rock bridge, and passed the millhouse just after it. The road, a narrow and twining little two-lane, wove first through pastoral farmland and then back into a shady woods. At the first split in the road, Vivian veered left and soon passed the arched entrance sign for Buckeye Knob Camp she'd been told to look for. The next turn was hers, a looping driveway that led her back to the farmhouse she had chosen to rent, for no better reason than because the picture had appealed to her.

She pulled her red Explorer to a halt and stopped to stare in delight. The house was even better than the picture had been – a rambling, white two-story farmhouse with quaint angles and deep porches set among a nest of shade trees. Sweeps of March daffodils grew along the side yard and clumps of yellow and purple crocus nestled along the walkway, ending in a colorful cluster beside the house. Many of the shrubs around the porch were in bloom – yellow forsythia, salmon pink japonica, and white bridal wreath. Bulbs peeked from underneath the shrubs and crowded the flowerbeds that decorated the yard.

An expanse of green yard spread around the farmhouse, and beyond the barn the land rose into woodland and right up the back ridges of the mountainside. Off to the right Vivian could hear a creek burbling behind a row of trees. A peaceful and quiet scene - with not another house in sight.

Vivian sighed contentedly as she got out of the car. "I've come to paradise," she announced.

Pulling her purse out of the car, she looked for the key the realtor had sent her. After digging it out, she climbed the steps and started across the porch, weaving her way between worn, wooden rockers and planters spilling over with more flowers. She tried the front door, and it opened easily. Right at her feet inside the door lay a floral hooked rug with the words "Welcome Home" worked into the rug's nap.

A slow grin spread across her face as she looked down at the little rug. "Well, well, this is really almost too perfect."

As if in agreement, a huge clap of thunder shook the sky, and a streak of lightning crashed down almost beside Vivian's red Explorer parked in the driveway. Vivian blew out a sharp breath and dashed out to her car to start unloading her luggage before the rains came.

Just as she dragged the last of her bags and boxes into the house, the sky completely opened up and the rain began to pour down in a torrent. As Vivian shook her wet hair and looked out the window at the darkening sky, another roll of thunder rumbled through the house, even rattling the windowpanes.

Vivian slammed the front door and peered out the window to see an ominous slash of lightning streak across the dark sky. The deep echo of thunder that followed reverberated through the wood floor beneath her feet. It was scary, and Vivian felt definitely spooked. She'd come here hoping for privacy and solitude, but right now she really wouldn't mind a little human company at all.

Wincing at the next bolt of lightning, she gathered her courage and squared her shoulders with resolve. "Time to check this place out."

As she started down the farmhouse hall to explore, a strange man cloaked in a dark green rain slicker stalked out of the back of the house directly into her pathway. Wherever had he come from? Vivian's heart leaped into her throat, and she put a hand up to her chest automatically. The man's clothes were dripping wet, and he was holding a rifle across his arm.

Chapter 2

Scott Jamison had had a long day. He owned and managed Buckeye Knob Camp in Wear's Valley, and he had been cleaning camp cabins. Spring was here, and he'd soon have his first corporate and group retreats using the grounds and facilities. Plus, visitors would be checking out the camp when they came to the Smokies over the coming months. He needed to start getting everything into shape after the winter.

He'd ended his workday when the first signs of the storm started and he'd come back up to the director's house where he lived. Scott had showered and then flopped onto the couch for a rest when the first bolt of lightning hit. It sounded like it almost touched down at his grandma's old house behind the camp. He looked out the back windows of his log home through the trees to see if everything looked all right over there. He could just see the side of the house through the woods.

A light was on. He could see it shining through the twilight. Someone was in the house again. Great. Scott sighed.

This was getting to be a real problem. The area teenagers had learned that the house was sitting vacant, and they had started to sneak into it to party in the last months. Of course, it wasn't any of the local kids. They all knew him and had known his Grandmother Jamison before she died. The kids breaking in probably lived over toward Sevierville. Who knew how they had heard about the house being empty. But they had. Several times, Scott had phoned the sheriff to come by and deal with them. However, the kids usually got away before the sheriff could catch them and take them in.

Scott dialed Sheriff Hershel Fields. "Hershel, this is Scott Jamison. I think there are kids over at Gramma Jamison's place again. I can see light through the trees. How far are you from my place?"

"Well, you're in luck, Scott. I'm just up the road at Blackbear having a bite of dinner. The wife Clara's having some kind of ladies' shower at the house and I was trying to make myself scarce for a while until it was all done. I can be over in about ten minutes. By the way, glad to hear you're getting ready to rent that place for a while. That'll put an end to all this. When are your renters coming in?"

"Next week some time, I think. It's some woman professor that wants to get away for a while to take a sabbatical and write a book or something. She's supposed to call the realty company when she comes in. Mother will probably bring her out since she's had all the contacts with her from the realty office. Nice staid academic type, she told me. Sounds like a safe bet for Gramma's place for a while."

"Well, I'm paying up with Sheila here at the cash register now, Scott. I'll see you in just a little bit. Maybe we can catch these kids tonight, so they'll get the idea that using empty houses around the valley isn't such a good plan."

Scott hung up the phone and went out to the hall closet to get his rain slicker. On the way he took down his .22 rifle from the gun rack.

The rain started coming down in a fury by the time Scott walked the short path through the woods and crossed the footbridge over Honey Lick Branch. The creek formed a boundary line between the camp property and the Jamison farm that had been his grandparents. Scott skirted around the back of the house to let himself quietly in through the kitchen door with his spare key. He could hear someone hauling stuff into the house and dumping it on the floor just inside the front door. Amazing that kids would even want to be out and getting into trouble on a foul night like this. There was one heck of a storm coming in now.

Scott stood waiting, dripping on the kitchen floor, until he heard Hershel's car starting to come up the drive, then he turned and started up the hallway of the farmhouse. A girl who had been coming down the hall stopped suddenly, startled at his presence in the house, her eyes growing huge as she caught sight of his rifle. Her hands flew automatically to cover her heart.

Scott raised his rifle and gave her a cold stare. "Party's over. Sheriff's on the way. Better tell your friends to get on in here, too, before the Sheriff comes. He'll want to talk to all of you about breaking and entering. This is private property, you know, not a place where you can hang out and smoke dope or get drunk. I want you to get the word out that this house isn't available for kids to party in."

The girl stood speechless for a few minutes, her breath heaving in and out in short gasps. She was obviously scared to death. Good, Scott thought. She had a right to be. The old farmhouse was still filled with all his gramma's old furniture and possessions. The last time a group partied here, they'd left a nasty mess Scott had spent a half-day cleaning up. Nothing had been stolen, but Scott figured his luck was about to run out on that option if the place stayed empty.

"Where are your friends?" he asked her curtly. "No one's going to get hurt here, girl. But none of you are going to be partying here tonight, and that's a fact."

"Who are you?" the girl finally rasped out.

"I'm Scott Jamison. I own Buckeye Knob Camp and the property next door. This was my Gramma Jamison's place, and this is Jamison land you are on."

The girl straightened up then, beginning to catch her breath. Then something in her expression changed gradually from fear to challenge.

She flashed him a defiant look. "I'm not a teenager here to have a party hour, Mr. Jamison. I have a legal right to be here, and I do not appreciate being nearly frightened out of my mind by you waving a gun around in here and threatening me."

Hershel came stomping into the house about that time. Seeing Scott with his rifle raised, he looked off down the hallways and into the parlor and the front bedroom, before joining Scott and the girl in the hall.

He took off his hat to shake out some of the water. "I don't see any more kids in here. Maybe they all took off when they heard me drive up."

"There weren't any more kids," Vivian announced primly. "And do you think you could ask your cowboy friend here to put his gun down now?"

Hershel gave Scott a look, and Scott lowered his rifle.

"Look here, girl," Hershel began. "This here's private property and …."

"I assume you're the sheriff." Vivian interrupted before he could finish.

"Sheriff Hershel Fields." He studied Vivian more closely now. "You're a little old for this vagrancy stuff, aren't you, girl? Usually it's teenagers that do this kind of thing."

"Thank you for noticing that, at least," Vivian snapped back. "And since you didn't ask my name, let me provide it. I'm Dr. Vivian Delaney and I'm the new renter for this house. I know I've arrived a little earlier than I'd been scheduled to, but I certainly didn't expect to be met with a gun and a threat. I paid March's rent in advance before I came, and legally I have every right to be in this house."

Hershel raised an eyebrow at Scott. "Is this your new renter?"

"I'm not sure." Scott studied the girl more intently, beginning to get an odd feeling about this whole situation now.

"I have identification in my purse on the entry table in the hall-way." She pointed behind her toward the door. "You can check it out if you like."

She smiled at them sweetly then, beginning to realize she had the upper hand.

Hershel grinned sheepishly back.

"There's California plates on her Blazer, Scott. Where did you say this professor renter of yours was coming from?"

"I didn't say." Scott frowned. "All I knew was that she was from out west."

"Well, California's out west sure enough. And I didn't see no sign that anybody broke in, so I'd say it's safe to say that this here is your new renter, Scott." He chuckled a little, seeming to enjoy the joke.

The sheriff turned to Vivian and held out his hand. "Welcome to the valley, Dr. Delaney. Sorry we got you confused and caused you a little undue stress tonight."

Vivian put her hand in his tentatively and then quickly withdrew it, not overly eager to be cordial yet.

"Some teenagers have been coming over here and causing trouble on the weekends," he explained. "And so, naturally, when we saw the lights we thought some kids had come over and broken in again. We was hoping to catch them."

Hershel tried another smile her way. "I hope you'll understand that it was an honest mistake we made catching you instead. I'd say the fault is a little yours as well, ma'am. You're early to arrive and you didn't call your realtor to tell her you were here. That realtor is Scott's mother. If you'd contacted her, she'd have called Scott, and Scott would have known that the lights in this house were legit. Might have saved us all getting out in the wet tonight."

"You have some very good points there, Sheriff Fields," Vivian conceded. "But, of course, Mr. Jamison could have simply asked me who I was before he pulled a gun on me, too."

Scott scowled in irritation. "Now, listen here. The last time a bunch of kids broke in the house, some of them were doing drugs and alcohol. Kids like that are dangerous to themselves and to others. I didn't want any trouble tonight."

"Well, it looks like you got some, anyway," she replied tartly.

The sheriff hid another smile with his hand and put his rain-drenched hat back on. "Well, I'll be off now. Scott, why don't you walk me out to the car? I'll need you to sign a report about my visit."

Scott trailed out behind Hershel and back into the rain again. The earlier torrent had now diminished to a slow drizzle.

"What report?" he demanded, as soon as they got out of earshot of the house. "I've never needed to sign a report about this before, Hershel."

"I was just needing an excuse to get on out of that house." Hershel laughed. "And I figured I might get you out of there, too, before she decided to scratch your eyes out. Whooee! That girl was mad! She was containing it real professional like, but she was mad as a wet hen. Too bad things are starting out so frosty between you and your new renter, Scott."

"Why's that, Hershel? She's just renting the house."

"Boy, you must be blind as well as stupid." He grinned. "That's one fine, gorgeous young woman you've got moving into your Gramma's place, not some old lady academic like you told me was moving in. I mean, I may be a married man, but I got eyes. And with that soaked down t-shirt and jeans, it was hard not to look. I didn't see no ring on her finger, neither." He laughed again and punched at Scott. "You sure were wrong about this renter being safe and quiet. I'll bet you the young men will be lining up out here to see her if her educational credentials don't scare them all off." He smirked again.

Scott pulled the hood of his slicker over his head with a jerk of annoyance. "I'm glad you're seeing this all as so funny."

"Aw, your pride's just wrinkled from being made a fool of." Hershel cuffed Scott on the arm with affection. "Happens to me all the time. It'll pass off, boy. Get on in out of the rain now, and try to make nice with your new tenant and make things up."

Hershel climbed into his car and gave Scott another wave goodbye before he closed the door and started up the motor. Scott watched him pull away before he slogged back up on the farmhouse porch. He reached for the door, and found it locked tight. His gun was now propped outside the door.

He sighed. It just wasn't worth the effort to push for more to-night. It was getting late, he was soaking wet, and he hadn't eaten dinner yet. It could wait until tomorrow. He picked up his rifle, headed back down off the porch, and started for home.

Chapter 3

VIVIAN WATCHED SCOTT JAMISON LEAVE from her position just inside the door. In one sense, she was relieved that he hadn't pushed his privilege and knocked to come back in again. But in another, she was disappointed. She'd have liked to give him another piece of her mind. The very idea of him coming over here and scaring the life out of her with a gun like that! Who did he think he was, anyway?

She leaned back against the hallway wall and gave a big sigh. God, she'd been scared. The sheriff was right - she should have called her realtor first. The man could have actually shot her, for heaven's sake. Or she might have stumbled upon some of those kids partying and found herself in an even worse kind of mess.

"Lord, when will I learn not to be so impulsive?" She rolled her eyes toward the heavens.

Another crash of thunder came, as if in answer, and the sky opened up even more with a sweeping new deluge of rain. Vivian sighed and went to check the lock on the front door one more time. As she did, she heard a scratching outside the door that made the hairs on her arms prickle up. She knew black bears lived in these mountains.

A sliver of fear crept up Vivian's neck as the scratching continued, and she found herself almost wishing she hadn't locked the door on Scott Jamison. She heard a high whine and a short bark then and found herself sighing in relief. It was a dog outside! She went over to the door and looked out the window beside it. A small, wet, tri-colored collie looked up at her with canine eagerness, lifting its ears in cute appeal and wagging its tail. The little dog scratched on the door and barked again.

Vivian cracked the door. "Oh, why not? How much more trouble can I have tonight?"

The collie raced in without hesitation, shook itself off, and then headed down the hallway toward the kitchen. Before Vivian could close the front door, a damp-furred cat streaked in right behind the dog. The calico shook itself as well, and after a plaintive meow of complaint, followed the dog down the hallway. Both animals seemed entirely too familiar with the house to Vivian's way of thinking.

Vivian shook her head and followed them down the hallway. "Well, great," she muttered. "Let's add one more unexpected complication to this night, a house that comes complete with resident pets."

The animals led Vivian straight into a large pantry and utility room off the kitchen. The cat jumped up on the washing machine to meow at an empty dish, while the collie pushed around a larger dish on the floor. Labels on the dishes let Vivian know the dog's name was Fritzi and the cat's Dearie.

While Vivian tried to decide what to do about the animals, the collie pawed at the pantry closet door impatiently. Opening the door, Vivian found bags of dry food for both the pets on the shelf.

"Well, I guess you're both staying for dinner." She laughed and poured out food for both. Having the animals there comforted her somehow.

She filled their water dishes, too, and, after finding some soup and crackers on the pantry shelves, decided to fix herself some dinner. She explored the kitchen to find a pan to heat the soup in, and when it was ready later, took her dinner into the adjoining country dining room to eat. The animals soon followed her and curled up around her feet for a nap.

While she ate, Vivian made calls to let everyone know she had arrived safely. She called her parents. She called Betsy's office line and left her a message. She called Roz at her office to do the same and to let Roz know her fax would be hooked up by morning for any communications she needed to receive. Then she called Tad at home, who, of course, claimed he was sitting by the phone waiting to hear from her.

"I'm here safe and well, Tad," she assured him, smiling in spite of herself.

Tad launched immediately into a tirade of worrying and fussing. After she assured him again that everything was fine, he moved on to update her on assorted news and office gossip. Vivian finished her soup while she listened.

Actually, she owed Tad a great deal for all the time he'd spent helping her through her recent spate of problems and making her arrangements to come to Tennessee. He'd located her new red Explorer, a better car for traveling than her old Honda. He'd mapped her trip out and arranged her stopovers. He'd helped her pack and had her California furniture put in storage. Also, Vivian had stayed over with Tad and his partner Boone for several weeks before she'd started her trip out to California. They had both been a terrific support to her through everything that had happened since this winter.

Now, in true Tad style, Vivian listened to him bombarding her with another sweep of maternal worries. She smiled with fondness at his genuine concern for her.

"Everything is fine, Tad," she assured him again, never considering for a minute telling him about her encounter with the local sheriff and her neighbor with the gun!

"I followed the map easily with no problem, and the farmhouse is simply charming," she told him.

Tad replied, "Honey, Boone and I just want to know that you have everything you need out there. You go walk through the house right now before we hang up, so if there is anything you don't have, we can get it right out to you. You know, Boone and I will both sleep better knowing that everything is alright there."

"Okay, okay," she conceded. "I'll go walk through the house right now and tell you all about it. And you can tell Boone. If you want, you both can fly over here and see it for yourself. Honestly, Tad, I'm sure this farmhouse is going to be a great place for me to work."

Tad interjected a comment then about an upcoming deadline. "You know I hate to mention it right now, Vivian, but I do need those edits by the tenth."

Vivian sighed. "Tad, I know I need to get some work out to you by the end of this week. And I will. Stop worrying. It's marvelously peaceful here. If I could get work to you while teaching full-time, I'll keep getting work to you now that I'm not teaching at all. I wish you'd just relax. This change is going to be a good thing for me. We agreed about that."

Vivian washed up her dinner dishes while Tad reviewed several other assignment deadlines that she'd already heard twice before, at the very least.

"Let's do this walk through, Tad," she insisted at last, when she could finally get a word in edgewise. "I'm tired, and I haven't even unpacked yet."

He apologized, repeating that he just wanted to know that everything was safe and acceptable before he hung up.

Vivian sighed. "Okay, Tad. You've already seen the outside of the house in pictures, and you know it's a rambling old two-story farmhouse. The property is truly beautiful – flowers and big shade trees everywhere, a bubbling creek nearby, the mountains close enough to taste in the background. I can't wait to explore outside tomorrow."

"You'd better watch out for snakes and bears and stuff," he put in.

Vivian laughed. "I know there are bears and snakes and spiders in the country, Tad. I grew up in rural California, remember? Stop worrying. You're the city boy. I grew up in little country towns. I know how to be careful."

Vivian got up and started to look around. "The downstairs of the farmhouse has three main rooms, a front parlor, a downstairs bedroom, and a big kitchen and dining room combination. The kitchen dining area is a lovely open set of rooms, full of light with big windows looking out into the backyard to a nice woods and a creek.

"It's very cheerful." She walked around to peer into china cabinets and corner shelves. "There's a wonderful collection of blue delftware here – indigo Spode and Blue Willow. I hadn't noticed that before. The owner must have been a long time collector."

Vivian walked up the hallway, looking around. "A big open hallway stretches from the front entry all the way back to the kitchen and dining area. There are paintings along the hall, a little half bath, closets, and a broad staircase climbing to the upstairs."

She peeked into the big living room at the front of the house.

"The front parlor has an old Victorian look with a deep bay window across the front. The color scheme is in rich, sunny yellows and deep blues. It's filled with antique cherry furniture, stern family portraits, needlepoint pillows, and hand-worked samplers. Somebody was really good with a needle here."

The bay window drew her attention, and Vivian walked into the room to look out over the front yard. "There are rockers and old wicker pieces with faded cushions on the front porch." She smiled. "I'm going to love it out here this spring and summer. It's so nice and homey."

Vivian listened to Tad's comments while she walked back down the main hallway and into a side hall leading to the downstairs bedroom.

She opened the door and peeked in. "Oh, how lovely. The downstairs bedroom is blue and white with soft striped wallpaper and a marvelous old white bedspread with a handmade flower-garden quilt at the foot of the bed. I can see a bathroom and a big closet off to one side. I think I'll stay in this bedroom while I'm here. It brings back memories of the room I had when I was a little girl before my mother died."

Fritzi bounded into the room, barking a greeting. Vivian had to stop and tell Tad about the resident pets while she walked upstairs.

Not interested in pet stories, Tad prompted her to get back to telling him about the house. "What's upstairs, Vivian?"

"Well, like a lot of old farmhouses, this one has three huge rooms upstairs off a broad hallway that looks down the stairwell. Probably these were once all bedrooms. People used to have big families when this old house was built."

"Is there a good room for an office up there?"

"There should be. One of the bedrooms is supposed to be a sitting room. Maybe that will work."

Vivian smiled as she peered into a large room at the end of the hallway. "I've found the sitting room, Tad. It's a wonderful room, painted a soft yellow, and it has a lot of light. This is definitely where I'll have my office. There's a desk here already, a big side table, a nice old striped sofa, and lots of bookshelves. It's cozy. I'll put my laptop and printer on the desk and my fax over on the side table. And I'll be all set."

"Is the room inspiring?" Tad asked.

She laughed. "You know I don't have to be inspired to write, Tad Wainwright. Writing is much more discipline than inspiration." She looked around. "But, truly, if a place was inspiring, this one would be tops on my list. In the daytime, I'll be able to look out the windows over the yard and see up toward the mountains behind the house."

Tad started talking to Vivian about upcoming deadlines while she walked down the hall to look at the bedrooms.

She interrupted him with excitement. "You won't believe these upstairs bedrooms. One is a boys' bedroom and the other is obviously a girls' bedroom. The rooms look just like they probably did when the kids lived in them. I wish you could see them. Even the children's toys are still here – dolls, trains, books. Everything has been left just the same, as though the children just went out to play or off to school yesterday.

"And get this," she added. "There are even hand-worked samplers over all the beds that tell the children's names. There were six of them, four boys and two girls. Wouldn't it have been wonderful to grow up in a big family like this one? It feels like such a happy home here."

"Maybe the house will stir some new story ideas."

"Maybe so." Vivian glanced around the girls' bedroom wistfully and then squatted down to steal a look into an ornate, Victorian dollhouse under the window. "You know, this girls' room is a dream. There is a big wooden dollhouse here that would make any little girl start imagining dramas. It is so sweet."

"You know, underneath that academic veneer, Vivian, I think you're really just a sentimental romantic at heart."

Vivian smiled at that. "You're probably right, Tad. But keep it to yourself, you hear. I want to keep my professional image intact."

Tad's voice took on a teasing tone. "Did you bring your own little dolls with you, Vivian?"

"You know I did," she answered him primly. "They've gone everywhere with me ever since I was a little girl. You, of all people, should know that. And you should know what they mean to me, too. They're all I have left of my real mother. Perhaps I'll settle them into this fine old dolls' house while I'm visiting here."

Vivian enjoyed Tad's laugh to that idea.

She stood up and yawned then. "Okay, Tad, we've been through the whole house. Will you let me get off the phone and unpack now? You know what my agenda has been like these last days. I'm really tired, and I'm ready for a hot shower and an early bedtime with a good book."

Vivian paused. "Thanks again for all you've done for me. I don't think I could have gotten through this time without you and Boone and Betsy."

Tad's voice was gentle then. "We love you, honey. We just want you to be happy."

"Just keep people from finding me, Tad. If you and Betsy want me to write, then keep people away from me. Keep me hidden."

"We'll do our best for as long as we can," he promised.

After hanging up at last, Vivian walked back down the stairs and started to retrieve her luggage and boxes from the entry hall. The wet footprints over the floorboards reminded her of her scare earlier with Scott Jamison and the sheriff. Her thoughts wandered back over those moments, almost making her heart beat fast again. The nerve of that man. Coming over here with a gun to threaten her and calling in a sheriff.

She stopped to think about it for a minute. Perhaps he had a right to be worried, she thought. As he said, there had been some ongoing problems with vandals. It had certainly turned out to be an incident. She wondered, suddenly, how Mr. Jamison had felt when he discovered she'd locked him out of the house and put his gun outside.

Vivian shrugged. Perhaps it would be a while before she had to see him again. To be frank, she hoped it would be a rather long time before he came by again, if ever.

Chapter 4

Scott stomped back through the woods after leaving his Gramma Jamison's house. He had worked himself into a nice little fit of anger, which was unusual for him. By the time he let himself in the back door of the cabin, he was completely soaked, as well, despite the heavy slicker. He toweled down in his bathroom, kicked off his wet shoes, and dug a dry t-shirt out of the chest of drawers, muttering the whole time.

Padding barefoot out into the kitchen, he poked around in the refrigerator looking for something to eat, while grabbing up the phone to punch in a familiar number.

"Hello, Scott," his mother answered. "How are you, dear?"

"Geeze, mother, I hate these new phones that tell people who's calling just by the number. It gives me the creeps to have someone know who I am before I even get a chance to say hello."

"You sound cross, dear," she remarked. "Is anything wrong?"

"Yes, a lot is wrong, mother. Did you know that professor woman was coming in early to Gramma Jamison's place?"

"No, dear, I thought she wasn't coming until next week. I'd have to check my notes at the office, but I'm positive that's what she told me. Is she here already? Did she come by to see the house?"

"She not only came by, she's settled herself right in. Why didn't you tell me you gave her a key, mother? I saw the lights through the storm and thought some of those kids were over there having a party again."

"Oh, dear," she answered airily. "I hope you didn't go over there and scare her."

"As a matter of fact, I went over there with my rifle and probably scared the pee out of her. And Hershel Fields came, too, all ready to arrest her before we figured out who she was."

"How upsetting that must have been for her!" There was an anxious edge to his mother's voice now.

"Upsetting for her?" Scott complained, coming close to shouting. "Listen, mother, it was pretty upsetting for me. I thought those kids were tearing up jack again at Gramma's place. I tromped all the way over there in the pouring rain to save the day and instead got royally embarrassed."

"Was Hershel upset with us, dear?"

"Oh, Hershel thought it was a great joke and razzed me about it," he told her in annoyance. "Honestly, mother, I just wish you had filled me in more on this renter. It might have saved me a bad evening here."

"Well, I did tell her to contact me before she went out to the house. Granted, I sent her a little map, but I never thought she would try to find the place on her own. The woman was coming all the way from California, you know. It's not like she would know the area or anything."

"This woman looks more like a girl than some staid old maid professor, mother. Are you sure she's going to be a suitable renter for Gramma's place?"

"She had wonderful references, son. And she has a PhD degree and has been teaching college out in California. She can't be that much of a girl with all that education behind her. Maybe she just looks youthful."

"She doesn't even look as old as I am, mother. Believe me, she's very young."

"Well, perhaps that will be nice for you, dear. Is she attractive?"

"That hardly has anything to do with whether she'll be a suitable renter or not, mother," Scott snapped in annoyance.

"No, but it might be nice for you to have someone young and smart and attractive so close by." Scott heard that speculative tone in his mother's voice. "And I don't think she's married either, dear. In fact ...."

Scott knew only too well where this line of thought was going. "Cut it with the matchmaking, mother. You have two of your sons married already and one with grandkids. Give it a rest. I've got the camp to run, and I'm not the least bit interested in settling down right now with anyone."

"You always were the one who liked to play the field," she replied with a wistful tone, drifting off into her usual reminiscences of Scott's early years. "And always so popular with the girls, too. They chased after you much more than after Raley and Kyle, perhaps because you were always such a handsome thing and so charming. Raley was my strong and determined child and tended to be a little forceful sometimes. I think he scared the girls a little bit in that way, don't you? And Kyle was always a bit shy. You usually helped him with his dating if I remember right. You introduced him to Staci, too. Such a wonderful girl and such a nice little wife. She's so good for him, don't you think?"

Scott rolled his eyes in exasperation. "Kyle and Staci are a great couple, Mother, but what does that have to do with this situation with our renter next door? I really want to know more about this woman, Mother."

"Now Scott, just because you got off to a bad start with our new renter, doesn't mean she is not a suitable one. I told you I checked all her references out, and they are excellent."

He frowned. "So tell me what you know about her." He tapped the counter with impatience.

His mother paused, obviously thinking back. "Well, my original contact with her came through Betsy Picardi. She's an editor out in California, lives in Sacramento. She and her family meet here in the area for family reunions periodically and they stay in some of our rental cabins up in the mountains. Wonderful people. Well, Betsy called me and said she had a client that she worked with in California that was going to take a sabbatical from her teaching to do some writing. Betsy has an interest in the book, of course, and she wanted her to have a nice, quiet place to work. Tennessee had come up because the client – that was Vivian, of course - thought she might have some relatives in this area. Betsy remembered us and called me to see if we might have a place she could rent long term, for six months to a year."

"And this Betsy Picardi spoke well of this woman?"

"Oh course, dear. And let's quit calling her 'this woman.' She has a name, Vivian Delaney. She's a professor, a writer, and Betsy also uses her to do some editing work for the publishing company. Honestly, Scott, I don't know how we could have found anyone more suitable. You know we're not ready to sell the place yet, and we don't want tourists renting it for short-term weeks with all Gramma's things still in the house. Ms. Delaney, or rather I guess we should say Dr. Delaney, has put her furnishings in storage out in California for a space. She was really delighted to find a furnished place to lease. I think she will be a good renter, Scott. I can't figure out why you are so uncomfortable about her. Perhaps it was just the storm and the identity confusion that has upset you so much about this."

"Maybe." He couldn't even say why he was so ticked off. There was just something about that girl that made him uncomfortable.

"I'm sure our new renter is just going to be perfect, dear," his mother assured him. "Why don't you go get a good night's sleep and see if you don't feel differently about everything in the morning? I'll try to drive over tomorrow to help smooth things over at the farmhouse. I'd like to see Aunt Mary, anyway, while I'm over there. It's been an age since she and I have had lunch and visited. Maybe I'll take her over to meet Vivian with me. I'll stop by and see you, too, dear, while I'm there. Do you need me to bring you anything?"

"No, I'm fine, thanks, Mother. And listen, I really need to get off and fix something to eat now. I haven't had any supper yet with all this mess that's been going on tonight."

"Yes, of course, Son. You go fix yourself a nice little dinner." She paused for a minute. "It's a shame things had to start this way with our new renter. You did apologize to the girl for all this, didn't you, dear?"

Scott's end of the line was quiet.

"No answer is a clear answer, Son. Perhaps in the morning you could stop over there first thing and make that apology. You know, she did have a right to be there, Scott, despite all this confusion. And I'm sure you and Hershel frightened her dreadfully. That's hardly the way we Jamisons welcome people to the valley, you know."

Scott listened to a few more platitudes of this sort while he dug around in the refrigerator for something to fix for dinner. Then he excused himself, by saying he needed his hands free to cook, to finally get off the phone.

"Some sympathy," he grumbled as he hung up.

He made a quick bacon and egg sandwich and took it into the living room to eat. With the lightning still crashing all around, he could hardly plug up the television again for company.

So he sat instead and looked out at the storm and watched the lights winking through the trees from his grandmother's house.

The girl was pretty, he acknowledged at last. Too pretty and too young. His grandmother's house was his responsibility now, and he was going to be back and forth there a lot. It would make it more awkward - dropping in on a single girl living alone. He didn't want her getting ideas.

Scott lounged back on the couch to relax, but then had to sit up to get the dog bone out from under the couch cushion. Oh, geeze, he thought. Fritzi and Dearie were out in this rain. He'd forgotten them both in all this confusion. Probably they were holed up under the green glider out on the front porch. It was a wonder they hadn't been barking and yowling to get in the house since he got back.

He checked the front porch and the back. Then he checked through the house to be sure they weren't already inside asleep somewhere. No luck.

Great. They'd never be out on a night like this by choice. They must have gone to the farmhouse. They missed Gramma Jamison, and to them the farmhouse was still their home. Scott had brought them both over to the camp with him after his grandmother died. He'd promised Gramma he'd take care of them, too. But the animals just didn't understand why they couldn't live on at Gramma's house like they always had. So they were back and forth all the time be-tween Scott's place and the farm.

Sometimes Scott stayed over there with them just for old times' sake and to please the little pets, as well. He even kept food for them, and for himself, at the farmhouse.

"Just a big softie," he muttered, glancing toward the window again.

It was a bad storm out. The rain was still coming down outside in sheets. Scott wondered if the girl would let the pets in. He knew Fritzi would scratch at the front door. And Dearie, despite her small size, had a big mouth on her. She could make herself a real nuisance with her yowling if she had a mind to.

He smiled at the little joke that played in his thoughts. The animals probably figured the family had just finally gotten sensible and found someone to live at the farmhouse to take care of them. His renter really had her work cut out for her if she didn't like animals.

Scott looked out at the lights through the woods again. If she didn't let the animals in, they'd probably come on back home when the rain let up. He'd stay up awhile and listen for them. He had paperwork to do, anyway.

Chapter 5

Vivian was standing on a step stool rummaging in a kitchen cabinet for a coffee maker the next morning when Scott came in the back door carrying a brown grocery bag.

"Good morning," he said pleasantly.

Vivian, startled by his sudden appearance, just barely caught herself from falling off the stool.

"Don't you ever knock on the door like ordinary people?" she snapped. "I almost fell off the stool, you startled me so."

"Sorry. Here, let me help you down." He put the bag of groceries on the counter and reached up to take her hand.

She took his hand, stepped down and stumbled, and suddenly they were too close. Something crackled in the air like the electricity of last night's thunderstorm. They stood silent for a moment, both caught off guard with it.

Vivian's blue eyes slid over him assessingly. Scott was glad he looked a lot better than he had last night, when he'd been draped in that wet slicker and carrying a gun. He knew he wasn't a bad looking man - tall with hazel eyes and dark hair that had just a touch of premature grey above the ears. His physique was lean but muscular, and he was nicely sun-browned from being out-of-doors so much.

That last girl, Jeannie, he'd dated said he had a sensual, boyish charm and that he was too good-looking for his own good. Scott had liked that description. She'd also said he looked like trouble on wheels for any sensible woman. Scott grinned, remembering that.

Vivian dropped her eyes and moved back from him. Then she busied herself moving the step stool back across the kitchen. Scott studied her at leisure while she did so, sweeping his eyes slowly over her from top to bottom while her back was turned.

Hershel had been right about her being a gorgeous woman. He'd been too riled up last night to really appreciate her looks. She had a serene, quiet beauty, almost regal. She was almost as tall as he was, long legged, looked athletic, with rich, dark chestnut-red hair, and indigo blue eyes that looked like the patterns in his Gramma's kitchen dishes. And, to be frank, it had been a long while since he'd been around a woman who gave him a real zing like she did.

He'd watched her pull her hand away quickly when she realized they'd been staring at each other too long. Now she was busying herself around the kitchen trying to act like nothing had happened. That meant she wasn't fast or forward. It also meant she was a little shy. If there was one thing Scott knew about it was women. They had always liked him, simpered and flirted with him, contrived ways to get his attention, and often came on to him. Sometimes it was flattering, and sometimes it almost seemed like a curse. Some girls were so blatantly sexually aggressive today that it embarrassed him. And he didn't embarrass easily, either.

Vivian leaned over, tucking the stairs back up into the step stool. Hmmmm. Scott found himself watching her more closely then, because he realized she wasn't wearing very much in the way of clothes. Just some kind of long t-shirt with little knit shorts peeking out underneath it. He watched her walk back across the kitchen and let his eyes drift up over her body. Apparently, she wasn't wearing a bra, or any kind of underwear that he could discern, and she was barefoot, too.

"What are you staring at?" she asked self-consciously, catching his gaze moving over her.

"Just trying to read what's on your shirt." He answered her casually, not wanting to let her know he'd been ogling her.

She looked down, as if trying to remind herself what she was wearing. Then she turned towards him so he could see the words across the front of her shirt.

"Chick with Brains," he read. "And accompanied by a badly

faded picture of a baby chicken wearing horn-rimmed glasses".

She smiled and shrugged. "It's an old shirt. I've had it forever. A friend gave it to me for Christmas one year." She pulled the shirt down nervously, making it clear to Scott that his observation about the lack of underwear had been a correct one.

He caught her glance and grinned. "Let me guess. You just got up and you haven't gotten dressed yet."

"It's only eight o'clock," she countered, misreading his message completely. "And I was looking for the coffeemaker when you came in and scared me again. By the way, do you know where it is?"

"Yeah," he answered, walking over closer to her and almost backing her up against the kitchen counter. "I do know where it is, and I brought breakfast makings, too, since I thought you might not have had time to get out to the store yet. But there's one thing I need to check out first." He moved still closer until he could look down into those deep blue eyes.

Zing. There it was again. That spark. Just like electricity. Lord, it felt great. Scott grinned a long lazy smile down into Vivian's indigo eyes.

"You're making me uncomfortable, Mr. Jamison." Vivian's breath came out fast after her words.

"Yes, I know, Dr. Delaney. In case you haven't noticed, we have some kind of nice little chemistry thing going between us whenever we get too close."

A cooling look came into Vivian's face and Scott watched her put on her professor's face and manner. "We have no *thing* between us, Mr. Jamison. Except perhaps a legacy of annoyance from the times you've come into my house here and tried to upset me."

"The name is Scott," he answered, as a slow smile crept over his lips. "And technically this is my house, not yours. Or at least my family's house." He looked down at her shirt again, his eyes lingering over the words on it and more precisely exactly where those words were situated. He noticed a physical change underneath the thin layer of material and began to feel a little physical change of his own.

"You know, Vivian," he said on a husky note, enjoying the sound of her name and how well it seemed to suit her. "If you are indeed a 'Chick with Brains,' I'd advise you to go get some clothes on while I start some coffee and get our breakfast going. Otherwise, you may *become* breakfast if we linger around here much longer. We valley men have a bit of the wolf in us that you need to be careful about. Running around in pajamas in front of us is not a good idea."

Her mouth set itself in a firm line and her eyes blazed back at him then. "If you'll remember, Mr. Jamison, you are the one who came walking in here this morning without an invitation. I didn't invite you in, and I certainly have not been parading around in front of you, as you put it. I live here now, if you'll recall ...."

He stopped her words by leaning over to put his lips against hers. "You know, you're just getting me more excited by being mad." His mouth touched hers lightly. She froze for a minute, just long enough for him to get a taste of her, a minty taste of morning tooth- paste with a touch of something strawberry on her lips. His head spun, and he knew she felt the jolt when it came again, because when it hit, she just fell into the kiss, her reason and anger slipping away for a minute.

Scott had a moment then to deepen the kiss and get sensually lost in the taste of her before she recovered and jerked back.

"You had no right to do that," she challenged, but her voice was a little shaky from the moment.

"I know, but it was worth it." He grinned at her, his heart still beating madly and his mind reeling. "You'd better go get dressed now, 'Chick with Brains,' before you tempt me to do it again."

She stomped out of the room, mumbling some sort of verbiage about how rude he was and that she was going to have to get a lock put on the door, but he didn't pay much attention to it. Instead, he watched her from the back, running his eyes down the long expanse of the back of her legs and up to the peep show of the bottom of her hips showing just beneath the pajama shorts.

"Whew." He exhaled out loud when she left the room. "Hershel was right. She's a stunner."

It was going to be a lot more trouble, or perhaps a lot more fun, than he had expected having her here. She was sweet, re- ally sweet, and there was something incredibly exciting going on between them. But she didn't want to like him. In fact, judging from her reactions, she was obviously fighting her attraction to him. He laughed over that. That just made the challenge better. He loved a new adventure and a goal to win. And he definitely wanted to find out more about Miss Vivian Delaney. To be honest, Scott couldn't remember feeling this way around a girl since he'd been a fresh-faced kid with his first crush.

A scratching on the back door interrupted his thoughts. He opened the kitchen door to a tail-wagging Fritzi and a streak of cat through the door as Dearie headed for the laundry room and her food bowl.

"Well, there you guys are." Scott reached down to scratch Fritzi's head behind her ears. "You two are a couple of traitors. It wasn't very loyal of you to come over here and leave me alone last night."

"They showed up just after you left," Vivian told him, coming back into the room. "Probably followed you over when you came."

She was dressed now, wearing old jeans and a faded navy t-shirt that set off the blue of her eyes. Her thick hair was still pinned up in that little bun in the back, tendrils wisping down her neck and little strands of her bangs flirting with her eyebrows. She hadn't fussed with her hair one bit since she left or put on any makeup for him. Scott liked that. She wasn't making any effort to please him or to attract his notice.

"You haven't started the coffee," she remarked tartly.

"No, I was greeting my traitorous friends here." He walked over to dig out the coffeemaker from under the counter and started to spoon coffee into it. "I assume they wheedled you into letting them in last night."

She nodded. "They're both yours?"

"They are now, but they belonged to my Gramma Jamison before she died. They still think of this place as home. I hope that won't be any trouble. They'll both probably be underfoot with someone staying here now."

"It won't be any trouble. I like animals. They're a comfort."

He started to work on the eggs now, while Vivian made herself useful finding plates and putting toast in the toaster. Scott liked the fact that she wasn't making a big deal out of the kiss. Most girls would have been simpering and making up to him now, assuming some big passionate love affair was getting started between them. Vivian was ignoring the whole situation and moving on. Like a professional. He grinned. She was a professional.

"Tell me about your grandmother," Vivian said, perching on the step stool.

"Margaret Mary Jamison was her name." He smiled at the memory. "But everyone called her Mamie. Born and raised not far from here in Townsend. Met my grandfather, Stuart Truman Jamison when she was sixteen at a Friday night square dance at an old barn here in the valley. They got married a year later and first moved into the starter house behind his parents' place and then they built this house."

"What's a starter house?" Vivian asked, interrupting him.

"It's a little house that Appalachian families used to build behind the big family home for newly married children to start housekeeping in. Sometimes the senior adults would move over to the starter house later in life, as well."

"How interesting."

"Here, take a plate over to the table," he said to her. "And see if you can find some jelly in the refrigerator on your way."

He took his own plate and the platter of toast she'd made into the dining room off the kitchen, and came back to pour two cups of coffee.

"Do you like strawberry?" Vivian held up a jelly jar in question. Remembering the strawberry taste of her lips suddenly, Scott almost spilled the last cup of coffee he'd poured.

"Yeah," he answered, keeping his back to her while he rearranged his thoughts. No need to start up anything else right now. He was enjoying the comfortableness of getting to know her.

They settled down to eat, and Scott noticed that she ate with relish. No picking at her food and talking about how many calories were in everything.

"So what happened next with your grandmother?" Vivian asked him, pressing him to tell her more of the story he had started.

"My granddad practiced law and farmed. He became rather respected around here for his fairness, and he became a judge later on. My grandmother ran the home and helped with the farm work, did her needlework, and raised six children."

"Four boys and two girls." Vivian's voice was almost dreamy. "The boys were – let me see if I can remember - Sterling, Franklin, Lionel and Warren - and the girls were Eugenia and Dorothy."

He looked at her in surprise. "So where did you pick all that up?"

"From the samplers in the bedrooms upstairs - one over each child's bed. Did your grandmother make those for each of her children?"

"Yes, she was always great with a needle."

"I saw her work everywhere when Fritzi gave me the tour of the house. I was just sure it was hers. She must have been a wonderful person, Scott."

Scott found himself almost misting up at that. He hadn't thought this much about his grandmother in a long time.

"You loved her a lot, didn't you?" Vivian said, watching his face.

"Everyone loved Mamie." He made an effort to sound casual, not wanting to give away his deeper feelings.

"That's not an answer," she pressed. "You loved her yourself and you loved her strongly, too. It comes out in the way you talk about her."

Her insight surprised him, but Scott could hardly deny her words. "Yes, we were really close, my Gramma and I. I came to live with her after Poppy Stuart died. My brothers were off in college then, and Gramma needed someone here with her. I'd stayed with her a lot in the summers anyway. I loved this place, and I liked to be around the camp. I've always loved the camp."

Vivian watched him with a little half smile and listened raptly. Scott found it oddly calming and comforting just being in her presence. She had one of those low, melodious voices, too, kind of like a newscaster's.

He studied her thoughtfully then. She stayed quiet while he did so but, after a moment, gave him a soft, slow smile. It flickered at some place deep inside him.

"How did you end up with the camp, Scott?"

"Well, the camp belonged to Bernie and Myrna Taylor for as long as I can remember." Scott settled back to continue his story. "A church affiliation owned it before the Taylor's bought it, but they worked with it even back then. Bernie and Myrna came to the camp as kids, then as counselors, and then as live-in directors. Bernie was great. I guess he was my hero growing up - a terrific guy. I still keep up with him and Myrna. They retired to Florida to live near their kids and grandkids."

He stopped to get up and get some more coffee for both of them.

Vivian took her cup gratefully and poured milk into it. "Did you go to camp there, too, when you were little?"

"From the time I was old enough to get in the door," he admitted with a grin. "My brothers and I went to Buckeye Knob Camp every summer, and often for several sessions of camp since mother worked with dad in the real estate business. It kept us busy and active a good part of the summer, and the rest of the time, we usually stayed here at Gramma's and Poppy's during the week. So, of course, we were often over at the camp then, too. When I got too old for camp, I worked as a counselor there. Even when I got quite a bit older and could have gotten better summer jobs like my brothers, I kept going back. I just loved the place."

He looked thoughtfully out the window. "You can't imagine how I felt when I learned that Bernie and Myrna were going to sell the camp. Land in this area has become more valuable over time, and I had a vision of the camp being demolished for streets of nearly identical Smokies rental cabins. I was torn apart to think about that."

"What happened?" Her eyes widened and she looked so riveted by his tale that Scott wondered if her interest was sincere or feigned now.

"Listen, you don't have to act polite and hear all of this old story." He drew back, giving her an opportunity to opt out gracefully. "It's probably boring to you."

"No story with heart and passion is boring, Scott Jamison. Don't you know that?"

He studied her again, sensing her sincerity, and felt an odd pull at his heart. She was such an intense little thing.

"What happened next?" she asked him once again. "Finish your story."

"Well, my grandmother said: 'Go talk to them, boy. Tell them you want the camp. Tell them you want to keep it going. They'll listen.'"

He looked at Vivian and smiled. "I hadn't even acknowledged to myself that I wanted the camp until Gramma said that. But then I knew. Just like that. I had to borrow money from everywhere and use my trust money. But I got the camp. That was four years ago. I worked with Bernie and Myrna that last summer they ran the camp to learn everything I could from them. Then I spent the next year renovating and, also, marketing and advertising the camp in every way I could."

He sat back then with a smug look. "That's my specialty area. I majored in marketing and advertising in college, and I had been working for LeConte Agency out of Gatlinburg doing just that type of work for companies all over the area since I'd graduated. I was good at it, too." He grinned at her. "Now I got to turn those nice skills toward growing my own business."

"And have you done that? Have you grown your own business?"

"Yes, I have," he answered with a touch of pride. "I've taken the camp from being a small summer camp that was losing money to being a large camp with a strong profit flow now. About 1400 campers can come to camp here every summer now and make the kind of memories my brothers and I once did. Plus, during the year, I have weekend conferences and corporate retreats coming in to use the lodges that Kyle and I added to the camp."

"Who's Kyle?"

"My younger brother. I'm the middle child. Raley, my older brother, went into the family real estate business with Dad and Mom in Sevierville and then opened a second branch up in Gatlinburg. But Kyle always loved the building end. He's a contractor now, specializes in log homes and vacation houses. He and his crew helped me renovate the first year I got the camp. We updated all the kids' cabins, built some new lodge houses, and expanded some of the area buildings we use. You'll have to come over to see it."

"I'd like that."

"Does that mean you've forgiven me for coming over here with a gun last night and scaring you?" he teased.

She gave him a prim look. "I don't recall that you offered an apology to that incident so I could consider whether I'd even want to forgive you or not."

He winced at that.

"Why is it so hard for men to apologize?" she asked him.

He shrugged. "Generations of species training in being the strong hunter and provider that does no wrong?"

She laughed. "Took your psychology classes in college, didn't you?"

"Yes, ma'am." He grinned back.

"That still doesn't let you off the hook from apologizing, Mr. Jamison," she added smartly.

"I really am sorry if I scared you, Vivian Delaney."

"Well, I'll give thought to getting over it." She paused to look at him. "A first impression's a powerful thing, Scott. You've showed yourself to be a somewhat impulsive person so far, and I haven't seen much since to dissuade me of that impression." She got up and started gathering up the dishes to take to the kitchen.

"The world needs impulsive people," he suggested. "Without the adventurous, the risk-takers, the people not afraid to follow their impulses, the world might have stayed a little stagnant. The Wright brothers might not have tried to fly that little plane at Kitty Hawk. Lewis and Clark might not have set out on that expedition to explore the west. Margaret Mead might not have ventured to other cultures to learn how differently people in other countries did things from the way we do."

"You think well on your feet, Mr. Jamison."

"And you like that?" He knew he was baiting her.

"I like articulate people who know how to express their ideas and thoughts. And you seem to do that very well."

She looked out the kitchen window then, studying the sky. "It's going to be a nice day today," she said, changing the subject. "Would you have time to show me around the farm before you go back to work? I'd like to feel a little more comfortable about the property. Not have any more surprises." She gave him a pointed look.

"I'd be glad to." He grinned at her, ignoring the subtle jab. "And, later, if you like, I'll show you around the camp, too. Possibly cook you dinner."

"Maybe," she replied evasively. "I still have some unpacking to do today. And then there are some calls I need to make."

He smiled to himself. She wasn't going to be easy, this one. For one thing, she had her own life going. She wasn't looking for some man to make her happy or complete. She already was complete. He'd have his work cut out for him chipping through her professional veneer and getting close to her.

"If you'll rinse up the dishes," she said, starting out of the room. "I'll go and put some shoes on."

Yep, Scott thought. Dr. Delaney was used to setting the tone and having control. He'd indulge her for now, but it would be fun to turn the tables on her later on to see how she liked having someone else strong around her. He wasn't one of her little students, and he had no intention of staying in his place.

Chapter 6

Vivian walked down the hallway and around the corner into the big downstairs bedroom she'd claimed as her own. Then she sat down on the bed and let out a big sigh.

"What in the world have you gotten yourself into, Vivian Delaney?" she asked herself. "Starting a relationship is not anything you can afford in your life right now. And neither is getting too close to anyone. Besides, you know that never works out, no matter how many goose bumps someone gives you."

She pulled her shoes out from under the edge of the bed and started putting them on. Frankly, even if she hadn't needed to put her shoes on, she'd have sought an excuse to get away from Scott Jamison's company for a few minutes.

"First he comes over here and scares the liver out of me with that gun," she said to herself. "Then he waltzes into my kitchen, nearly scaring me to death again. And then he gets me up against the kitchen counter and kisses me before I have time to figure out what he is doing." She blew out a long breath again.

"And I let him." She shook her head in disbelief. "In fact I almost encouraged him. I don't know what came over me. It was like something short-circuited my reason."

She still remembered with wonder the intensive feeling that had rushed over her with that kiss. When she'd fled the room to get dressed she'd thrown cold water on her face just to get herself back together. You'd think she was a little teenager again with her first boyfriend from the way she was acting. Vivian shook her head firmly to clear her thoughts.

"Scott Jamison may have a nice boyish charm about him, but there is a sensual danger about him," she told herself. "Undoubtedly, he's a big ladies man. Which makes me wonder why he's bothering with me. Usually his type stays away from the smart girls and finds some silly little blond with big boobs to run after."

She shrugged. "I'm just going to have to be careful. There's a lot at stake while I'm here. And I have a lot of work to do. I don't have time to give Mr. Scott Jamison a diversion."

Vivian squared her shoulders then, and went into the bathroom to brush her teeth before going back to the kitchen.

Scott had washed up the dishes and was sitting with a cup of coffee in the dining room looking out the window when she returned.

"That dogwood out there is going to be a mass of blooms this time next month." He pointed out the window. "It has a lot of buds already. I think this is going to be a banner year for the dogwoods and redbuds."

She glanced out at the tree, loaded with buds now, that stood beside a concrete birdbath. "You like nature?"

"I love it, and I love to be out of doors." He smiled at her. "I don't think you could run a camp successfully if you didn't, do you?"

"Probably not," she responded guardedly, reluctant to share too many of her personal thoughts with Scott. She needed to keep her distance. "But I guess it would help if you also liked kids and enjoyed working with them."

"Fortunately, I love kids." He gave her an impish look. "And I was an Eagle Scout and a Scout leader. Were you a Girl Scout, Vivian Delaney?"

"No, Mr. Jamison, but I was an avid Campfire Girl. That's about the same thing in California where I come from." She looked at him consideringly. He was trying so hard to be polite and charming, and she was being almost rude and abrasive in her efforts to stay aloof. She shook herself mentally. There was no need to get carried away, she told herself judgmentally. She could be nice, too.

"I do love the outdoors, too, Scott," she admitted then, offering him a smile. "And like you, I went to one sort of camp or another about every summer after I was ten."

"And what about kids?" He sent her an easy smile. "Do you like kids, Vivian?"

"I don't know very much about kids. My work is with college students, and I was an only child."

He got up, put his coffee cup in the sink, and started leading the way out the kitchen door for their tour.

"Does that mean you're going to tell me all about your life now?" he asked teasingly, as he started down the back porch stairs.

Vivian shot him a cool glance. "I might at some time, but now I think you should tell me what I need to know about the farm."

Unruffled, he shrugged. "This was supposed to be my mother's, the realtor's, job, showing you around the place here."

"It still can be," she told him matter-of-factly. "I have her phone number. I did ask if you had time for this."

"Don't get prickly, Vivian." He raised one brow. "I was just kidding around. I'm pleased to show you around. I love this place."

Scott started to walk through the yard behind the house toward an old barn Vivian could see beyond a stand of trees. He talked as he walked, and Vivian followed, listening to his verbal tour.

"This farm originally had a lot more acreage than it does now." He spread his arm in a wide gesture as they started up the farm road. "The Jamison farm, which is what most people call the farm here, is only about an acre across and three acres back to the property line up against the mountain. The boundaries are easy to note, two creeks on each side, the road in the front, the mountain ridge behind. Honey Lick Branch is the smaller creek over toward our left there. It separates the farm from Buckeye Knob camp. There's a low flat bridge across it not far from the back of the farmhouse that takes you right over to the camp.

"The creek on the other side is deeper and swifter," he continued. "It's the one you can hear rushing along its way when you sit out on the porch in the quiet of the evening. It separates the Jamison farm here from the other piece of the original farm property. Everybody calls that section of the farm Spring Farm now, because a little spring comes out of the mountain up behind it. A shallow rill runs from the stream down the mountain to form the western boundary of the old farm property where my great grand-parents used to live."

"Is that the one that has the starter house?"

"That's it." Scott nodded. "Unfortunately, the old farmhouse burned down one summer. But the starter house remained. When my Uncle Leo started to think about retiring from his law practice, he and my Aunt Mary bought Spring Farm from my grandparents and built a house on the old foundation right where the original farmhouse once stood. It's a big, white, two-story place, a lot like the first farmhouse was, but much more modern inside. Aunt Mary's not much for roughing it."

"I don't remember a Leo as one of the Jamison boys' names," Vivian interrupted.

"Leo is a nickname for Lionel."

"Oh, I can see that," Vivian replied, smiling. She was really enjoying Scott's story-telling ability and this new aspect of him being revealed. Perhaps he had more to him than the playboy image she'd originally labeled him with.

"So who lives in the starter house now?" she probed.

"You ask a lot of questions." Scott's eyes met hers.

She kept her voice casual. "I'm interested to learn all I can about this house and the family that lived in it. I like family stories. Just indulge me, okay?"

He raised his eyebrows suspiciously.

She smiled at him again, encouraging him to continue by offering yet another question. "Does anyone live in the starter house now?"

"My cousin, Nancy, does. She's Mary and Leo's daughter."

"And is she just married and starting out?" Vivian asked, charmed by that idea.

"No, unfortunately, Nancy is divorced." He scowled. "She married a resort salesman who proved to be unable to stop selling him-self to every female who crossed his path even after he was married. You get my drift?"

"Yes," she answered him. "He cheated on her and he hurt her."

"That he did. And he also hurt two great little boys, Jordan and Martin. After trying many times to give Doug Wilkes yet another chance, Nancy finally left him and came on back home here with the boys. She moved into the starter house so she and the boys could have their own little place and a little privacy from Mary and Leo."

"Is she alright?"

"Very much so now. Thanks for asking." Scott reached down to pick up a stick in their path, snapping it and tossing the pieces over the fence beside them. "In fact, I was the lucky one out of the separation. Nancy is a terrific office manager. That's how she met Doug in the first place; she was managing the resort office where he was working in sales. I had just bought the camp when she moved back home four years ago, so I hired her to run the camp office. She's great; I don't know what I would do without her."

Scott sent another of those quick, charming smiles Vivian's way. "Keeping books, organizing records, and running an office day to day are not my strong suits." He shrugged. "But they are Nancy's. She's been a real asset to me. You'll meet her and the boys eventually, and I'm sure you'll meet Aunt Mary and Uncle Leo, too. They are your next-door neighbors on the left, although there's a longer walk from the farmhouse over to their place than to mine. I'm more directly on your right."

He kicked a stone as he walked along. "To be quite frank, Vivian. There aren't many neighbors down here on Stoney Mill Loop. It's pretty quiet around here. There's just the camp, this farm, Leo and Mary's place, and the Greenes' house on around the bend in the loop."

Vivian caught the new name Scott mentioned. "Are the Greenes your family, too?"

"No. They're a young couple. Haven't lived here long." He stopped to lean up against the fence beside the barn now. "He's a doctor. Just opened a practice up the highway. She's got a child and stays home right now. I'm sure you'll meet Ellen and Quint soon. Actually, if you know anything about country people, you'll know that most everyone nearby will eventually find some excuse or other to stop by to see you. They'll bring a jar of honey, a cake, a welcome plant, or just stop around to see if there is anything they can do for you."

She smiled at him. "That's nice that people are so cordial and welcoming."

"Well, that's one way to look at it," he replied. "Some people might see that type of country custom as simply nosey. It certainly makes it really hard to have any secrets or any privacy around here. People in the valley have a way of finding out things."

A little chill passed over Vivian at those words. She thought about her own reasons for being here and her attention wandered away from Scott for a moment as she did. When she came back to herself, she found Scott watching her thoughtfully.

"Hope you don't have any secrets you want to hide." His words sounded probing and he seemed to be watching her expression with interest now.

She walked past him to peer in the barn door instead of answering him.

Posing another question, she purposefully shifted the conversation to a more neutral topic. "Do you keep any animals here?"

"Not now," he answered her, allowing her to change the subject on him. "My grandparents used to keep a few cows, horses, and chickens here, but after Poppy Stuart died, Gramma let them go. There are only farm machines and storage items here, now, and maybe a few possums and bunnies hopping through."

That boyish smile lit up his face again. "You may see those guys sometimes, Vivian. They're not very fearful of people. Sometimes the possums come right up near the porch in the evening, but they won't bother you. They're just curious."

Vivian struggled not to stare at him like a silly school girl. He was so cute and he was really hard to ignore. Especially when he smiled. He smiled so easily and freely, too, and it literally lit up his face every time he did so, crinkling up the corners of his eyes. Yet his body movements were so relaxed and easy, like he didn't have a care in the world. Honestly, he was so charming without any effort, Vivian thought. She wondered if he had always been that way.

Scott was walking along the fencerow beside the barn now, and he stopped the journey just where the fence line started to turn the corner. He pointed down a well-worn path that followed on beyond the turn of the fence. "If you followed this path on along the fence line and away from the barn, you'd soon start up a trail through the woods and then connect to another trail that winds over the lower ridge of the mountain. The back line of the property is up that way. We'll walk there someday, if you like, and I'll show you Slippery Rock Falls beyond the ridge. There's a great cascade further up above that, as well."

Scott turned around suddenly to start back and ran right into Vivian who was following almost too closely behind him.

"Oops!" she said, starting to laugh. But her laugh stopped quickly as the electricity, that always seemed to happen whenever Scott got too close to her, prickled up her spine again and then simply flooded over her.

Almost stunned, she looked up into Scott's face and found him grinning over her reaction. He obviously was delighted. Vivian backed up, annoyed with herself that her emotions could be so easily discerned by him.

Whatever in the world was wrong with her? Her heart was hammering again. Her breathing had quickened, and all over a silly bump against a man.

She really ought to have more self-control than this. After all, he was just another pretty boy. She'd seen enough of those in her day. She couldn't imagine why she was letting herself be so affected by this one.

She turned away, trying to pretend that nothing was different and trying to ignore the steady gaze of Scott's hazel eyes on her. Vivian felt a flash of irritation. She didn't like being uncomfortable in social situations. And Scott made her uncomfortable. It seemed like the man was always watching her, assessing her actions and reactions like a biologist watching an interesting bug.

He looked away then, giving her a moment to recover.

"Do you know what these marks mean on the fence rail here?" He pointed out some carved marking on the fence posts, pretending like nothing in particular had just happened between them.

Vivian felt relieved that Scott wasn't going to pursue the obvious intimacy of their situation. She turned to study the markings carved in the wood, giving herself a little more opportunity to regulate her breathing and get herself back in control.

"These little circle marks here?" She traced her fingers over two little circles with a line underneath that someone had obviously scratched into the fence with a knife.

"Yeah, that one and these other little cross marks here on the rail below it." He pointed out a second set of marks. "The hobos and travelers put these marks on the fences a long time ago. The circle signs with the bars underneath mean *You can sleep in this farmer's barn.* The cross marks mean *Good place for a handout.*"

"Really?" she asked, fascinated as she always was with new knowledge and almost forgetting her discomfort of a minute ago.

"Yes, really," Scott answered, teasing her a little for her enthusiasm. "Foot travelers through the countryside used to leave marks on the fence posts to let other travelers know what kind of folks lived in the houses along the way. This was especially common during the depression years when times were hard and when so many people were on the road trying to find a better life somewhere."

"So these signs told travelers your grandparents were good people who would give them a handout and let them sleep in the barn over night if they needed to," Vivian replied thoughtfully.

"That's it," he answered.

"What if the hoboes wanted to warn someone about bad people? What would they put then?"

Scott shrugged. "Well, I've seen danger signs a few times, like a poison sign mark. Once I saw a dagger carved in a fence. Poppy Stuart said it meant *Dishonest man, don't ask for work.*"

"How absolutely fascinating." Vivian smiled in delight, beginning to study the fence rail to look for more markings she might not have seen.

"Well, only you would think so. It doesn't seem to take much of a story to get you whipped up and interested." Looking up, she found him watching her.

"Well, I am a teacher and a bit of a writer," she returned. "We teachers and writers like stories. We like to hear them and we like to tell them."

"And what do you write, Vivian Delaney?"

"Academic articles and things." Her reply was evasive. "You know, like most professors write about the things they research and teach."

"What do you teach in college?"

"British Literature, English composition, that sort of thing. You know." She shrugged nonchalantly.

"No, I don't know," he answered her teasingly. "It's not my field, so you'll have to enlighten me a little more, professor."

"Well, besides teaching basic English composition, usually for freshmen, and a British Literature sequel that sophomores or juniors take, I also teach an upper level course on Victorian Women Writers, plus courses in European Folklore."

"Ahhh," Scott said. "That latter sounds more like the sort of person who would be interested in the fence carvings of hobo travelers."

"I do like legends and stories." She smiled at him. He really did have a nice side.

"What did you do your big dissertation on, Dr. Delaney? I know enough about doctoral studies to know you have to do some sort of major research work before they'll give you your PhD."

"I wrote my dissertation on Andrew Lang. He was a Scottish writer of the late 1800s and early 1900s best known for the incredible number of folktales, ballads, and stories he collected and published."

"The fairytale guy?" he asked her. "The one who wrote those color books?"

Her face lit up. "That's the one." She was surprised that Scott even knew who Andrew Lang was. Most people didn't.

"Lang was fond of naming his collection books after colors," she told him, warming to her subject. "Like *The Red Book of Heroes* or *The Blue Fairy Book*. He published many fairytale book collections, thirteen with color names like the yellow, red, violet, and green fairy books ...." She trailed off and shrugged.

"I can see you getting excited about something like that." He smiled at her. "Are you doing some more of that kind of work while you're here on your sabbatical?"

"Sort of," she answered, evasive once again, and turning to study the fence rail markings while she talked. "I'm really doing some work on several things while I'm here. Including project work for my editor. Editors have things they need you to work on sometimes for a publisher. Specific assignments, you know. This project was going to take a little more time than I could manage while teaching full-time. So I took some time off."

Vivian turned to find Scott studying her again. He made her nervous the way he was always watching her.

"I need to get on to work now." He looked at his watch. "I have a plumber coming over to the camp this morning to check out some problems we've had from the winter."

"Oh, of course," Vivian replied lightly, trailing along behind him back toward the house, glad of a change of subject once again. "I'm sorry I took so much of your time this morning. But I appreciate you showing me around."

As they came closer to the house, Fritzi came frisking out to meet them.

"Well, where have you been?" Vivian reached down to pet the little collie, who then circled around Scott's legs until he properly acknowledged her, as well. They found the cat, Dearie, curled up asleep on one of the front porch rockers, but she didn't do more than open an eye sleepily in welcome as they came up onto the farmhouse porch.

"I appreciate the breakfast, too, Scott," Vivian added politely, turning to hold out her hand as if to shake hands with him before they parted.

"No problem." Scott avoided taking the hand she offered.

You know, Vivian," he observed. "I've always had a gift for discerning truth from lies. It has come in handy in business and in working with the camp." His eyes narrowed. "You'll excuse me for being impolite, but you're not a very artful liar. I don't know what really brought you all the way from California to Tennessee but I know that it's more than you're telling me. People generally come to isolated places back in the mountains because they're running away from something."

He paused, watching her a moment, a little frown creasing his brow. "You know I operate a children's camp next door, Vivian, and I hope you're running away from something honorable. I'd like you to give some serious thought to telling me what you're really doing here in the mountains, especially before I have my summer campers and counselors coming in here. If it's honorable and not illegal, you'll find that I'll keep it to myself and that your confidence is safe with me. I'm an up-front person, Vivian, and I don't much care for lying as a character trait even for a good reason. It's my belief that generally the truth is always the best story to tell."

Vivian felt the blood drain out of her face. She dropped the hand she had held out to Scott and backed away from him.

"The offer to see the camp later on is still open." He kept his gaze locked on hers. "Take care of the animals, Vivian. I think they're likely to hang around at the farmhouse now that you're here. This place feels more like home to them than mine."

He started away from the farmhouse, and then turned again as an afterthought. "There's a small grocery store near here on the valley highway and a larger one on back toward Sevierville. If you'll stop by the camp office, Nancy will give you a map of the area. It will help you in getting around. She also can tell you anything you need to know about the surrounding area. She grew up around Sevierville, and she's a native."

He studied Vivian again with those thoughtful eyes.

"I'll see you," he said at last, when she didn't say anything at all in return to him. "You know where to find me."

Vivian stood rooted to the spot until he had walked around the farmhouse out of sight, and then she dropped herself down onto the porch step. She was shaking and seething at how outspoken Scott had been. But she knew she was scared, too.

She'd chosen to come so far away from home so that no one would be likely to ask questions about why she was here. So that no one was likely to probe into her personal life. Betsy assured her that people wouldn't question her story of taking a sabbatical from college teaching. "Professors do that all the time," Betsy said.

Now the first person Vivian had gotten to know was already questioning her story. And, blatantly, calling her a liar. He'd even used the word liar to her face. Vivian fumed at that. He had no right to be that forthright, or that accusatory. As if she was some common criminal that might hurt the children at his camp! Her pride burned at that thought, especially. What could she do? She didn't know. She'd obviously have to think of something else to tell him. He was going to expect a further explanation. Vivian sighed deeply.

"Lord, what am I going to tell him?" she asked in a silent prayer. "I don't want everyone here to know about me. If I tell everyone all about myself, there will have been no point in coming here. And I need this time away."

Vivian sat quietly with her head in her hands hoping for an answer to her prayers. No answer came right away, but Vivian wasn't overly discouraged. Something would come to her in time, she thought. It always did. God would help her know how to handle this.

There just had to be a way to make this work out. Surely she didn't miss it totally in coming to Tennessee at this time. It seemed so right when the idea had come to her. Besides, she wanted to search to see if she had any old family ties here. Her father had always talked about this area, and she knew he'd grown up here. Perhaps there were still some Delaneys around somewhere. This was another little piece of her mission in being here.

She sighed again and got up resolutely. She'd been through worse. She'd get through this. She'd call Betsy and get her ideas on what to do. Betsy always had good advice.

Her natural optimism began to return to her as she went into the farmhouse. She liked it here. Despite the problems with Scott, she loved the house and the area. It stirred her creative juices in a way she hadn't expected. It was going to be a good place to write. Surely, she could work this thing out with Scott Jamison. And maybe she needed to work on her storyline about being here a little more carefully before she told it again. Evidently, it wasn't very believable as it was.

Chapter 7

$\mathcal{B}$Y LATE AFTERNOON, VIVIAN HAD calmed down and settled in more comfortably at the farmhouse. She had unpacked the rest of her suitcases and boxes, set up her office in the upstairs sitting room, and gone over to the market on the highway to pick up some groceries. After her shopping trip, she also made some needed phone calls. She talked to Betsy, who had given her some sensible tips on how to handle this new situation with Scott Jamison, and, together, they worked out a better story to present to the locals who quizzed her about her background.

Throughout the morning, Vivian fumed and worried over the situation with Scott. His harsh words often replayed through her mind, as did his acts of thoughtfulness and his obvious attraction to her. What a mess. Her feelings about him were totally confused and she had no idea what he really thought about her. Vivian liked to get things, and people, tidied up in her mind, but this situation was one that just wouldn't sort itself out readily. By noon, she'd decided that some hard work was the best answer to get the whole Scott scenario out of her mind for a while.

Now, at nearly three, she was sitting out on the front porch with her laptop, writing. The porch curled all the way around the front section of the farmhouse, and there was a sturdy metal table toward one corner of the covered porch with several cushioned chairs that matched. This made a great outdoor office, and, besides, Vivian thought it was simply too pretty a day to work inside.

A huge golden forsythia bloomed just below her table on the porch and Vivian could hear the bees humming around the blooms on the bushes. It was great background music and she found her thoughts were flying as she wrote.

A car coming up the driveway interrupted her flow of thought, and soon two older women were getting out of a silver luxury sedan. Both waved cheerily.

"You must be Vivian," called the woman who had been driving. "I'm Stella Jamison with Jamison Realty - the realtor you've been communicating with, dear. And this is Mary Jamison." She gestured to the other woman who was climbing out of the other side of the car.

The women looked remarkably alike, both blond, still relatively slim for their years and almost the same height. Both had fresh, peachy ivory complexions in stark comparison to Vivian's olive skin and outdoor tan.

Vivian closed out her computer program as they came up on the porch to join her. This was Scott's mother, she thought nervously, pasting a welcoming smile on her face and wondering how this meeting would go.

"Spring is certainly here," commented Stella, looking around and smiling. "And the old place is starting to bloom out already."

"Yes, I really need to get over here to get a start from a few of Gramma Jamison's plants before too long," Mary added. "You know the volunteers are always popping up this time of year. It's a good time to transplant before things get too big."

Stella put a white box down on the table as she sat down. "We went up to Auntie Em's for lunch before we came, dear. And we brought some drinks and one of Em's homemade desserts over here to share with you."

Mary giggled like a girl. "You'll just die and go to heaven over Em's triple layer carrot cake. Stella and I got a whole cake so you could keep the rest." She opened the box. "I'm going in the house to get us a knife and some glasses for these colas. We got diet soda to compensate for all the calories in the cake, dear, so we can all say we're watching our figures." She laughed merrily at her own little joke over this, and Vivian started to wonder if these two women weren't both just a little light-minded.

"Scott told me about what happened last night when you came," Stella said to her candidly after Mary had left. "That must have been terribly frightening for you, dear. I'm so sorry you had to meet our family that way. Men are so terribly impulsive sometimes. Especially the Jamison men. I hope you're not dreadfully bitter toward us for all of this. And I hope that boy of mine came over here this morning and offered you an apology, too. He certainly owed you one."

Vivian found it hard to know which of her comments she should reply to first.

"Scott did come by with his regrets," she answered at last, as Stella settled comfortably into a chair at the table. "He was also thoughtful enough to bring breakfast and to help me find the cof-feepot, which went a long way toward helping me get over the night before."

Stella laughed. "I can hardly function before my coffee in the morning."

Mary came back with a knife, several small plates, and three glasses of ice on a small tray. "Don't you just love all this blue Delft-ware in Gramma Jamison's house?" She set out three china plates, all in patterned blue floral prints. "Really, Stella, we needed some-one to stay here at the house just to keep the Delftware safe." She laughed heartily at her own little joke again.

"It's a beautiful collection," Vivian commented, relieved that the conversation was going so well. Obviously, Scott had not confided his suspicions about her character and honesty to his mother.

Mary sat down in a chair beside Stella's. "Gramma Jamison just adored Delft and any blueware, and she collected it for years."

"Mary," Stella interrupted. "Vivian told me that Scott did get over here to apologize to her this morning."

"Well, good." Mary nodded, obviously pleased to learn that. "That whole episode must have been dreadful for you, Vivian. Especially with Scott and Hershel wielding guns around. I don't know why men always think they have to get guns involved in everything. They're just such violent creatures sometimes, don't you think?"

The two women chatted on together while cutting the cake and pouring out the diet sodas.

"You know, you two look a lot alike," Vivian finally put in.

Stella smiled. "Oh, honey, we're sisters. Didn't Scott tell you?"

"No." Vivian shook her head. "I think he just mentioned that you were married to brothers."

"Well, that, too." Stella looked thoughtful. "There were four of those Jamison boys and all of them so good looking. I met Franklin when I took a job in his real estate office. Lord, that place was a mess when I first came. Franklin had just gotten the business off the ground and he'd been doing most of the office work himself and hiring temps when he needed any day help at the office. I organized that place from top to bottom the first week and then I organized myself right into his life." She said the last with a tinkling laugh. "Lord, he was a tall and handsome man. Still is. And I think the Jamison men age so well, don't you agree, Mary?"

Mary nodded.

"I met Leo at Stella and Franklin's wedding," Mary told Vivian, picking up the tale. "It took me a year of finagling before I finally got him to ask me out. And the rest is history. Leo and I have two children, a boy and a girl, and Stella and Franklin have three boys."

"Isn't it your daughter that lives in the starter house and works with Scott's camp?" Vivian asked conversationally.

"Yes, that's my Nancy." Mary's pleasant face clouded. "She married a handsome scoundrel that we all took to at the start, before we realized he had no sense of commitment toward a marriage. It was really hurtful for Nancy, but she is doing better now."

Stella reached out to pat Mary's hand. "I'm always hoping there will be someone else nice for her out there. Nancy deserves another chance at happiness."

"You don't have to be married to be happy," Vivian offered, and then realized from the faces of Stella and Mary that she had not said quite the right thing.

"Well." Mary raised her eyebrows. "Careers are nice, dear, and I know the young girls really like those today. But a career doesn't keep you warm at night." She laughed at her own joke again and Stella joined her.

"We don't mean to tease you." Stella sent Vivian an appealing smile. "But we've been very happy with our Jamison men. And women of our generation were more interested in home and family, I suppose. Family always came first before career then."

"But you've always worked, too," Vivian reminded Stella, seeing a bit of a contradiction in her words. "Scott said you have always worked in the realty office with Franklin."

"Well, yes, I suppose I have." Stella seemed surprised at the idea of her job at Franklin's agency being thought of as a career.

"Have you worked also?" Vivian asked Mary.

Stella answered for her. "Mary will say no, dear, but she's a caterer. It's always Mary that we get to do all the showers, wedding planning, and special events around here. She's just wonderful with it."

"But I seldom do it for money," Mary argued. "So you couldn't really call it a career. I just so enjoy planning and arranging things that I always find myself involved somehow whenever something is happening. Also it gives me the most marvelous excuse to shop and spend someone else's money." She laughed merrily again at her own humor and Stella laughed along with her.

These two are a case, Vivian thought to herself in amusement.

"Now, dear, you'll have to tell us all about yourself." Stella leaned forward, ready for a good gossip. "All we know is that you're here on a sabbatical from your teaching to write some sort of book and that you work with Betsy Picardi. Franklin and I are so fond of Betsy."

She turned to Mary and added, " Betsy Picardi and her family have stayed several times at our rental cabins up in the mountains and Betsy is just the most delightful person."

Vivian took a breath. She planned to do better with her story this time.

"I'm fond of Betsy, too," she said, plunging in. "And, actually, what you know about me already is just about all that there is to know that's of any importance. I was raised by two professors, and it seemed logical that I became one, too. I was an adopted child. I lost my own mother when I was nine, and I lost my father even earlier. He was in the military and was killed abroad."

"Oh, how tragic for you, dear." Stella shook her head sympathetically.

"Yes, but I was lucky." Vivian smiled. "Dorothy and Roger Owen took me into their home after my mother died."

She'd made up that last name for Dorothy and Roger simply on the spur of the moment. Being creative was certainly a useful gift at times.

"Dorothy and Roger couldn't have any children of their own," she continued. "And they gave me a good life. Delaney is actually my family name, though, and I like to use it now. Vivian Leigh Delaney. I was hoping in part to try to find some of my relatives by coming to Tennessee for this sabbatical year. I can remember mother always telling me my father's people were from around here. But I never met any of them. After my mother died, no one knew of any names here to contact. My mother didn't have any family left I could go to. So I went to the Owens."

"Delaney, Delaney." Stella repeated the name out loud thoughtfully while she was thinking. "There's something familiar about that name, dear, but I can't remember any particular contacts just now. Can you, Mary?"

"No, not right off," answered Mary. "But we'll ask around for you, Vivian. It's always good to track down your roots and know your people."

Stella and Mary began to talk about family then and about genealogical ties they had to this family or that in the valley.

Vivian felt an instant sense of relief as the conversation shifted. Evidently Stella and Mary had accepted her story on face value. Perhaps she had enough details in it now to satisfy most people and to make it sound believable. Actually, she had added in much more of the truth of her life in this telling. Scott was right. The truth was best whenever one could tell it. She just couldn't afford to tell all of the truth right now.

Chapter 8

*O*VER THE NEXT FEW DAYS, Vivian settled in at the farmhouse, and began to familiarize herself with the community. Stella had brought her a map of the area at her visit, and Mary and Stella had filled her in on where the closest large grocery store and shopping centers were. While out exploring, Vivian drove around the local streets and learned the small shops and stores that were nearest to her. She discovered several places to eat that were not far from the farmhouse, a country buffet restaurant called The Blackbear, Auntie Em's, a little luncheon café close to the entrance of Stoney Mill Road, and an interesting stone restaurant set back along a stretch of cascades along Cove Creek called The Creekside. She'd tried them all when she had been out and about.

March seemed to be offering up an abundance of sunny days, and Vivian often did her writing out on the front porch. She was writing on her laptop out on the porch today. And she was even wearing shorts, the day was so warm.

Scott was right in telling her that many of the local people would come to call on her. Each day some new visitor appeared but Scott did not come again. Once she saw him out in the yard. He played with the animals for a while and got something out of the barn, but he didn't come up to the house. Vivian supposed she should be relieved about that, but instead, she found herself annoyed that he didn't even stop by to say hello.

As she looked up from her laptop now, she saw a young woman coming across the yard from the log bridge at Deep Hollow Creek. She had short brown hair and was wearing cut-off jeans and a T-shirt. Beside her skipped a small girl with flaxen blond hair caught up in a ponytail.

"Don't get up," the woman called. "We'll come up on the porch."

Vivian closed out her computer while they climbed up the stairs.

"I'm Ellen Greene." The young woman held out her hand in greeting as she reached Vivian's table. "And this is Chelsey, my daughter, who has just turned five."

Vivian reached out to take Ellen's hand. "I'm Vivian Delaney."

"I heard you'd come," Ellen said. "I've been dying to get over to see you, but Chelsey was sick with a cold and that kept me in for a while."

Chelsey grinned and hung back a little behind her mother's legs.

"Since when have you been shy, Miss Chelsey Greene?" her mother teased her. "Why don't you give our new neighbor the gift we brought her?"

The child held out a little basket. "It's our soaps, Miss New Neighbor." Her voice had a childish lisp but she gave Vivian a squinty smile of greeting.

Vivian smiled back at her.

"I make homemade soaps," Ellen explained. "I brought you a variety to try."

"How wonderful." Vivian started looking eagerly through the colorful bars of soap - each packed in excelsior inside the wire basket. "Thanks to both of you."

Ellen settled down in one of the porch chairs, propping her feet up on the empty chair across from it.

"Can I go swing on the swing?" asked Chelsey excitedly, jumping a little on one foot and then on the other. "Please, please, please."

Ellen waved a hand in answer. "Yes. But stay where I can see you."

Chelsey headed across the yard toward an old wooden swing hanging from a huge maple tree in the front yard. Fritzi trotted after her to keep her company.

Ellen brushed a loose strand of hair behind her ear. "Chelsey loves that swing. She's always asking to come over here to Mamie's and swing. It's hard for her to understand that Mamie's not here anymore. She misses her."

"I think everyone misses Mamie," Vivian offered. "She must have been such a remarkable person."

"She was, and as good as gold. I spent a lot of nice times out here on this porch talking to Mamie. One of her favorite sayings was *'Good porches make good friends.'*"

Vivian smiled. "That saying is on a sampler just inside the doorway."

"I remember, and I love that sampler," Ellen confided, smiling back. "In fact, I love all of Mamie's samplers. Did you know she wrote most of the sayings on them herself? Another favorite of mine says: *Yellow and blue like sun and sky; make the days pass blissfully by.*"

"That one's in the front parlor," Vivian recalled.

"Mamie said it was her own personal philosophy for having her house all decorated in blues and yellows. She said yellow and blue make a person feel happy."

Vivian grinned at that. "She has a point, you know. There is something about those colors around you all day that lifts the spirit."

The girls talked companionably about small things for a few minutes, getting acquainted.

"God, I'm glad you're here," Ellen confided at last. "I really needed a woman friend, and it will be wonderful to not be the only educated, professional woman around here anymore. They call me *That Pharmacist Woman with All Them Science Degrees.*" She wrinkled her nose. "I earned that exalted title because I have an undergraduate double-major in chemistry and physics and another master's degree in pharmacy. And then, I guess, because I worked as a hospital pharmacist in Knoxville until Chelsey was born. Big deal. It's only two degrees, for heaven's sake."

Ellen stopped and made a face. "I know it may sound awful and snobby to you for me to talk like this. But so many people around here think it's downright queer for a woman to have degrees in chemistry and pharmacy. Mr. McFee told me one day that I had 'an awful lot of book-learning for a woman.' And Mrs. Rayburn asked me if they 'really let women major in things like chemistry and physics today.' She said she thought science-stuff like that was only for boys."

Vivian muzzled a giggle. She understood the feeling of being thought odd for having a lot of education.

"Don't be so quick to laugh too hard, Vivian Delaney." Ellen wrinkled her nose. "They're already calling you *That Professor Doctor Woman* that lives down at the Jamison place. Everyone gets a label around here of one sort or another. Your other label is *That Woman that Writes Things*."

Vivian laughed out loud then. "I suppose I'd rather be labeled for those two things than for some other awful thing. I guess you're also *That Woman that Makes Soap*."

"Yes, I am," Ellen admitted with a grin. "But that one carries more respect around here. Valley people honor crafting and people who are skilled with their hands in the old crafts. However, I have to admit, as much as I love it here, that I sometimes get hungry to be around someone who doesn't think it's peculiar to have a few degrees."

"So what brought you here to the valley?"

"Quintin and I both got restless for a less yuppie suburban life. Quint's a family physician. He wanted to start his own practice, and he learned that the only doctor in this area was retiring and selling out his practice. We could have lived closer to Knoxville and the city life there, but we started looking around here at country houses in the valley. When we found the old Graham place we just fell in love with it. Have you seen it?"

"Is that the brick house set back from the road past Leo and Mary's place?"

"That's it." Ellen smiled with pleasure. "The house is only a block or two from your place, and shorter, if you cut across the creek instead of taking the road. It's called Maplewood, because the house is set back in a grove of maple trees. It's a wonderful place, a big two story with a white-pillared porch, rambling rooms, and tall ceilings. It felt so much more like a real home after living in the McMansions suburb where we lived before. Ugh!"

Ellen made a face. "All the houses there were so much alike. It was almost creepy."

"I'll have to walk over to see your place one day," Vivian said. "I love old houses, too. They have so much more character."

"Well, this is a fine one. And there is a big barn and a couple of sheds behind the house. That appealed to me, too, because of my soap-making."

"How did you get into doing that?"

"As a hobby." Ellen shrugged. "I'd done undergraduate work in chemistry, if you remember, and I've always liked to cook up things on the stove." She laughed. "I've blown up a few things, too, experimenting. I got into soap-making as something safer to play with after I was married. The process of it is really chemical. Here in the country with the barn and sheds behind the house, I've been able to expand a little hobby into a small business."

She pulled one of the soaps out of the basket and showed Vivian the label. "I call my soaps Greenellen Soaps. You know, like Ellen Greene reversed. This one is Lavender soap."

Ellen passed the bar of soap over to Vivian. "After the basic process of soapification, that's getting the soap started with oils or fats, plus distilled water and lye, you can add whatever colors, fragrance, and textures you like to make the bars pretty and unique. I added lavender buds for texture to this one. When I can find them, I add hibiscus to get a natural purple color or I use artificial colorings. The lavender oil I use is primarily what gives this soap its wonderful sweet scent. See?"

"Ummmm." Vivian held the bar up to her nose to sniff. "What are the other soaps you make?"

"Sunflower, Vanilla, Peppermint – about thirty different kinds." She smiled. "I've put a variety of the soaps I make in your little basket there. Plus a container of my liquid soap I use for dishes. You'll like that, and it's better for your hands than the store bought kind."

Vivian looked through the soaps. "Did you make the little labels yourself, Ellen?"

"No. I had a graphic artist friend make me a stencil stamp with that little herbal logo and the fancy lettering of Greenellen. I couldn't have created that myself. I'm real inventive but not very artistic. With the stamper, all I have to do is stamp my design in dark green ink on the brown wrappers I put around each bar."

Vivian studied one of the wrappers. "It's a nice cottage industry look."

"Thanks," Ellen said. "I usually make soap on Tuesdays and Thursdays. If you're interested, you can come over and watch for a while."

"I'll do that."

Ellen called out to Chelsey to check on her, while Ellen continued looking through the soaps. She picked up a bar of soap swirled in green.

"What's this pretty one?" she asked, when Ellen sat down again.

"That's my Camp Soap." She grinned. "It was one of my first experimental soaps and now it's one of my best sellers. It's my secret recipe. It has no fragrance and no fatty oil build-up and it's great to help keep the bugs away. I work a natural repellent oil blend into it. Scott Jamison started letting me sell it in the camp store at first, so I named it Camp Soap. Now I sell it in hiking and outdoor stores, too, and in most of my shop accounts."

She paused. "Scott Jamison is great, you know. Have you met him?"

Vivian nodded.

"He has a wonderful way with kids and he is so personable. I've never known an easier, more natural person to be around. Quint and I just love Scott. It's incredible what he's done with the old Taylor camp, too. Have you seen it?"

"No, I haven't gone over yet." She dropped her eyes, not wanting Ellen to read her thoughts.

"Well, I'm surprised Scott hasn't dragged you over there already. He just loves to show off the camp, and he has every right to be proud of it. Chelsey is already asking me when she'll be old enough to go."

Vivian looked up. "What's the earliest camp age?"

"Seven years old or getting ready to start the second grade. So Chelsey has got a ways to go. But Scott's so sweet. He takes her around the camp and lets her see where she'll stay when she's old enough. And he lets her play in the pool when the camp isn't in session. She just worships him and so do Nancy's boys, Martin and Jordan. Martin is seven now and he's getting ready to start camp this summer for the first time. Jordan and Chelsey are only five and they are just green with envy."

Ellen had propped her feet up on the table while she talked. She had on old, battered tennis shoes with no socks. Ellen was probably five six to Vivian's five eight. She had a little sturdier build than Vivian's but looked fit and healthy. Her hair was cropped in a short cut and her face was clear of make-up, with a slight sprinkling of freckles across her nose. She was unaffected and natural, and Vivian liked her.

"Got anything to drink in the house?" Ellen asked her.

"Colas and tea. And some chocolate chip cookies I picked up at Auntie Em's yesterday. Want some?"

"Tea would be great." Ellen grinned. "And Chelsey will want tea and some cookies, too, if it's alright. Look in Mamie's pantry and see if you can find Chelsey one of those plastic glasses Mamie used to keep in there for the kids. I don't like her wagging real glassware around. It's too likely to get broken as active as she is."

They all shared a snack then. Afterwards, Ellen helped Chelsey tie the dandelions she'd collected into a dandelion crown to wear around her head. When Ellen suggested making a necklace to match, Chelsey ran out to gather more dandelions out in the yard. This gave the two women time to visit a little bit longer.

"How did you end up here in the valley?" Ellen asked.

Vivian filled her in on the same details she'd given to Stella and Mary.

Ellen listened with an easy interest, her feet propped up on the porch rail. "Well, to my way of thinking, this is a great place for a sabbatical." She smiled broadly. "And I'm certainly glad you'll be right next door to me."

Vivian smiled back, relief sweeping over her. So far only Scott had challenged and questioned her about her reasons for being here. Everyone else was very gracious and accepting, just as Betsy had suggested they would be. This puzzled Vivian. And she still wasn't sure what she wanted to say to Scott at their next meeting.

"All right, tell me who's been over to see you," Ellen demanded. "Besides Scott, that is. And besides Scott's mother and Mary Jamison. Mary has already told me she stopped by and that you were, in her words, 'just a darling girl.'" She said the last in exactly Mary's voice tone, and Vivian couldn't help giggling over it.

"Well." Vivian searched her memory. "Mrs. McFee and Mrs. Rayburn came by one day. They brought me great homemade jelly and pickles. And Mr. and Mrs. Miller came by to tell me if I was ever sick that they would deliver anything I needed from up at their market on the highway. I thought that was so nice. Mary brought her husband Leo over. Clyde and Edith Harper stopped by. He told me he mowed and kept up the property here and over at the camp. Clyde didn't have a lot to say, but his wife Edith was real chatty, and she brought me a great pound cake. Then yesterday, the minister's wife, Susan James, came over and brought her mother with her. Her name was Ruth Hart, I think. She said she used to be a really good friend of Mamie's …"

"And they invited you to church, of course," interrupted Ellen. "You'll have to go to church somewhere, you know, or you'll get a reputation of being a heathen around here. You're not a heathen, are you? Although I'll still like you even if you are." She gave Vivian a teasing look. "I'll like you even if they start calling you *That Woman That's a Heathen.*"

"Well, I'm not in the heathen category, so don't worry." Vivian laughed. "In fact, being by the camp here has reminded me that I first came to know the Lord in a meaningful way at a church camp up in the California mountains. I think mountains have always been special to me ever since. It seems like you can always feel God's presence so strongly in the mountains. Do you notice that, too, living here by the Smokies, or is it just me?"

"You, me, and a lot of other people." Ellen shrugged. "I think it's one of the things that draws people to come to live here in this area. Don't you?"

"Well, I like that idea better than another one I heard," Vivian observed, remembering Scott's comment that most people who came to the mountains were running away from something.

"If you want to go to a great place for a mountain-top experience, we can hike to the top of Buckeye Knob one day. It's that first tall mountain ridge you can see behind the farm. It's really gorgeous up there. You can sit on this big rock at the top of the knob and look out all over the valley."

"That would be fun, Ellen. I really want to see a lot of places around the area while I'm here."

"Well, I'd better warn you that if we take Chelsey, it's less likely to be serene and peaceful." Ellen laughed and pointed to Chelsey hanging upside down by her knees from a big tree limb in the front yard.

As if on cue, Chelsey's excited shrieks pealed out across the yard.

"Scott! Scott!!" they heard her exclaim as she dropped out of the tree and started to race across the yard to the tall man coming toward them.

A big smile flashed across his face as he caught sight of the little girl and soon he was picking her up to swing her around in the air. Something tugged at Vivian's heart at the sight.

"I told you she was crazy about Scott." Ellen waved a greeting at Scott from the porch. "Look at how he plays with her. He's such a terrific guy. You just wait until you see him with his campers this summer. They adore him and follow him around the camp like he was the pied piper. He has such a way with the kids. Truly charismatic."

Ellen stopped to motion Scott to come up on the porch before continuing. She grinned at Vivian then. "And he's darned handsome, too, don't you think?"

Watching him, Vivian had to agree in spite of herself. Her heart had started to pump already just at the sight of him.

Chapter 9

Scott tossed Chelsey up on his back and let her ride to the porch with him, bucking her every once in a while to make her shriek with delight.

"Hi, heartbreaker," Ellen said, getting up to give him a kiss on the cheek. "I haven't seen you for awhile."

He grinned at her. "That's because you haven't asked me over to dinner lately. If you want to feed me tomorrow night, I'm yours for the entire evening."

"You're on." Ellen laughed. "Quint's been looking for an excuse to cook ribs out on the grill. You can come help him with the basting."

"I'll be there." He slipped Chelsey off his back and watched her run back out to the swing. "What can I bring?"

"A bottle of wine and Vivian, if she'll come join us," Ellen said. "She hasn't been over to the house yet. And I'm dying to have Quint meet her."

Scott raised his eyebrows and looked Vivian's way. "It's fine with me if it's okay with Vivian." He gave Vivian a *'now it's in your turf'* look.

He watched as she hesitated, but her hesitation was only for a minute.

"I'd be delighted to come." She gave Scott a smile and a serene *'so there'* look in return.

Obviously, Scott observed, Vivian hadn't told Ellen anything about their little discussion of a few days ago. That surprised him. Most girls babbled out any little upset that came their way to anyone who would listen, particularly to another female. As far as Scott knew, none of Vivian's other visitors had been told anything about their altercation, either. Even his mother and his Aunt Mary had had nothing to tell, and those two always loved a good gossip story. Vivian had actually been amazingly discreet. A cool professional right down to her toenails, Scott thought.

"I'm so glad your mother found Vivian to stay here at the farmhouse." Ellen patted an empty chair, encouraging Scott to sit down. "She's fantastic. We had the best time getting acquainted today. I decided we're going to be great friends while she's staying here. I'll probably grieve terribly when she goes home next year and then mope around morbidly for weeks afterwards."

Scott grinned as he settled into the chair beside Ellen. One of the things he'd always liked about Ellen Greene was her candor and her quirky, offbeat sense of humor. She was always so much fun to be with.

He'd met Ellen and Quint the first week they'd moved into Maplewood, and they'd hit it off right from the start. Quint was a comfortable man to be around, and Quint and Ellen loved to entertain and have fun. Scott spent a lot of time with them whenever he could.

"Scott, I can't believe you haven't taken Vivian around the camp," Ellen fussed. "It's so great over there. Besides, I want her to come sit out at the pool with me when you open it up and maybe see if she can beat me across the lake in a canoe race." She turned to look at Vivian then with a mischievous sparkle in her eyes. " I do hope you learned canoeing at your summer camps, Vivian?"

"Yes, I did." She looked up happily, a faint smile playing on her lips. "But it's been a long time, Ellen, and I doubt I'd be much competition in a canoe race after all these years."

"Oh well, I'll give you a head start until you get back in form. And wait until you see Pine Lake, Vivian. It's the centerpiece of the whole camp. Honestly, Scott, you've just got to take her over there. It's right next door, and it's silly for me to describe it when she can walk over there and see it for herself."

Scott put out an offer. "We can go over right now if Vivian wants. Martin and Jordan are over at the HQ with Nancy. Chelsey will be glad to see them."

"Don't you dare even mention that idea to her," Ellen threatened. "She's had a nasty little cold, and she's just now feeling well enough to get out at all. I really need to try to get her back to the house now to poke some medicine down her and see if I can induce her to take a nap. If you say one word to her about going over to the camp, I'll never get her back home. So you just wait until after I leave with her and then you can take Vivian on over to the camp. I really want her to see it."

After a few more minutes of talk, Ellen called to Chelsey and then stood up to say her goodbyes.

"I'll see you both tomorrow night. About sixish, if that's alright." She gave Vivian a hug goodbye and then gave Scott one, too.

Pulling back from Scott, she gave him a warning look. "You be nice to Vivian. I want her to be happy here so she won't leave. I am just stoked to have a real woman friend around here at last."

"I'm always nice." Scott offered her one of his charming, public relations smiles.

Ellen put her hands on her hips. "You know what I mean, Scott Jamison. I know all about your fast reputation with the ladies."

She turned to Vivian then and grinned. "You watch out for him. These handsome ones are trouble sometimes."

"I'll be careful." Vivian looked thoughtfully over at Scott. "He looks like the troublesome kind."

Ellen laughed and joked while Scott and Vivian walked her out into the yard to start home with Chelsey.

Chelsey hugged Scott goodbye around the legs and began to whine to stay longer.

Scott pulled her ponytail playfully. "I heard you've had a cold. But you know, Chessy Cat, if you go home, take your medicine and get a nap today, you might be well enough for me to come over to have dinner with you tomorrow night."

"Really? Can he really come?" Chelsey asked Ellen, dancing up and down in front of her with a pleading look. "Can he? Can he?"

"Well, I think so if you'll do the nap and the meds like he said." Ellen gave Scott a smile and a conspiratorial wink. "We can't have

Scott over if you're still sick."

Chelsey studied her shoes for a minute. "I'll be good and do it if Scott can come."

"Well, then, that's great. And I might even invite Vivian to come, too," Ellen added as another incentive.

"Okay." Chelsey considered her. "She must be nice if she lives at Mamie's."

Chelsey looked up at Vivian. "Do you know Mamie?"

Vivian remembered Ellen's words about Chelsey not understanding clearly that Mamie was gone. She smiled at the child. "I've heard only the nicest things about Mamie. And I love Mamie's dollhouse."

"Me, too!" Chelsey said, her eyes brightening up.

"Do you have some dolls at your house?"

"Yes, two baby dolls and two doll beds." She stressed the twos.

"Will you show me those if I come over tomorrow?"

"Yes, and we can play," Chelsey added with enthusiasm.

A little more chatting about dolls and dinner went on, and then Ellen finally got Chelsey started across the yard toward home.

After they'd gotten out of sight, Scott turned to look at Vivian. "You don't have to come over to the camp just because Ellen brought it up."

"I'd be delighted to see the camp," she said, surprising him. "Just let me go put away my laptop and the glasses we used from our snack first."

"I'll help you if I can snitch a cookie and some tea before you put everything away."

Vivian smiled her answer and Scott followed her back up to the house.

After they walked up on the porch, Scott noticed Vivian was quick to pick up the laptop and secure it under her arm before he could make a move to put his hands on it. He wondered about that, but then he got occupied in sampling Auntie Em's chocolate chip cookies and carrying dishes back into the house.

Soon they cut back through the yard behind the farmhouse and headed toward the camp. As they walked along, Scott considered bringing up their conversation from the day before to possibly clear the air, but then he decided against it. She might get into a tiff again if he did, and despite his reservations about her, he still wanted to have more time in her company. He'd thought about her every day, which surprised him. And some of his thoughts had been rather physical ones.

"Here, I'll give you a hand," he said, as they came to the log bridge across the creek. "We've never put a rail here because this stream's not very deep."

Instead of arguing, Vivian let him take her hand to help her across the bridge. Scott avoided looking at her as he did so, afraid she would realize how touching her again affected him. He thought it might be best to play it a little casual today.

"You were right that I would have a lot of visitors," she told him, making an effort at conversation.

"My guess is that you've met most of the people that live close around you now." He grinned at her. "I'd say you've met at least a representative of the McFee family, the Rayburn family, the James family, and the Hart family by this time."

"It must be the valley ritual." Vivian laughed and Scott loved the throaty sound of it. "The only ones you missed mentioning were the Millers and the Harpers. Mr. Harper said he did the mowing and the maintenance for the farm and for your camp. I wanted to be sure that was accurate."

"Yeah, that's right. Clyde Harper is a good man." Scott snapped a dry twig off a tree as he passed. "I was fortunate to get him as maintenance for the camp. He worked with a big contracting business for years, and he can build or fix anything. I'd heard he had retired, gotten bored, and was looking for a part-time job. He's just in his late sixties, and the man works like a trooper. Makes me tired just to watch him some days."

"So tell me about the camp," Vivian prompted.

"Better, I'll show you. Kind of like the old saying, a picture's worth a thousand words. It's better to see it than to hear about it. I'll show you around, and you can ask what you want."

They climbed a well-worn path from out of the woods now. To the right a large log house sat up on a slight hill and down to their left a parking area surrounded an even larger wood structure.

"What are these buildings I can see now?" Vivian gestured.

"Up on the hill to the right is my place, usually called The Director's House by the campers, and down here on our left – where we're stopping first – is the camp business office and the camp store, usually called the HQ - obviously for headquarters."

They swung around to the front of a rustic stone and log building. The building stood just inside the arched camp entrance sign that Vivian had seen from the road the first day she arrived. Inside the HQ, Vivian met Nancy Wilkes, Scott's cousin and office manager, and her two boys, whom she had put to work unboxing items for the store.

"We're getting paid *real* money for working," five-year-old Jordan told Scott proudly.

"That's a dumb thing to say," seven-year-old Martin interjected. "What kind of money did you think we'd get, Jordan? Play money?"

"Martin's making fun of me again, Mom!" Jordan wailed.

"Well, Martin may find he might not get paid anything if he continues that." Nancy offered this response calmly, not even looking up from her paperwork.

"Sorry, Jordan," said Martin quickly.

Martin looked up at Scott with a big smile then. "This will be my camp t-shirt this summer, won't it Scott?" He held up an orange t-shirt with a bear on it, the words Buckeye Knob Camp across the top.

"That's it, kid," Scott said, ruffling his head. "You'll be a Blackbear camper this summer and you'll get to stay over in the cabins behind the lake."

"No fair," grumbled Jordan.

"Your turn will come." Scott gave him an affectionate hug. "And I think you're old enough to help your mother with the camp store some days this summer, if it's alright with her."

"For real?" Jordan asked, brightening up.

"Well, I think you can come over at store hours and we'll see how you do," his mother said, careful not to promise too much, but smiling at Scott with appreciation.

Vivian poked around the camp store for a few minutes while Scott signed papers for Nancy and looked over a few pieces of correspondence she wanted to ask him about.

As they left the HQ a little later and started down the main camp road, Scott talked companionably about the camp. "We're already starting to get applications in for the summer. I've already hired my counselors – some are returning from last year. I'll be doing interviews this month for others. For each camp unit I have here, I hire a college-aged Senior counselor, an older high school Junior counselor, and two junior high or early high school CITs - CIT stands for counselor-in-training. The latter come mostly for the fun and the chance to keep coming to camp after they are too old to be official campers any longer."

"How many counselors do you hire altogether?"

"Counting the CITs, I have 24 counselors, four for each of my six camp units. I believe it's important with a kids' camp that you have enough counselors and that you hire first-class ones. I work hard to get really good, talented people."

Scott had started to lead her around the main loop road in the camp now.

He looked at Vivian questioningly. "Did Martin give you a camp map like I asked him to?"

"Yes," Vivian answered, pulling the pamphlet out of her pocket. She opened it up, pausing a second to look at it. "Cute graphics," she said.

He smiled at her. "Presentation is important. This is the map we send out in our information packets. I wanted it to be eye-catching so it would make people want to come."

"Well, it's colorful and very charming," Vivian told him, offering him one of her slow soft smiles that really melted him. "If I got this, I would want to come here so badly. And what's neat about the map is that you can really use it for finding your way around the camp."

She stopped and studied her map intently for a minute. "That building," she said, pointing excitedly to a large two-storied log building ahead on their right. "That's White Oak Administration building and the other big building after it with the big porches is Spruce Hall where the dining hall is. Is that right, Scott?"

"You're a good map reader," Scott teased, pleased with her enthusiasm and interest.

"Oh, look! Now we're coming up on the lake!" she exclaimed as they walked on. "And just look at it! It's so big! I had no idea such a big lake was so close to me and to the farmhouse. It's simply wonderful."

Pine Lake spread out before them, a broad almost circular lake, big enough for canoeing and a lot of water sports. There was a winding road curling in and out picturesquely around its boundaries.

"You'll have to help me practice with my canoeing so Ellen won't beat me too soundly in a race." Vivian smiled warmly at him, so caught up in her new adventure exploring the camp that she seemed to have forgotten their awkward times from before.

Scott was glad she wasn't holding a grudge and pouting, and he relaxed and began to enjoy his time with her. Vivian skipped ahead of him, heading down to the covered dock at the edge of the lake. Scott followed along behind her, enjoying watching the back of her long legs and the shape of her hips under her shorts. She really had beautiful legs. His brothers teased him about being a leg-man, but, admittedly, legs were one of the first things Scott noticed in a girl. Followed by the overall package and the eyes. Scott always found that eyes revealed what was going on in the soul. And he had always been good at reading eyes.

"I love it here," Vivian announced with delight. She sat on the dock now, swinging her feet back and forth and gazing out over the lake.

He dropped down to sit on the dock beside her. "The sun's bringing out all the highlights of your hair." He studied her admiringly.

"My hair always looks red in the sun," she complained, making a face.

"Your hair's not red, Vivian, it's chestnut – like the coat of a chestnut mare. And the highlights are golden on it in the sunshine. It's really beautiful."

A little flush rose in Vivian's cheeks, but she looked back at him steadily. "You have gold highlights in your hair, too, Scott Jamison, and your eyes look more blue than hazel here by the lake."

"Well, if your eyes were any bluer, Vivian Delaney, a man would fall into them and get lost."

She studied him. "We're doing a nice job of flirting here by the lake, aren't we Scott?" she asked softly, a little smile starting at the corner of her mouth.

"Yes, as a matter of fact we are." His eyes moved to her mouth thoughtfully as he began to consider kissing her again.

"Well, no more romantic talk for now." She pulled herself quickly to her feet again, seeming to read his mind. "Our day's getting away, and I want to see the rest of the camp. Are there any other places as beautiful as this?"

Chapter 10

SCOTT SMILED AT HER BACK as she started up the dock toward the road again. He watched her get out her map and start to study it again. All business now and romance put neatly aside.

There wasn't much pretense with Vivian sometimes, Scott thought. She tended to call a spade a spade. Which only confused him more about all the secrets he knew she had and was concealing from him. She acted so charming and guileless, that Scott found it hard to imagine any secrets she had would be really bad ones. Surely, they couldn't be illegal ones. Yet, why else would she always be changing the subject, hiding her laptop away from him, and giving evasive or untruthful explanations to his questions? He wondered if she knew how her eyes darted around anxiously whenever she told a lie. She didn't have much of a poker face. Perhaps she had just been hurt in the past, he thought. Maybe she was running away from an abusive or failed relationship. He hoped she would talk to him about it soon. He had meant it when he told her he didn't like lying.

"What are those big buildings over on the other side of the lake?" she asked him now, pointing again.

She had such expressive hands, he noticed, and she gestured with her hands while she talked, especially when she was animated or excited. She also lit up like a Christmas tree, as delighted as a child, when something interested her.

"You're watching me again," she told him, turning to find his eyes on her. "Quit that, and tell me about your camp."

He shook his head again at her candor. "Those buildings are the guest lodges. Kyle and I built them, situated here in the center of the camp around the lake, for the retreats I had in mind during the year. A camp ordinarily only makes money during the summer when the kids are present, but I thought a camp located in a setting like this near the Smokies could make money throughout the year if there were some comfortable accommodations for adults. Most grownups, you know, have lost the desire to sleep in bunk beds or in a cabin with no heating and air-conditioning. They also don't have any desire to walk to the latrine in the night with a flashlight."

Vivian giggled. "You're right about that. But, I remember it was fun and exciting doing all that when I was young."

"Did you tent camp or cabin camp when you were a girl?" Scott liked these times when Vivian was so interested in his life and his work. And he liked these easy times when she revealed things to him about her own past, too.

"Oh, both," she answered him. "I tent camped with Campfire Girls and stayed in hogans and cabins with church camps. Sometimes, when I was older, I went to retreat weekends that were in mountain lodges, somewhat like yours."

She stopped to study her map. "Take me and show me where your kids stay now." She flashed him an encouraging look.

"Alright," he said. "We'll go to the upper camp. It's where the older campers stay. It's really pretty up there." He turned to catch her eyes. "Are you sure you're not getting bored with all this?"

She wrinkled her nose at him. "I'm not bored, Scott. Remember I'm the one who asked for this tour. But you don't have to take me around if you don't want to."

"Are you kidding?" he replied. "Give me a bandbox and a subject I enjoy and I love to expound!"

She gave him a cute smile. "I like to listen to you expound."

"Well, then we're a match made in heaven," he teased, but he was secretly thrilled that Vivian liked listening to his accounts and stories. Maybe it was because she wrote stories herself that she was so interested in everything.

He led the way back down the main road but soon turned off

onto a side road to their left.

"Across the lake from the dock, where we were before, are the camp units for the younger kids who are only seven and eight. I try to put the littlest kids the closest to the main buildings and down in the flatter area of the camp."

They came to a rock bridge crossing a stream now, and Vivian stopped to hang over the bridge rails to look down at the little cascades and rills below.

"This stream is called Laurel Prong." Scott stepped closer and stood beside her at the rail. " It runs all through the camp. It's a tributary from out of Honey Lick Branch, the stream that we crossed near the farm. Actually, most of Honey Lick diverts over here to become Laurel Prong, and the part of Honey Lick that goes on down by the farm is quieter and much more shallow."

"Come on." Scott reached out to take Vivian's hand in his. "I'll take you up to Falls Camp now. It's the camp area for the oldest girls, eleven to twelve years old."

To Scott's surprise, Vivian let him take her hand, and they walked along companionably holding hands, until Vivian pulled her hand free in excitement to point at something along the way again.

"Oh, there's the swimming pool!" she cried. "What a lovely setting!"

Vivian took off down the hill toward the pool. It spread below them in a broad open area. Scott followed along behind telling her about the camp swimming area.

"As you can see, there are two pools here – a shallow beginner's pool and a deeper and longer pool with a diving area for the better swimmers. By having a beginner pool and a main pool like this, we can have several ages of campers here at one time. Usually we have Boys' Swim and then Girls' Swim, with three age groups of campers in the pool at once – but all of the same sex."

He grinned at her. "It cuts down on the boys watching the girls so much in their bathing suits at swim period. And it just makes the whole lesson aspect easier to have sexes segregated for swimming."

"That's sensible." Vivian gave him a prim look as she started back up to the road.

"Over there - that's Head House across from the pool." Scott pointed to a nice-sized cabin set under a giant tulip poplar tree across the street from the pool area. "My main camp director and assistant camp director stay there."

"Have you already hired them?"

"Yes, and you'll be happy to know that I was able to hire a woman and man team this summer. Mainly because my past directors, Alec and Andrea Capuni, agreed to come back again. Alec and Andrea met here two summers ago when he was camp director and she was a senior counselor. They got married, but they've returned two summers now to direct the camp. They love it here, and I was tickled when they agreed to come again. The kids call them the A-Team. They're both wonderful with the campers. I'll introduce you this summer."

At her request, Scott took Vivian into Head House to look around, and she insisted on going into every room to ooh and aah over the rustic furniture, iron beds, and framed mountain art.

"Oh, it must be wonderful to work here for a living all the time," she exclaimed. "To be a part of all this camp fun every summer."

She looked up at him then with a glow on her face, and Scott found himself suddenly almost dizzy. He put a hand against the door frame to casually steady himself. This woman had the most amazing effect on him. Fizzling his blood, dizzying his senses, zinging him with sensations. He'd simply never felt anything like this before around a woman. Whenever she looked at him in a certain way, he felt like a moth being drawn toward a flame. It was exciting – oh, yes, it was exciting - but it felt dangerous, too.

Vivian was too preoccupied with her tour to notice Scott's reactions. She walked out the door of Head House studying her map and deciding where to go next on her tour. Scott took a deep breath before following her out.

"What are these camp areas off to the right and left down these little side roads?" She pointed and gestured again as they started up the camp road. Scott smiled to himself, loving her excitement about his camp. He knew he had a big ego and Vivian had a way of playing to it that was sweet and uncontrived.

"Those are the camp areas for the middle age campers nine to ten years old, Pine Camp for the boys and Dogwood for the girls."

Vivian looked wistfully down the wooded roads leading back into the camp areas.

"Come on, Vivian." Scott grinned at her and took her hand again. "The cabins in all the camp areas look just the same. And I want to take you on up the hill here through the woods to the older kids' camping area. I promise you'll like it there."

"Okay," she said reluctantly. "But will you show me all of it some day? I don't want to miss anything."

He looked down at her and kissed her nose casually. "You, Vivian Delaney, underneath all that grown up body and those degrees, are a child that never grew up."

"I know," she told him in a conspiratorial whisper. "But don't let it get back to the university. I'm in enough trouble there already."

She turned back with eagerness to start up the camp road, not seeming to even be aware of what she had just said to him.

Scott raised an eyebrow. He started to ask her 'what trouble?' but then he bit his tongue. It would all come out in time. He could wait a little longer.

He took her up the Rock Hill Road through the woods where the lower ridges of Buckeye Knob began. They passed by the outdoor amphitheatre and playing field at the base of Rock Hill with its old rock stands built right into the hillside. It had been at the camp for longer than Scott could remember. Then they wound their way up to Falls Camp where the older girls stayed.

"You are going to let me explore the cabins here, aren't you?"

Scott shook his head indulgently. "Any of them you like. But you'll quickly see that once you've seen one camp cabin, you've seen them all. They all have basically the same layout. The only difference is that the counselor cabin in each camp area is bigger with two small bedrooms off each side and a small sitting area in the middle. The camper cabins are all just one big room with four sets of bunk beds in each."

Vivian went clambering up the stairs of the first cabin, built high up from the ground on stilt foundations. There was a deep, covered porch on the front, and inside was a large open room, just as Scott had said.

"Isn't this wonderful?" she exclaimed. "And it's neat for the cabin to be up on stilts. It's almost like being in a tree house. Are all the cabins up high like this?"

"Pretty much." Scott leaned against one of the bunks while she looked around. "Although the cabins for the youngest campers are built right down on the ground. Nobody wanted any of them falling off the porches. In fact, I guess these upper cabins here on the ridge are the highest off the ground. But you almost have to build them that way to make them work on the slopes up here."

"I like the built-in bunks in here." Vivian walked over to examine one. "You wouldn't mind sleeping in the top on one of these. You can get up easily because there are good sturdy ladders on the side, and the mattresses don't droop down toward the bed below on saggy springs."

Scott laughed. "That was one of the biggest renovation expenses Kyle and I indulged in for the camper cabins. We got rid of the old metal bunks and lumpy mattresses that had been at the camp for as long as we could remember, and we put in these built-ins. Drawers underneath and on the sides give the campers a little more room for their things, too. We kept the old wood tables and chairs and the chest-of-drawers in each cabin, but we refinished them."

"And you put nice comforters on the beds." She reached over to run her hand over a sky blue one on one bed. "That was a nice touch."

"We bought in bulk for that and it helped with expenses. All the spreads in Falls Camp are blue, just like the Falls Camp shirts. Every camp unit area has a different color theme. That way you can spot a kid in the wrong unit right away. He'll be the kid in the orange shirt among a sea of blue."

"Tell me the colors. " Vivian sat down on one of the chairs in the cabin and looked up at him, her face animated.

"You really don't want me to go through all that, do you?"

"Absolutely," she insisted. "It makes it all more alive to me."

Scott shook his head at her.

"Remember, I'm a writer, Scott. You have to humor writers and their imaginations." She gave him one of her slow soft smiles again.

"Fine," he said, indulging her. "Blue here for the older girls at Falls Camp, grey for the older boys at Hill Camp on the other side of the ridge, green for the middle years boys down at Pine Camp, a coral pink for the middle girls at Dogwood Camp, yellow for the little girls at Lake Camp, and orange for the youngest boys at Blackbear Camp."

"So in summer there will be a rainbow of children running all over the camp." Vivian sighed dreamily. "I can't wait to see it."

"Well, you'll have to wait to see it," Scott said practically, hauling her out of the chair. "Camp doesn't start until June, and it's only March now. Besides I need that time between now and then to get ready. And we need to head back down the mountain. It's late, and dark is starting to fall. There's no electricity up here yet, and I didn't think to bring a flashlight. Any more exploring will have to wait for another day. Dark falls quickly in the mountains."

They left the cabin, hiked down the dirt trail leading away from the cabins, and were soon headed back toward the main camp road. Vivian looked back longingly.

Scott grinned at her. "You're too big to be a camper now, Vivian. But I'll let you come over to help some this summer, if you want."

"Could I?" she asked, her eyes shining up at his.

"How could I refuse?" He leaned over to kiss her nose again and thought about pulling her up against himself to kiss her more thoroughly.

Seeming to sense his intent again, Vivian distanced herself artfully and then flashed him a smile. "Thanks for taking me around the camp, Scott. It was really fun. I'd almost forgotten how wonderful camps are. I always loved them when I was little. I guess I still do."

"Well, I enjoyed spending time with you today, Vivian." He meant it more than he could express. His camp was his pride and joy, and he was pleased by her interest in it. "In fact, for your enthusiasm, you get the reward of having some of my home-cooked spaghetti when we get back down the mountain. I cook great spaghetti, and you can see my place while I cook. Maybe I'll even let you make the salad."

He expected her to hedge a visit to his place, but she did more than merely hedge. She aggressively balked. All the way down the mountain, she tried to convince him why she needed to go on back to the farmhouse and why he needed to get on back to his place to get work done, having spent so much time with her this afternoon.

By the time they got to Scott's house and the entrance of the camp, Vivian had become almost surly.

"I really do want to go on back to my place now," Vivian

told him almost frostily, as Scott started up the path toward the Director's House. "And you don't have to walk back with me. I remember the way."

He turned and played his trump card then. "Listen, Dr. Delaney – or should I say more accurately Dr. Mero? – you and I have some things to talk about. And I intend for for the two of us to discuss those things now. Do you understand me?"

Vivian was shocked into silence for a moment, and then she flared into life.

"You have no right to go snooping into my life, Scott Jamison," she blazed.

He gave her a steely look. "I have every right. You're staying in our family's home, you're living beside my camp, and you lied to me. I think that justifies the little inquiry I made this week. I wanted to see if you were who you said you were. And I've found a small discrepancy. I think you owe me an explanation for that, don't you?"

"Who else have you told about this?" Vivian's face had paled and she was breathing more rapidly. Scott could see that she was both upset and scared, even in the twilight.

"I've told no one, Vivian," he said softly. "In case you haven't figured it out yet, I like you. As I told you before, any secrets you have are safe with me unless they are illegal or dangerous to others. But I will have an explanation. And I want it tonight. Or I will do some more calling and some more checking until I can get the answers I want on my own. Now, I suggest, very nicely again, that you come on up to the house where you and I can talk about this congenially over dinner."

She stood there for a few minutes, simply staring at him, and then she finally spoke.

"Your little sign here going up to your house says Fox Place, not Director's House." She laid her hand across a wooden sign staked beside the path. "Why is that?"

Her comment was completely out of context, and it wasn't what Scott had expected her to say. However, Vivian never seemed to do or say what Scott expected at any time.

"Fox is a family nickname of mine," he answered. "My brothers and I all have nicknames like that. My oldest brother is Raley

Hawkins Jamison; we call him the hawk. He has a real hawk nose, too." Scott smiled in spite of himself.

"My younger brother Kyle Berringer Jamison is the bear. It's a great name for him; he's a big lovable guy. My full name is Scott Foxworth Jamison; so I am the fox. We came up with these nicknames one summer fooling around with family middle names, and they stuck."

He watched her tracing her hand over the sign, obviously collecting herself while he talked. "When Kyle was working on the camp renovations and making new signs to put all over the camp, I came back to my house one afternoon to find this sign he made for me stuck in the ground. I didn't have the heart to take it down."

Vivian was silent again for another minute or two. Her brow was furrowed; she was obviously thinking.

Scott stepped in to bridge the silence. "You see how cooperative I am in answering your questions? I'm just asking for a little cooperation from you in return, Vivian."

She sighed deeply and then looked up at him with a cool stare. "Fox is an appropriate nickname for you, Scott. Foxes are known to be crafty and sneaky."

Scott laughed and led the way to his house, aware that she was following along after him, if somewhat reluctantly.

"Welcome to my lair, Vivian," he teased, holding the door open for her, and letting her walk in ahead of him.

Chapter 11

$\mathcal{I}$NSIDE THE HOUSE, SCOTT DIRECTED Vivian to the guest bath, while he went down a hallway in another direction to wash up. Vivian thought for a moment of making a run for it, but realized she had no place to run to. Besides, running wouldn't solve her immediate problem now anyway.

She went into the bathroom and studied her face in the mirror over the sink.

"Now what?" she asked herself. "However did he find out I am Vivian Mero?" The next obvious question was to wonder just how much more he knew about her background.

Vivian sighed. Years of teaching and working with students, faculty, and administrators had taught her not to be hasty in actions or words. She seldom leaped to conclusions anymore or acted on impulse alone. She thought things through now, listened to all sides, collected all her data, and then decided on her actions and words.

"We'll hear what he has to say and find out what he knows first," she told herself. "Then it will come to me what I have to say in return."

After finishing in the bathroom, Vivian wandered out into the hallway again and over into the big living area of the cabin. Like most mountain cabins, this one had broad halls, open spacing, beamed ceilings, and chinked walls. Rustic sofas and chairs circled in front of a large rock fireplace and Vivian could see a large kitchen and dining area next door. The décor was in blues, rust, and gold, and there were a lot of pictures of foxes on the walls. Vivian shuddered.

"You don't like foxes?" Scott asked, coming around the corner.

"They're cute to look at, but often a lot of trouble to people. "

Scott raised his eyebrows. "So, you think I'm cute to look at?" he teased.

"We were talking about foxes, not you." Vivian refused to be baited. "Where's that spaghetti you've been raving about?"

He grinned, obviously pleased to see that she seemed less upset now. "The sauce is in the freezer just waiting to be heated up. I'll get that and the pasta started right now. Do you think you could make a salad and get some French bread buttered and ready to put in the oven?"

"Sure thing," she assured him. Nothing could be gained by being uncooperative.

They puttered around together in the kitchen making a quick dinner for the next twenty minutes. Vivian had little to say, but Scott chatted away cheerily, regaling her with camp stories and trying to get her to laugh. He was making an obvious effort to be congenial, but Vivian found it hard to relax, knowing an inquisition was lurking just around the corner.

"Good spaghetti," she commented finally, as they started to eat together.

"Thanks," he said.

As they finished their dinner, Vivian noticed Scott was watching her from across the table.

She looked up at him. "You're staring at me again."

"You're a beautiful woman to watch." He flashed her a charming smile.

Vivian sighed heavily. "Why don't you tell me what you've learned, Scott?" she asked, tired of the suspense now.

He crossed his arms, ready to cut to the chase, too. "I had some concerns when you wouldn't tell me about yourself over at the farmhouse. I waited a few days, hoping you'd decide to come over and talk to me like I asked you to. I knew you were lying to me about why you were here. When you've been a camp director long enough, you begin to get good at telling truth from fiction. As I told you, I don't like lies."

"So you've said," Vivian replied.

He studied her for a moment. "My mother came by after her visit with you. She said she and Aunt Mary were simply charmed by you. She was chatting away merrily about you having been adopted and having lost your parents at a young age. She told me about the family that took you in, Dorothy and Roger Owen, and how you said they had been good to you. She thought it was such a shame you'd lost your people and thought it was so sweet you wanted to come back here for your sabbatical to look for your father's family. Was any of that story true, Vivian?"

She gave him a blazing look. "Actually, it all is, except that Dorothy and Roger's last name is Mero. I'm being protective of people I love right now, Scott. And I have a right to keep my private life private, if I want to. It's not my obligation to tell you or anyone else what I don't want known about any aspect of my personal life. I don't have anything dark or illegal or shameful in my background, and, to be quite frank, I resent you snooping into my past as you have. You have no right to do that."

"It is my view, Vivian, that whenever a person lies, they give others the right to look into their lives to learn the truth." His eyes narrowed dangerously. "As I told you, I have a camp full of kids here every summer. I have to be protective of that. I also care a great deal about my grandmother's place, and I want to keep it safe."

Vivian gave him a surly look. "When I discussed renting your grandmother's house, no one suggested that a full background search would be needed."

"Well, I decided to conduct one anyway." Scott sent her a pointed look. "It wasn't that hard, Vivian. I decided to assume you really were a professor, and I started with small colleges in northern California. Mother thought she remembered the town Betsy said you lived in, so it didn't take much searching to find the names of the colleges around that area. I called each one telling them I was trying to locate a Dr. Vivian Delaney in their English department who I wanted to consult about some research I was doing in British literature and folklore."

"Evidently, you know how to lie well, too," Vivian put in nastily.

Scott shrugged. "At Armitage College, when I was transferred

over to the English department, this nice little receptionist said a
Dr. Vivian Mero had taught in those subjects in the last year, but not
a Dr. Vivian Delaney. I acted as though I must have had the name
wrong and gave a description of you to try to verify that Dr. Mero
was indeed who I was looking for. The receptionist said Dr. Mero
had not been working at the school since last year, but that your
description matched the picture in their college yearbook. I asked
where I might get in touch with you, as I'd heard you might be on
sabbatical, and she said that you had left the college's employment
and that you were not on sabbatical."

"And?" asked Vivian angrily.

"And she told me conspiratorially that she thought there might
have been some kind of problem when you were on staff, but that
the department head got mad whenever she tried to ask about it.
So, now it's time for you to fill me in on the rest," said Scott. "You
have obviously left your job or have been terminated, and you are
obviously using a false name here as a lessee. I think I found out all
I needed to know for now."

An anxious thought hit Vivian then. "You didn't call my adopted parents, the Meros, did you?"

His eyes locked with hers. "No, I thought it was time for me to
talk with you a little more first."

Inwardly, Vivian heaved a huge sigh. He knew some, but not
all. She needed to think now how she should respond. And she
needed to be as truthful as she could be. Obviously, Scott could
smell a lie a mile away.

"Aren't you going to serve me dessert?" she asked, stalling for a
little more time to think.

"I thought you girls were always watching your weight and skip-
ping dessert," he said, teasingly.

"Only sometimes," she responded dryly. "But some days in life
seem to call for dessert, and this is certainly one of those for me."

Scott laughed.

"Besides." She smiled at him. "I saw chocolate ice cream in
your refrigerator when I was getting the ice out for the drinks, and
it's been calling my name ever since."

Scott went in the kitchen to dish out some ice cream, which
gave Vivian time to clear her mind and plan what she wanted to tell

him next.

After spooning down a few bites of ice cream, she looked up at him candidly and began. "All right, Scott. Your information was accurate. I was basically terminated from my job at Armitage. It's not something I'm exactly proud of or interested in telling everyone about right now. In one sense, I am on a sabbatical while I decide if I want to go back to another university to work a year from now. I could teach again, Scott. I have good credentials."

"Why were you 'basically terminated' from your job at Armitage?" Scott parroted her words back to her in a sarcastic tone she didn't like.

She glared at him for that. "Because basically, the college disagreed about how I should conduct my outside personal life."

He raised his eyebrows archly.

"Not that type of conduct," she snapped at him. "It wasn't that kind of personal matter. I did some fiction writing the department didn't think highly of."

"Something controversial?" He leaned forward with interest. "Something racy and sexy?"

"If you'll quit asking me questions, I might just tell you about it," Vivian told him testily. "And I don't want you to make any more calls to people about my life, Scott."

She frowned and stopped to jab at the last of her ice cream. "I think I'd better go back a little ways with this story first."

Vivian looked up to find him watching her intently

"I want to be sure you're satisfied that you have enough information about me to make you happy." Vivian lifted her chin and met his gaze squarely. "First off, I really was born Vivian Leigh Delaney. My father was a Delaney, and that is my real birth name, Scott. The Mero's were good to me and I agreed later that they could adopt me. This changed my name legally to Mero, but I am still Vivian Delaney, too, in a sense. I mostly told the truth there, Scott. And the other things I told your mother and your Aunt Mary were true, also. My life is really not as complicated or as intriguing as you want to believe."

Chapter 12

"So, is this where I get your whole life story now?" Scott asked teasingly.

She glared back at him testily. "Yes, this is where you get my whole life story." Her mouth tightened in irritation. "It seems to be the only thing that will satisfy your fervent curiosity."

"Good. That's exactly what I want to hear, Vivian." He grinned smugly.

Vivian felt like kicking him.

"Want some coffee?' he asked her, changing the subject. "I'll start making it, if you just keep talking."

"Fine." She bit out the word with resignation. There was no going back now.

She sighed and began her story. "The Meros were both college professors at a liberal arts college outside of Redding called Sierra Vista College. They were an older middle-years couple that had never had children. Roger Mero was a dean who worked in the Education Department, still teaching the occasional class, and Dorothy was a professor of Children's Literature in the library science program. It was a nice fit for me moving in with them. My mother had owned a little used bookstore in Mendocino that she had inherited from her mother. We lived above it in a cozy little apartment. I loved her and I loved the store. She'd always said she would leave it to me someday when she died. Unfortunately, she died a little too soon for that to happen."

"That must have been tough." Scott put a cup of hot coffee down in front of her.

"It was," she said, stirring in sweetener and cream before continuing her story.

"But there were positives," she told him. "I'd been raised around books, was already academically bent, and I thrived in the college environment where the Meros worked and lived. Their conversations were always about college, classes, students, books, and their ongoing research. Dorothy was always bringing home children's books for me to read and would ask my opinion about them. Sometimes I went to class with her or to the office with Roger. I missed my mother dreadfully at first, but, gradually, I came to love living with the Meros. Children adapt."

"I'm really sorry you lost your family, Vivian."

She smiled at Scott. "Thanks," she replied. "It was a hard time. But it could have been worse for me. The Meros had a nice place - a big brick house in an old, established neighborhood that was only two blocks from the college. I could walk or bike over to the campus or down to the little township between. Redding is a pretty place. Often I missed Mendocino and living by the sea, but I learned to love the mountains." She paused. "Have you ever been to California?"

"No. But I've been out west before and to Tahoe, which isn't too far away. Go on with your story."

"All right," she said, sipping on her coffee again.

Obviously, she wasn't going to shift his attention off the subject this time. "I soon made a friend, Jan Paulton, on the next street over, which really helped my life at this time. We became best friends from then on. We played on the streets in the suburban neighborhood around the college together, biked to the library and the park, went down to the drugstore to get a shake, and went to school together. I often stayed with Jan's family when the Meros were at campus meetings or away for trips. Her family was like a second family to me. She had two older brothers and a baby brother, and her Grandmother Hester lived with them, too. Her father was the minister of our church, and her mother was our Campfire

Girls leader. So, you see, I was just a nice, normal girl growing up, Scott – nothing scary for you to worry about with your campers." She looked up to find him watching her steadily. "Did you stay with the Meros until you graduated from high school?"

"Yes, I did, and then Jan and I both went to college right there at Sierra Vista. I stayed with the Meros through undergraduate school, too. Professors' kids got free tuition, and I was leery of going off on my own just yet. I finished at twenty-one with a BA in English and then received a Graduate Assistantship to California State in Chico, just 80 miles below Redding. I could drive home easily when I had a long weekend or a holiday or I could take the Amtrak."

She stirred her coffee idly remembering. "At California State, I was an RA, or resident assistant, in Blair Hall, the Honors College Dorm on campus. I worked with the students in the dorm, tutored English comp on the side, and graduated at twenty-three with my master's in English. The Meros were proud of me. Roger said I needed to branch out then, go out of state for my PhD, so I took an offer for a Teaching Assistantship to get my doctorate in English at The University of Oregon in Eugene."

Vivian stopped to laugh at herself. "It was the closest school offer I got that was also out-of-state. I really wasn't very bold then. But I grew a lot in confidence in those years at Eugene. Grad assistants get a huge load of classes to teach, so I quickly got over being shy and realized that I loved to teach. I also loved my students."

"And how many of the boys fell in love with Professor Mero?" Scott asked, grinning at her.

"Oh, there were a few that flirted." She looked up at him, knowing this was one answer she could be truthful about. "But I really didn't have much time for young men or dating. My doctoral workload of teaching, taking classes, and then doing research and my dissertation were exhausting and took all my time. It seems now that those years just flew by, even though the days seemed long then."

"Want another cup of coffee?" Scott asked, getting up to get himself one.

She sighed. "I probably shouldn't, but yes. Too much coffee sometimes keeps me up at night."

"Then we'll switch to wine next," Scott said, passing her a grin. "And get sloshed."

Vivian giggled. It was good to laugh for a minute.

Scott came back with their coffees and sat down again.

"So you got your doctorate and started job hunting." He caught her glance. "How did you end up at Armitage College? Was it because it was close to home?"

"Perhaps, and because I felt comfortable with the environment," Vivian admitted. She had decided that the more readily she answered all of Scott's questions tonight, the less likely he was to probe further into areas of her life she still wanted to keep to herself. The point was to appear cooperative.

She smiled at him. "Armitage wasn't too far from Redding, and, it wasn't too far up the coast above Mendocino where I'd spent my early years. Plus, it was a small liberal arts college more like Sierra Vista where I'd spent so many happy times."

"So what happened there to screw it up? Surely just writing some fiction books couldn't get you fired."

"I never said I was fired." Vivian fidgeted with her spoon on the table while she talked. "But I was pressured to resign and I did. As the head of my department put it, I had a conflict of interests."

"Tell me about that," Scott pressed.

Vivian sighed. "Okay, if you like. I came to Armitage to replace Dr. Norman Beeker, who had just died. I never knew him, but the kids called him "The Beek". Seeing his picture later, I understood why." She giggled.

"To be frank, I entered a very stuffy English Department at Armitage." She looked up at him with candor. "I didn't fully pick up on that fact at my interviews or I might have considered another school. The department had distinguished itself over the years in the English field by many scholarly publications, textbooks, and in-depth studies on prominent writers. My master's on Andrew Lang attracted their attention. They were hoping, of course, that I would carry on the department tradition. And in my first year, I did have several related academic publications in some noteworthy journals. So they were pleased with me. I also was a very good and beloved instructor. My student evaluations were always excellent and students stood in line to get into my classes. This proved to be both good and bad."

"How could that be bad?"

"Not all professors are as good with people as with their books and research. My department seemed to have an overload of scholarly individuals who were generally not beloved by the students. This made me different from the norm."

"I imagine you were great." Scott grinned. "And I can remember a lot of my own past professors that were not. So why didn't they like your fiction?"

"The head of the department, Dr. Percy Wright, was an expert in literary criticism, and he taught courses by the same name. He had an academic disdain for what he called 'trashy, modern fiction and the people who perpetuate it.' The associate head of the department, Dr. Stillman, agreed with his views. He had published several textbooks and multitudes of articles, many attacking the poor vocabulary and writing styles in the bulk of secular novels. The two other full professors in the department were in harmony with the first two, in general. A snobby sort of disdain for secular literature exists in some academic arenas. And all of these faculty members were in their fifties or above and were a closely knit set of colleagues."

"Were you the only young professor on staff?" Scott raised an eyebrow. "Sounds like a snobby bunch."

"I guess it was a snobby bunch," Vivian conceded. "The other associate professors close to my age were Dr. Fleenor Amons and Dr. John McCampbell. Amons was a chubby, bald, and very shy man in his forties who taught Rhetoric and Technical Writing, and McCampbell was a pompous, overly dramatic, and outspoken young man in his thirties who taught Drama and Shakespeare and had once been a short-term actor. He thought so well of himself that it was just painful to spend time with him."

She laughed and so did Scott.

"So who did you run around with? Surely not that drab bunch."

Vivian smiled at him in spite of herself. "Well, I lived in this wonderful old Victorian boarding house up on the cliffs by the coast and near the college. I had a great little apartment there, and the rest of the house was full of students and local hippies, artisans, and shop owners. We would sit around on the big porch in the evenings while some played guitar and sang. It drew other students and locals from around the neighborhood. I was a comfortable part of that group."

"Why was that a problem with your faculty?"

"It's silly, but they seemed to resent the affection the students and the locals seemed to have for me. Students would call out to me when I was walking across campus, stop by my office for advice or tutoring, or just come by to visit." She stopped to think for a minute. " I was the only faculty member in the English department who didn't have an unpleasant nickname."

Scott laughed. "They were jealous of you."

"No, I think I was just different from them." She sighed. "They seemed to think it was a mark of softness or weakness if your students were too attached to you or too familiar with you. I was often spoken to about that. But I couldn't seem to be any different. It just wasn't in me to brush off my students or not take time to talk to them. They'd come by my house many evenings and sit out on the porch with everyone. My department called this fraternizing with the students. This was frowned on, too."

"So you think this writing thing was really just another way for them to get at you when they were already upset with you about other things?"

"Oh, no." Vivian shook her head. "The other they might have been willing to continue to overlook. They often said these problems, as they termed them, were because I was so young, and that I would toughen up over time with the students. No, the writing was an entirely different thing."

Vivian stopped to consider this quietly for a while.

"Well, are you going to just sit there and think about this all by yourself or are you going to tell me about it?" Scott demanded, interrupting her thoughts.

Vivian looked up and smiled at him. "You caught me woolgathering. Doing all this talking has gotten me to thinking about everything again."

Vivian sipped at her coffee.

"You know," she said, thoughtfully. " I believe there was a part of me that was still like my mother even then, a fanciful woman that adored fiction, high drama, and an imaginative story. Sometimes academics began to feel very dry to me and, on the side, I wrote fictional stories just for fun. Actually, I started weaving stories even as a girl in little notebooks. Later, when academics wearied and drained me in my masters years at California State, I began to write some of my old stories and ideas into books."

"How did your stories get published?"

"An editor, Betsy Picardi, and one of the family owners of a small California publishing company called Picardi Press, came to speak at our college." Vivian smiled, remembering. "I was the Grad Assistant assigned to pick her up at the airport, entertain her, and see that she got to all the conference meetings on time. Somehow, she and I got to talking about books and writing, and I told her about my little books. She insisted on seeing them, took them back to her agency in Sacramento, and before I knew it, I was working with Betsy to get the books edited and press ready for publication."

"That's great." Scott cocked his head to one side. "I still don't see what could be wrong with that."

Vivian shook her head. "It's the kiss of death for a rising academic to become known for secular fiction. The focus of an academic is supposed to be on research and publication in scholarly journals. Betsy published my little books under a pseudonym to protect me. The readers liked them, even though my college department probably wouldn't have. Also, the publications paid me a nice little side income, which came in handy in those lean years of grad school. I was making my own way then and didn't like asking the Meros for money.

"And to be perfectly honest," Vivian added, smiling a little. "I really had fun writing those books. And once they began to sell, I had even more fun writing more. However, I never neglected my academic work to do it. It was just my leisure activity, my avocation, like some people play golf or research their genealogy or something. But I never told anyone about them."

"Ahhh," said Scott, the light coming on at last. "You didn't reveal that you were a secular fiction writer to Armitage College when you were interviewed and offered a job there?"

Vivian nodded and sighed.

"But they found out."

"Yes." She looked up at him now. "And they were as mad about my *not telling all* as you have been. They saw it as dishonest and deceiving that I hadn't told them I was publishing in other fields under another name. Even worse, they disdained the type of light fiction I'd been writing. I had numerous very heated conferences with Dr. Wright and Dr. Stillman, and with others in the department. Also, I had conferences involving a few higher administrators at the college, as well. I wasn't tenured yet, you know, and although no one suggested firing me, a number of veiled threats made it clear that this would reflect on my opportunities to become tenured at Armitage in the future. After all, as Dr. Wright said at least a hundred times to me, 'We have our reputation to consider.'"

"Haven't you figured out yet, Vivian Delaney Mero, that telling the truth is often better than telling a lie? Even lies for a good reason?" Scott frowned at her. "Lying never profits. Never."

"I think you're wrong." Vivian bristled at his criticism. "If I had told the truth to Armitage in the beginning, Scott, they probably would not have hired me at all. And if they had hired me, they probably would have insisted that I give up my outside writing entirely."

"Do you think most other colleges would see it that way?"

"Yes, I do." Vivian's reply was emphatic. "I've been around academia all my life, and I know the rules of the game."

"But I thought you told me that you could go back and teach if you wanted to," Scott said to her, reminding her of a comment she had said to him earlier.

"Well, now at this point, I could go back more easily simply because my novels have become rather well known." She smiled. "A little fame and recognition in any area makes its own way regardless of the rules."

Scott sat up in surprise. "Did I hear the word fame used in there?"

"Yes," Vivian answered him quietly.

He grinned and gave her a teasing look. "And are you going to tell me who this famous person in my kitchen is?"

"Only if you make me tell you by threatening to make more calls to my friends and family because you don't trust me," she told him candidly, looking up at him with an open appeal in her eyes.

Vivian watched several emotions pass over Scott's face at that. Annoyance, confusion, and perhaps hurt as well. Then he focused his gaze out the window.

"Look at me, Scott," she said to him. "I came all this way to these mountains, just as you suggested, to run away from being rather too well known once my pseudonym came out. It changed everything when people knew that I wasn't just Dr. Vivian Mero. They acted differently around me. And people invaded me. I couldn't get my work done. I couldn't have any space or any peace."

Vivian stopped to look down at her hands.

"The college sort of gave me an ultimatum," she said. "Choose the college and give up the writing or choose the writing and give up the college. I found I couldn't bear the idea of giving up the writing. It's a vital part of me. If I go back to teach again, it will be to a school that won't expect me to give my writing up at all. A school that will realize I can be both a good professor and a good fiction writer. I need to teach at some place that will accept the fact I need both things in my life."

Scott sighed. "And you don't feel that you can trust me with who this other side of Vivian Delaney Mero is yet?" Vivian could tell that he was disappointed that she didn't want to tell him more, but she had told him far more than she wanted to already.

"I'd like you to enjoy me for just what you see and have come to know." She bit her lip anxiously. "Just for who I am and who you see every day."

"Vivian, why do you think knowing what you write will make any difference in what I think about you?" Scott asked her, scowling. "I believe you've really told me the truth with this story, but I don't understand why you don't want to tell me the rest."

"I have my reasons," Vivian insisted, lifting her chin. "You're the only person I've even told this much to here. I'd like to keep it that way for now, if it's okay with you."

Vivian could see the war of emotions cross over Scott's face again, frustration, annoyance, and even a little hurt.

"Let me think about this for awhile." Scott pushed back his chair and started gathering up their coffee cups to take into the kitchen. "We'll hit the bathroom and then move into the living room. I need some time to digest all you've told me."

Vivian complied, giving him a little space.

He paced restlessly off down the hall and into the back of the house.

Vivian went into the kitchen and washed up the cups, then explored around the living area to look at pictures on the wall and books on the shelves. She'd always believed you could tell a lot about a person from how many books were in their house and what those books were about. Scott had an interesting and eclectic collection.

A little later, Scott came around the corner of the living room and walked right up to her, almost like he had done that day in the kitchen. He put his hands on the wall on either side of her as she turned to greet him, capturing her tightly between his body and the bookshelf behind her.

"I'm not really comfortable with all of this," he told her candidly, looking down into her eyes. "I'm a real open person, Vivian. I'm not comfortable with secrets. I feel that although you've really let your hair down to me in one sense, that you've left out all these other pieces in your story you don't want to share with me yet."

"I've told you that I didn't want to share everything," Vivian said softly. "That was honest, Scott."

"Well, I think there are more pieces you've left out than just your writer's pseudonym. And, quite honestly, Vivian, I don't like being left out of your life in any way, because you've started to matter to me. You've started to invade my senses in a way no woman has ever done. You are on my mind and thoughts too often, and I don't like there being secrets between us."

He cupped her chin with his hands and tilted her face up until her eyes met his. His voice was husky when he spoke. "I dare you to tell me, Vivian, that you don't feel what there is between us."

"I feel it," she whispered. And she did, sizzling down to her toes and back up again. Any time this man got close enough to touch her, she felt it.

"It's like lightning," she said to him softly. " Like the lightning in the air the first night we met."

That was all she got to say, because Scott's mouth closed over hers possessively. And she felt dizzy, like her feet would fall out from under her.

Their kiss deepened, Scott's lips warm on hers, his body pressing against her, stirring all her senses. Their breathing grew fast and ragged, and Vivian's heart started to race. Somehow, Scott got her over to the couch and lowered her into the cushions while still kissing her. He started to touch her softly then, up her arms, on her neck, under her hair. His hands were surprisingly soft and gentle, not grasping. It felt like he was exploring her with his fingers. Sensations rolled over her like waves crashing on the shore. And there seemed to be a crashing in her mind. Vivian's normal defenses felt shattered, and she felt drugged, almost unable to think. All she could feel was a whirl of sensations.

She heard soft sighs and little whimpers and recognized with alarm that they were hers. A side of her mind realized she was slipping slowly out of control, but she didn't seem able to stop herself. The feeling of Scott's mouth moving softly across her own mouth was just too wonderful. She didn't want it to stop. She didn't want to think rationally.

Scott teased at her lips with his tongue until she let him begin to slip it inside her mouth just a little, touching his tongue against her teeth, touching it against her own tongue. How gentle and sweet he was in his exploration. He didn't press and grope as so many other boys in her past had tried to do. He didn't try to take off her clothes or grab at her. He just seemed to be tasting and reveling in her.

She opened her eyes to look up at him, and he smiled lazily down at her.

"It's good, isn't it?" he asked her huskily. "It's really good between us. I thought it would be. It's been on my mind a lot, Vivian."

She nodded and sighed, too overcome for words.

"Touch me, too, Vivian," he coached her, putting her hands up on his face and moving them around behind his neck.

His skin seemed to tingle under her fingers, and Vivian soon found herself wanting to continue her exploration, touching his hair, running her hands down his arms and over his back. They seemed to be playing a child's finger game, touching everywhere they could that was acceptable, seeing how each place felt, reveling in the sensations.

Somehow in all the touching, they went from sitting up to lying down, and soon their bodies were touching, too. It was the most marvelous feeling. Vivian had had boys hug and hold her before, but she had never felt with them the way she did with Scott now.

Her mind drifted lazily away in a haze of feeling, only to surface again when Scott rolled over on top of her. How sweet it felt it to have him there. But how dangerous, too. Vivian wasn't a child anymore, and she knew how aroused they both were becoming.

She began to shake her head and struggle.

"No, Scott," she said, her voice only seeming to come out in a whisper.

"Oh, Vivian, don't say no," he whispered. "Say yes. You know you want to say yes." He kissed her again, and her mind whirled.

"No, Scott." She struggled a little against him now. "Really, no."

He looked down at her with agony in his eyes.

"Is it because I've hurt you checking on you, calling your college?" he asked her hoarsely.

She smiled at him. "With all of these wonderful feelings," she answered softly. "All of that went right out of my mind, Scott."

He groaned. "Let me make it go away some more." He leaned down to run his lips softly and tantalizingly across hers again.

Vivian felt like she could purr contentedly if she were a cat.

"Oh, you're good at this." Her words came out in a hoarse whisper.

"Yes, I am," he told her softly and with a little laugh of pleasure. "And this is only just the beginning, Vivian."

His mouth found its way under her hair then and to her ear, and then he was kissing her ear and doing some sort of erotic nibbling thing with her earlobes.

"Oh, Scott, stop," she whispered again, all her senses reeling.

"Why don't you stop fighting what you feel, Vivian?" he encouraged her seductively. "I promise you it will be good."

She managed to push him back a little more, trying to clear her head.

"Scott, it's not because it's not good or that it doesn't feel wonderful. Or because I don't think I'm beginning to care more than I should." She sighed against him. "It's just because I believe people should wait. Because I haven't ever ..."

His words cut her off. "Now don't tell me you're trying to convince me you're a virgin and that you've been saving yourself?" Scott asked her a little mockingly. "Come on, Vivian, you've told some tales in the past, but this one won't hold water. This is the twentieth century now and you're almost a twenty-eight-year-old woman and I'm a thirty-two-year-old man. We're not a couple of kids here. And we're past the age of consent."

Scott's irritation woke Vivian up from the fog of sensation she'd been wallowing in. She pushed her way out from under Scott, and got up from the couch.

"I'd like to go home now." She straightened her back, offended at his words and tone.

"You said before you could find your own way back." His voice was cross and irritable and he was scowling at her.

"All right," she said, looking out at the darkness now. Surely she could find her way through that little woods and over the creek even in the dark.

She started toward the door.

"Thank you for the nice dinner," she said softly, remembering her manners.

Scott groaned and muttered something that sounded like profanity.

Vivian let herself out the back door and started picking her way down the pathway from Scott's house. It was really dark now, and there were no street lights here in the country.

Suddenly, a friendly bark met her in the night, and Fritzi came up the path to rush around Vivian's legs.

"Oh, Fritzi, I'm so glad to see you." Vivian sighed with relief. "Will you help me get back home? I'm really scared to go alone. I'm so glad you're here."

"I'll walk you home, Vivian," said Scott's voice behind her. "Disappointment doesn't mean that I get to forget my manners, either."

Vivian didn't say anything, letting Scott step ahead of her to take the lead down the path.

She looked ahead into the dark. "Don't you have a flashlight?"

"I don't need one." His voice was snappish. "I've taken this path a million times, and we have a moon for light."

As Vivian's eyes adjusted to the dark, she could see a full moon shining in the sky above the trees. It was pretty and shed some light on their path, but she still would have preferred a flashlight.

Carefully, she kept pace with Scott so she could follow in his footsteps. She could tell he was angry because he was taking long strides, where usually he strolled easily when he walked.

Fritzi dashed up on the porch ahead of them when they got to the farmhouse. And Dearie was there already, meowing as soon as she saw them to let them know she was ready to be let in.

"Thanks for walking me back," Vivian said quietly, as she started up the steps.

"I thought for a minute tonight that I might be falling in love with you, Vivian," Scott said softly to her back.

Vivian whirled around to face him, anger slicing over her mind.

"I won't let that little remark go by, Scott Jamison." She straightened her shoulders, irritation flooding her. "And you will not make me feel guilty throwing that remark out at my back here at the last. I can assure you that you weren't even getting close to falling in love tonight. People who are falling in love don't push others to give more than they are ready to give physically. They don't ask for more than someone is ready to share. And they don't make fun of someone they think they care for just because they have different moral beliefs about sex before marriage or because they might be inexperienced. In addition, they don't make that person feel stupid or call them a liar when they try to tell them the truth about it. Maybe you should think about all that a little, Scott Jamison. You've spent a lot of time questioning my ethics here lately; maybe you should spend some time examining yours. You're not such a perfect knight in shining armor yourself."

With that, Vivian let herself in the farmhouse door behind Fritzi and Dearie and slammed the door shut soundly.

When she heard Scott start away from the house, she leaned against the wall and started to cry. How could he have gone from being so sweet to being so hurtful? It was just another reason to avoid men altogether, she thought.

"Let's go in the kitchen and make a snack," she told the animals, still sniffling. "And then let's all go to bed."

At the word snack, both the animals headed for the kitchen.

Suddenly, Vivian felt exhausted. It had been an emotionally tiring day and who knew what the next would bring. She remembered suddenly that Scott had never said if he was satisfied with her story. And he'd never promised either that he wouldn't look further into her background. This brought on a new rush of frustrated tears. She didn't know if she could take much more pressure from Scott Jamison. He could be so difficult at times and so arrogant and insufferable.

Chapter 13

SCOTT STALKED OFF THROUGH THE darkness to take a long walk around the lake before he went back to his place. It was two miles at least, but he needed to walk off some of his frustrations. This woman, Vivian Delaney or Vivian Mero, or whoever else she was, was driving him crazy.

First she lied to him, then she told him all about herself so sweetly that it made his heart melt. Then she drew the line and wouldn't tell him anything more about herself. Who the heck was she? Someone famous, she said. Was she making that up? Was all this mess a game just to intrigue him? Was she even telling him the truth now after all her lies?

And, now this new whopper. That she's an inexperienced virgin at her age. That just wasn't realistic in this day and age. Girls didn't save themselves anymore. He wasn't stupid. He knew his statistics. It was a rare thing for a girl not to have had sex by the time she graduated from high school these days. Why couldn't she have been her usual outspoken self and simply told him she didn't like him enough?

He tripped over a tree root, and said a curse word before he thought. Scott didn't believe in using profanity. He'd not been raised that way. But this woman took him to the point of forgetting all his morals and good manners.

He walked fast and hard around the lake road in his anger. He wasn't used to having girls and women turn him down. In anything. He didn't understand this woman, who he could tell enjoyed him, but drew the line at further intimacies. It frustrated him.

He heard his mother's voice in the back of his mind suddenly. She ripped him up royally not long ago for dumping the little daughter of one of her good friends. "You're so spoiled to getting your way with the girls, Scott. What are you going to do one day when you run across a girl with real spirit, with someone who can just say 'no thank you' to your handsome looks and charm? Well, you're going to get a taste of your own then, that's what," she'd said. "And I hope I'll be around to see it."

"Well, come check out the great downfall of your son," Scott announced to the dark bitterly. "Here's one who seems to have no trouble saying no to me at all."

He walked about another mile fuming before his anger began to cool. As he came around the lake, he let the moon on the water draw him back down to the dock beside the lake. To the same place where he'd sat with Vivian, watching the sun on her hair, watching her swing her feet and look out over the lake with such delight. He threw a rock in the water in irritation.

Back at his own place later, Scott's anger finally cooled down and he began to think a little more rationally. Could Vivian actually have been telling the truth about her inexperience? As he sat on the couch in the dark, he remembered that Vivian didn't even know how to respond when he tried to French kiss her.

"I actually had to ask her to touch me," he grumbled to himself. "And when she did, she just put her hands tentatively on acceptable areas. In fact, even though she acted eager, she was really awkward in intimacy. She didn't seem to know very well what to do." He frowned then, remembering that she'd never aggressively tried to flirt with him or seduce him with her actions before.

"I always assumed she was just playing it cool, keeping her professional distance." He punched a sofa pillow hard with his fist. Surely this woman couldn't really be an innocent at her age?

Scott flopped back on the couch, trying to think logically.

"What if she was telling me the truth?" he said to the dark. "If she wasn't lying, then I was an abominable heel."

He groaned. She had been so sweet. And whenever he was with her and got close to her, he went sort of crazy. He just wasn't his usual self.

"Every playboy has his day," his older brother Raley had teased him once. "Even the great fox will have his."

Scott got up and paced the floor. He usually knew how to handle women. He always had. But he didn't know what to do with Vivian. He really didn't. He alternated between never wanting to see her again and wanting to go over to see her again right now. She was like a disease that had gotten under his skin, like poison ivy or something. And he was miserable with the itch.

Scott slept fitfully through the rest of the night, and by morning he wasn't in a much better mood.

His brother Kyle came over to work with him on a cabin that needed repair at the camp. And he found himself almost unsociable.

"What's ticking you off today?" Kyle asked, marking off some pieces of lumber they were going to cut and use to replace some shelving.

"Nothing," Scott snapped, hitting his finger with a hammer at about the same time, and letting out a string of unacceptable words.

Kyle grinned at him. "Better not let mother hear you say that."

"Mother can go to the devil," Scott mumbled. "If it hadn't been for her letting that renter in to Gramma's I wouldn't be in this mess."

Kyle, never known to be slow, picked up on that mumbled bit of news and smiled to himself. He'd heard from his Uncle Leo, and from his mother, that Scott had been having a bit of trouble with the new renter at their grandmother's place. Obviously, there was a little more trouble afoot than most everyone knew about.

"I hear we've got a new renter over at Gramma Jamison's place," Kyle said conversationally, throwing out his baited line on the water.

Scott slammed some boards around in answer, and Kyle couldn't help grinning. The one most consistent hallmark of Scott's personality was his good nature. That he was cross and out of sorts probably just meant one thing. Kyle remembered it well. He had been miserable himself when he had been falling in love with Staci Graham.

He stopped measuring board to look over at Scott with a smile. "You want to talk about this, Fox?

"Talk about what?" Scott shot back.

112

"The renter. Girls. Whatever's bothering you." He raised an eyebrow.

"No thanks," Scott replied curtly. "And don't be making something out of this that isn't there, Bear. Nothing's really bothering me. I just didn't get much sleep last night, that's all."

"All right." Kyle turned to measure off another board, hiding a smirk.

"Where's Fritzi?" he asked, changing the subject. "She's usually following us around like a shadow while we work?"

"Hanging out over at Gramma's, smitten with the new renter, the little traitor."

He slapped a board down in front of his skill saw, banging a few more boards around in the process.

Kyle smiled to himself again. And Fritzi's not the only one smitten, he thought.

Raley stopped by later, and the three of them went up to the Blackbear for lunch. They liked to get together whenever they could fit it into their schedules, and several weeks ago they had planned to meet at the Blackbear when they knew Kyle would be over at the camp working.

While Scott took a phone call, Kyle filled Raley in on why Scott was in such a foul mood. The two had a good laugh over it.

At the Blackbear later, the three brothers settled down at a long table where all the locals usually ate when they stopped in for a meal. The brothers waved a greeting and said a few hellos to Reverend James and to Charles Hart, who were already sitting at one end of the table. Then they pulled out chairs at the other end.

"You know, Scott," said Raley, digging into the Blackbear's meat loaf special. "One of these days your turn is going to come to meet someone you can't seem to get off your mind. I remember Daddy always telling me that when the Jamison men fall, they fall hard."

"Lucky women that get us to fall." Kyle looked up with a grin. "Aunt Mary says we're all a bunch of sexy devils."

"Or a bunch of over-sexed devils," Raley countered back, laughing.

Scott looked up with a cross scowl. "Can't we talk about something else besides the prowess of the Jamison men today?"

Raley shrugged. "Sorry. It's usually your favorite subject, Foxer.

And you're usually razzing the two of us about all that we're missing since we settled down and got married."

"Well, you make us sound like a bunch of immoral animals," Scott groused. "We're good men, you know. We went to Sunday school and we were raised right."

Raley and Kyle raised their eyebrows at each other.

"We don't push women to do anything they don't want to do," he continued, seeming to almost forget they were there. "And we don't disrespect morals, either."

Raley and Kyle tried not to smirk now.

"You know the toughest thing for an old playboy like me," Raley put in. "Was when I met a really nice girl like Beth for the first time. Boy, that really put me in my place. Remember that, Scott?"

Scott looked up at him. "All I remember was that you weren't fit to be around for months when you were dating her. We couldn't figure out why you kept going out with her. You seemed to be mad at her about half the time."

"Love hits some people funny." Raley forked up some meatloaf off his plate. "And I fought the idea real hard."

"Do you trust Beth?" Scott asked, unexpectedly, out of the blue.

Surprised, Raley answered honestly and without any jest. "With my whole heart and life, Scott. Why?"

"Well, I just think that's important in a relationship, don't you?"

"Well, sure," Raley said tentatively.

"But trust is a big leap," added Kyle intuitively. "Like loving. I don't think most men want to go there willingly. Life just sort of drags us there."

"I sure to gosh had to drag you there with Staci." Scott looked up and smiled at Kyle in remembrance. "It was obvious to everyone that she was perfect for you, but you couldn't seem to see it at all."

Raley reached for another roll. "Well, we Jamison men are a little slow on the count sometimes to things that are really important, even though we're quick about the rest of things in life."

Hershel Fields came in the restaurant door then and called out to them as he walked across the room.

"Well, hey," he said congenially. "Haven't seen you Jamison boys together for a long time like this." He shook hands all around, while putting in some nice catch up remarks to Raley and Kyle, whom he saw less often than Scott.

"Did you ever get things straightened out with that red-headed renter of yours, Scott?" Hershel asked at last, slapping Scott on the back.

"To some small degree and with no thanks to you." Scott's reply was grumpy. "And her hair is chestnut, not red."

Hershel grinned widely. "And here I was thinking you weren't very observant about that girl. Looks like I was wrong, you havin' noticed just the exact shade of her hair by now. Bet you could tell me the exact color of her eyes, too, couldn't you?" he teased.

"Stuff it, Sheriff," Scott shot back. "I've got enough trouble without any crap off of you today." He got up, pushed his chair back with a crash, and stomped out of the restaurant.

"Whoo-ee!" Sheriff Fields said, pushing back his hat, and looking after Scott. "Looks like that boy's got it bad." He shook his head. "I reckon I feel sorry for him for it, too. That's one hell of a woman he's tangling up with."

Kyle and Raley cracked up then, unable to hold their laughs and guffaws in any longer. The Sheriff joined them, and then he pulled up a chair and told them all about Scott and Vivian's first meeting. He also gave them the lowdown on what he knew of Vivian from all the local gossips around the valley.

Scott peeled his truck out of the parking lot of the Blackbear, and then started to feel like an idiot after a few miles down the highway.

What was he thinking of to snap off at the sheriff like that? To walk out on his own brothers in a fit of anger? And right in front of the minister and his neighbors and friends in a public place? Whatever was wrong with him anyway? He turned around and headed back, trying to come up with a plausible excuse to explain his behavior.

"That woman's driving me crazy," he told himself again.

As much as he hated doing it, he offered them all an apology when he got back to the Blackbear.

"I don't know what got into me. I haven't been myself lately," he tried to tell them when he sat down at the table again a short time later. "And last night I had some problems that kept me up." Their smirks of understanding made Scott want to belt them, but he managed to get on through the rest of the meal somehow.

It helped the occasion when Kyle announced that he and Staci were going to have a baby. This news brought back slaps and congratulations all around and, thankfully, took the focus off Scott for a while.

After finishing lunch with his brothers, Scott worked for the rest of the day at the camp, trying to sort out his feelings.

At about four in the afternoon, he remembered suddenly that he was supposed to pick up Vivian and take her over to dinner at the Greene's later.

"Great," he told himself sarcastically. "Just great. This is just what I need."

He had at least wanted to sit on all of this for a few days before he saw Vivian again. Now he would have to confront her and smooth over this situation before they went over to Quint and Ellen's. He didn't want the Greenes picking up on his emotions like his brothers had and razzing him around the dinner table in front of Vivian.

No, he wanted back in the catbird seat. Hadn't he said that was the way it was going to be with Vivian? That he'd show her what it was like to be around a strong person with authority and confidence of their own? That he wouldn't act like one of her little college students?

Scott listened to some of his best motivational tapes while he got dressed later in the day. He worked hard on getting himself pumped up and reminding himself of who he was, what his goals were, what he wanted in life. Goals and aspirations beyond getting Vivian underneath him. That's all that was going on with her, he told himself. Pure lust. He'd experienced that before, and he would undoubtedly experience it again.

He'd have a few practical words with Vivian when he went to pick her up. Be calm and adult. Put their relationship on a new friendship level. It seemed like she had enough problems without him going after her like a conquest right now. Plus, she'd made it clear she didn't want that with him, anyway. Scott scowled over that remembrance. He admitted to himself that this irked his ego. But he could pull back and play it cool, too.

Vivian wasn't a bad sort in general and she was actually good company. There wasn't any reason to avoid her and make this situation more awkward. He was a grown man; he could deal with this. Scott even acknowledged to himself that he actually liked Vivian most of the time. So maybe they could just have some good times together. Be friends. After all, she was only going to be here for a year. Maybe he'd take her around and show her some sights. They'd keep it light. Yeah, that was the way to play it.

Scott looked in the mirror. He looked good, and he felt more like himself now. He was pumped up; he could handle this little situation with Vivian. He was the fox.

Chapter 14

VIVIAN SPENT A BAD NIGHT and a bad day after her encounter with Scott. Looking back, she knew her impressions of him had been accurate ones. He was an impulsive and reactive individual, and she didn't like impulsive, reactive individuals. She preferred more thoughtful people, people more in control of their minds and emotions. Vivian hated how Scott had caused her to react in anger at the end of their evening. But he had truly deserved it. The very idea of him trying to manipulate her emotions by posing the idea that if she slept with him their relationship might go further.

What had he said there at the end? She let his words play again in her mind: 'I thought for a minute tonight that I might be falling in love with you.' Hmmmph. As though love only existed after a fulfilled sexual act. She had begun to think better of him. And now she was disappointed in him.

"I'm really disappointed in your Scott Jamison," she told Fritzi, repeating her thoughts out loud. Fritzi took little notice, bounding on up the road ahead of her.

Hoping a walk outdoors would alleviate some of her built-up stress, Vivian and the collie had set out around the loop road in front of the farmhouse. Now they were following the creek as they strolled up a side street called the Wildwood Road. It led eventually to a white church on a hillside by the same name, and Vivian decided to explore the old cemetery beside the church before starting back.

She found many familiar names among the gravestones - Harts, Millers, McFees, Harpers, Rayburns. Vivian located Mamie's grave there, too, along with other Jamison tombstones. Even on a walk, she couldn't seem to escape from the Jamison family. Under two large shade trees at the back of the cemetery, Vivian found a concrete bench. She sat down for a minute before noticing a saying engraved across the back of it. It read: *"Spend time with God here - and your answers will become clear."*

Vivian sighed. She needed some answers, all right.

All morning, Vivian had found it difficult to focus and write for the minimal four hours she expected of herself every workday. She had written anyway. After all, she knew she didn't have to be inspired to write.

She reached down to pet the collie's head. "I learned a long time ago, Fritzi, that when a person has work to do, they just have to do it – not wait to be inspired or motivated. And when people have a writing gift – and I know I have that – they just have to make a space for that gift to flourish in. It's a theory I've tested time and time again and found to be true."

The collie lifted her ears and seemed to look up in genuine interest.

Vivian smiled at her. "My problem today was that I never moved over into what psychologists call *flow* – the state in which you lose yourself in the writing and in which time seems to just magically slip by. In fact, I had to fight to keep my focus and concentration at all. I watched the clock the whole four hours I was working, and the time simply dragged by minute by minute."

Frizi put a paw up on Vivian's knee sympathetically. Vivian petted her again, glad of her company.

As the little collie took off to chase a passing butterfly, Vivian closed her eyes to enjoy the quiet and relax her mind.

"Lord, I hope the saying on this bench is true, because I need some clear answers." She picked up a leaf to twist it in her hand. "I don't know what to do about Scott. He is different from anyone I have ever known before. I admit that I'm attracted to him. No man has ever made me feel like he does, Lord. I know he likes me, but I don't just want to be just a conquest for him. I'm sorry I made him mad, perhaps let things go a little too far. He would be so easy to love that way. I've never wanted so much ever before to... uh, well ..." She stopped and sighed.

"But I hated that he made me feel so stupid because I haven't done that before with someone else. What is so wrong with that anyway, Lord? Why is that practically made fun of today?"

She stopped and thought for a minute. "It's odd, Lord. Once adultery was thought to be wrong. In the story of *The Scarlet Letter*, Hester was forced to wear an embroidered *A* on her chest for succumbing to passion inappropriately. Today if an unmarried woman Hester's age didn't yield to her passions, she would probably be required to wear a big *V* on her chest for still being a virgin." Vivian shook her head and smiled at the humor of her own thoughts in this. "We've gone from one extreme to another. It's hard to know what is right sometimes with so much pressure."

Vivian hung her head. "I hated Scott being so angry at me for saying no, Lord. I also felt I might be starting to fall in love with him a little, too. Do you have to sleep with a man to have love today, Lord? Is that the only way anymore?"

She kicked at a stone on the ground. "I almost wish I never had to see Scott Jamison again. I hate all these confused emotions. After all, I came here for peace – not more turmoil. Maybe I just ought to leave."

A noise startled her, and she looked up to see a man coming across the cemetery from the back of the church. Catching her gaze, he smiled and waved as he came nearer.

"I'm Reverend James." He smiled and held out a hand. "Gilbert James. I saw you through my study window at the back of the church." He pointed behind him to indicate. "I don't think we've met, so I thought I'd just come out a minute and say hello. Besides, it's the sort of day that keeps wanting to draw me out into the sunshine. Ever since I got back from lunch at the Blackbear, I've had trouble concentrating on my work. Do you ever have days like that?"

He was a comfortable-looking man, probably in his early forties, his hair receding slightly on each side of his forehead. He wore glasses, khakis and a white shirt, and he had a nice smile that made Vivian feel relaxed.

Vivian took his hand and smiled back. "I'm Vivian Delaney. I'm staying down at the Jamison place."

"Ah, yes," he answered. "Vivian of the chestnut hair. My wife Susan and my mother-in-law Ruth Hart called on you. I wasn't able to come that day, had a hospital visitation. I'm pleased to meet you now. Mind if I sit down here with you a minute?"

Vivian moved over and gave him space on the bench.

"I was looking around the cemetery," she said. "The bench attracted me as a nice place for a rest before starting back. Do you think it's true what the saying on the bench says?"

"That if you spend time with God here your answers will become clear?" He gave her a kindly look.

She nodded.

"Well, I have two responses for that." He pushed up his glasses thoughtfully. "First, local legend has it that many an important and needed answer was found right here on this very bench. So the bench has developed a certain regional appeal. A lot of folks come to sit here on this bench when they need to find an answer to a problem. Some swear by it."

Vivian smiled. She liked folklore.

"My other answer is that when you spend time with God in any place, on this bench or in any other place, your answers are more likely to become clear just from the time spent with Him. Do you see the little scriptural note carved underneath?"

Vivian looked behind her. "Isaiah 65:24," she read. "I don't think I remember that one right off."

"The scripture reads: 'And it will come to pass, that before they call, I will answer; and while they are yet speaking I will hear.'" He smiled. "You see, God is eager to answer; it's just that all too often we don't ask."

"Do you think God has changed over time in what He expects of people?" Vivian frowned as she asked this. "It's a different world today from the days of the Bible. A lot of people think some of the expectations of that time aren't relevant for today's time."

Reverend James folded his arms over his chest as he considered this question. "Well, in thinking on that, several thoughts come to mind. First, like the Word says, there's really nothing new in the world. Most joys and wonders we know, and most sins and temptations we experience have always been around. The beauty and wonder of the clouds on a day like today, or the troubling of a man or woman's heart when they're tempted with a roll in the hay and yet know it's wrong in the eyes of God. Both are as old as time, I'd say. That's the way it is with most things. The times don't change basic joys or temptations much. I find that the rationalizations for sin are about the same now as they always have been, from Biblical days to today."

Vivian, at first enchanted with his words about the timeless beauty of the clouds, found herself almost in shock after he mentioned the temptation of a man and a woman. She kept her eyes down and avoided his. Did the man read minds?

He seemed unaware of her thoughts, and continued on congenially. "So the first part of my answer is that people and times haven't really changed that much in the essence of things." He paused a moment. "And for the second part, I don't think God has changed, either. The Word says He's the same yesterday, today, and forever more. People are always trying to update God, change Him around, revise His ideas, and modernize Him. But think for a minute about why people do that. It's generally to rationalize sin and wrong-doing, don't you think?"

He turned to her with an inquiring look.

"It's my belief that deep down, those that really know the Lord know what's really right." He stopped to study on that for a moment. "But there are times that all of us get confused and upset, that we wonder if we've got it right. This is particularly true when some new life situation or person challenges our beliefs in some way. We question ourselves then. It's entirely human. We do that even when, deep down, I think we already know the answer."

He smiled at her more broadly then.

"Perhaps that's why this bench seems to work for folks." He patted it affectionately with his hand. "When they sit here long enough, the truth they already know just rises up and becomes clear."

"Maybe so." Vivian ran her fingers over the print on the bench thoughtfully.

As she looked out over the shady cemetery, a quiet, peaceful feeling settled over her. "You know, talking with you reminds me of my chats with my girlhood pastor, Reverend Paulton, back home. He was my best friend's father and I spent a lot of time at the

Paulton's house growing up."

Pastor James nodded and leaned down to pick up a stray twig on the ground. "If you could be back home and could ask Reverend Paulton one thing right now, Vivian, what might you ask him?"

Vivian didn't answer at first, but Reverend James just sat there patiently on the bench, looking out over the cemetery and the green lawn. The birds sang in the trees overhead, the bees hummed in the flowered bushes nearby. A cow mooed off in the background. It was such a pleasant, peaceful place.

"I'd ask, how do people know when they're in love?" she said at last.

"Hmmm, that's a hard one." Gilbert James scratched his chin, obviously thinking it over. "Even the Word says it's one of the great mysteries, the ways of a man and a maid. But my thought is that there is the stirring of the possibility of love from the start. And sometimes those stirrings and thoughts aren't always comfortable. We're used to our singular ways. There is a selfish reluctance in all of us to begin to think of some other individual as much as ourselves – or more highly than ourselves. So in that sense, I think the beginnings of love are often uncomfortable."

"That's an interesting idea." Vivian picked up a leaf that had fallen from the tree overhead and traced her fingers across it. "What about the movie idea - seeing a stranger across a crowded room and knowing right away?"

Reverend James smiled. "Well, if I recall that film, there were enough difficulties getting that couple together to make a whole Technicolor musical."

"Yes, there were." Vivian laughed. "In fact, both of the romances in that movie had problems."

"It's another little theory of mine," he said. "Just a theory, mind you, that people resist love in the same way they resist letting God into their hearts. It means giving up an aspect of self. Sharing, trusting, giving another first place in one's thoughts. It means sacrifice and change. People resist that. I often see people testy and cross when they are near to conversion. I often see people testy and cross when they are near to loving."

Vivian turned the leaf over in her hand as she thought about his words. "That's an intriguing idea, too, Reverend James."

"I thought you might appreciate it, being an academic." He grinned at her.

Vivian smiled back. "I've met your wife, Susan. She's very nice. Tell me how you fell in love with her. How you knew."

"Well, since everyone in the valley knows this story, I guess there's no reason not to share it." Reverend James chuckled. "I came here as a young pastor to replace Reverend Charles Jackson Hart, lovingly known by all as C.J. He had pastored the church since he was a young man, and it was a hard act to follow, coming after him. But the congregation felt strongly, after my initial visits to meet the people and preach, that I was the one meant to follow. I did, too. I'd been an assistant pastor in a larger church, done evangelistic work and traveled, and I was ready for a church of my own."

He paused a minute. "When I first came, Ruth Hart – that was C.J.'s wife – insisted I stay in her home for a season while I looked for a place to live. She has a big farmhouse down the road behind the church, so it was close for me, too. Her children were all grown and gone except for one of her girls just out of high school, and Ruth Hart had plenty of room. After I lived with Ruth for a few weeks, I found myself all too conscious of her young daughter, Susan. I was just mortified, believe me. Here Mrs. Hart was offering me her hospitality and I was finding myself thinking unpastoral thoughts about her daughter. It was a terrible time for me."

Vivian laughed. "What did you do?"

"Well I fought it, of course. In my natural mind everything was wrong about it. She was young. She was the daughter of the man who had pastored the church before me. And I was boarding in her mother's house. I hadn't even settled myself into the valley, and I thought it would be the kiss of death on my new ministry to get involved with Susan Hart."

"What did Susan think?" Vivian was fascinated, as always, by the beginnings of a good story.

"I had no idea," he said, laughing. "There were times I thought she was flirting with me, times I thought she was watching me, and other times I thought she was just being nice to me. It didn't get my ministry in this area off to the easiest start. There was all this turmoil going on inside of me, and I didn't feel that I could talk to anyone about it. Unfortunately, I was also having trouble finding a rental property in the area that I could afford at the time. And, believe me, I was eager to get out of that Hart house."

"What happened?"

"An episode that changed everything." Gilbert looked over and gave Vivian a boyish grin. "Ruth sent Susan and me over to Mrs. Rayburn's to take food and visit after she had been in an accident. Since it was a fine summer's day, we walked. As it turned out, we got caught in a rainstorm on the way back, had to take shelter in a barn, and my righteousness took a back seat to my flesh. I found Susan more than eager to meet me halfway."

Vivian looked shocked.

"Now, now," Reverend James said with a smile. "It was just words and heated kissing. But I knew then my feelings were returned and how things would be. The Lord created passion, Vivian, and it's one of his very fine creations. Ellen Greene told me once she believes the Lord brings a chemical reaction between two people so they'll know they belong together. She maintains it's different with different folks. But when the rain quit that day, I went home an engaged man."

"How did Ruth Hart take that?"

Reverend James laughed and shook his head. "Said she'd wondered how long it was going to take the two of us to figure it out!"

Vivian laughed with him, and then a memory made her feel sad.

"It takes some time knowing." Reverend James twirled his twig thoughtfully in his hand. "And you have to be willing to take the risk to see it through. At one point I thought it would be easier to run. I'd just come to the valley. I believed falling in love with Susan was inappropriate. I thought a number of times about just leaving to avoid the problem."

Vivian dropped her eyes. "Do you think the Lord knows who He wants each person to be with?"

"How could you look around at the order of His world and think He wouldn't?" Gilbert asked her. "But then I'm a big believer of purposes and plans and destinies."

"So am I."

"Well, the Word says over and over again that blessings come to the righteous. So I tell my congregation that walking in righteousness and virtue is a key to receiving blessings in any capacity. When temptations or confusions come about, that's the key to remember – to stay on the right track so everything will work out as it should."

"That's a good thought." Vivian looked up at him and smiled.

Reverend James stood up and dusted off his pants. "Well, come to church on Sunday at ten o'clock and maybe you'll hear some more." He gave her a warm smile and offered her a hand. "And come back to the answer bench anytime, too. Or come by the office if I can ever help you with anything."

Vivian took his hand and stood up, also. "You and the bench have both been a help today. Thank you."

As she started away, Frizi jogging along beside her, Reverend James called out to her. "Vivian …"

"Yes," she answered, turning back around. She saw him standing beside Mamie Jamison's headstone with his hand laid casually across it.

"Remember what we said about it being hard for some to come to terms with yielding to the idea of love? Some bloodlines are gentler and some are more hot-blooded. Remember that patience is a virtue and to let patience have its perfect work. It's more needed with some. And so might be self-restraint."

He patted the tombstone fondly and started back toward the church. Vivian stood for a moment flabbergasted, trying to take in what he had said.

"I'm going to have to watch out for him," Vivian told Fritzi as they walked away from the cemetery and headed back toward the farmhouse. "That man's got a way of knowing just a little too much about what's going on with me. He's dangerous."

Despite that, Vivian felt better and lighter for getting out and for having met Reverend James at the cemetery.

She reached down to pat Fritzi's head fondly. "You know, I think there really is something to that bench. Old legends are often truer than fact, you know."

She walked back to the farmhouse with a lighter step, took a long bath in a scented tub of bubbles, and put on her favorite navy slacks with a cerulean blue blouse to wear to the Greene's. She knew it was an outfit that made her eyes appear even bluer.

Looking in the mirror at herself in the bedroom, she smiled. "Well, if there's anything starting to develop with Scott Jamison, we might as well look our best."

Vivian rarely wore her hair down, but tonight she chose not to bind it up into her usual professional bun. She let it fall down her back instead.

"You need every wile you have to catch a fox," she said, smiling at herself softly in the mirror. "We'll just see how things go. And, as Reverend James said, be patient."

Chapter 15

SCOTT FELT MORE LIKE HIS old self when he showed up at Vivian's door later that night. He knew he looked sharp, and he was ready for a comfortable evening with the Greenes. He'd picked up a bottle of Quint and Ellen's favorite red wine, a Merlot that went well with grilled ribs. After a hard day at the camp, he'd worked up a good appetite as a plus. Scott was, by nature, a social being, and he was ready for a good time.

When Vivian opened the door, he, admittedly, had to take a quick breath. She had let her hair down. He'd never seen her hair down, and it rolled over her shoulders like the rich mane of a chestnut mare. Dark blue slacks hugged her long legs and she was wearing some sort of soft, silky blue blouse that set off the deep blue of her eyes perfectly. He wondered if she knew that.

"Good evening, Vivian." He made a courtly half bow in her direction. "I was wondering if you would remember that we were to go to the Greene's tonight."

"Of course," she replied with an easy smile. "How could I forget when Chelsey was so excited about it."

Vivian started down the porch steps without waiting for him to take her arm, and Scott found himself relieved. She didn't appear miffed tonight; she wasn't pouting or sulking over what happened last night. Those were two of the things Scott hated about most girls. They usually never let a slight go and they sulked for days over it. But Vivian was just walking along casually, talking about how the blossoms on the white snowball bush glowed in the twilight.

"I've never seen anything like this before," she said, pointing toward the snowball bush. "Is it only that shrub that does that? Is this just a Tennessee thing?"

Scott picked up his pace to keep up with her. "A lot of white shrubs hold the sun's light and glow for a short time in the twilight. Look over there at that baby's breath bush. It's got a shine to it, too."

"Not as much as this snowball bush." Vivian stopped to look at it more closely. "It's just like magic, isn't it?"

He gave her a teasing grin. "Is that some of your Andrew Lang fairytale talk?"

"No." She lifted her chin. "But I can visualize fairies liking a bush like this, carrying the blossoms like lanterns to light their way."

Scott grinned. "It amazes me how a professional academic woman like yourself can be so fanciful. You teach dense literature that most of us labor to read through and then talk about fairies carrying blossom lanterns in the next breath."

"Perhaps I'm like a line from Whitman," she explained. "*You will never know who I am or what I mean, but I will be good health to you nevertheless ...*"

"*And filter and fiber your soul*," he finished.

"Very good, Mr. Jamison." She smiled at him warmly.

"Thank you professor." He sent her a smile back. "We're not all illiterate up here in these mountains."

"I've never said you were." She gave him a frosty look. "People always assume professors are mentally weighing everyone they meet to see how they measure up. It's not true, you know. In between the job, we're just people. Actually, it's nice to get away from having to carry that role of evaluating and grading whenever possible."

"Good point. I'll remember that," he said.

They walked along in companionable silence for a while, enjoying the evening, listening to the outdoor orchestra of creek frogs and tree locusts.

"Vivian," Scott said into the silence. "I think I was a little out of line the other night. I want you to know it's fine with me for us to just be friends. In fact, I think it's better. You've got your work to do and you're only here visiting in the area temporarily, and I've got my camp season coming up. It's not a real good time for either one of us to get heavily involved, and it complicates things."

Vivian didn't say anything for a few minutes. Nor did she show by the reaction on her face what she was thinking. It made Scott a little nervous waiting for her to respond.

"And you think?" he finally asked her.

"I don't recall you asking me what I think," she said diplomatically and without giving away even a trace of emotion in her voice.

"Well, of course I want to know what you think." He scowled, feeling cross that he had to explain himself. This wasn't going at all like he had planned.

"The idea of friends sounds fine to me." She reached out to casually pluck a honeysuckle blossom off a shrub by the path and lifted it to her nose to sniff. "We'll see how that goes. I'd like to make some friends while I'm here, have some people to share good times with. Like visiting with the Greenes tonight."

"Well, all right then." Scott blew out an inward breath of relief. She was okay with them just being friends. He was glad of that. Hadn't that been what he wanted? For her to agree with him? For them to put their relationship on a new level? And yet there was a bit of irritation in his mind that she had agreed so easily. She hadn't brought up any of the details of the night before, expressed any regrets. He waited to see if she would do that. He tried to watch her face to read her emotions. But she just walked on along with those long graceful strides of hers, keeping pace with him easily, seeming relaxed and comfortable with herself and enjoying the evening. He found himself feeling oddly provoked.

She asked him some polite questions about the camp then. They made some small talk, and the awkward moment passed away. Or it seemed to.

The walk to the Greene's place was a short one. Ellen and Quint's house was a big, brick two-story at the end of a U-shaped drive in a grove of maple trees. The wide front porch had tall white pillars and Ellen and Quint had left all the front porch lights on to guide Scott and Vivian down to the house.

Scott noted with pleasure that Vivian was quickly enveloped into the goodwill of the Greenes as soon as the door opened. Quint was round-faced and friendly, with the easy smile and ways of a family physician. Ellen was practical and warm-hearted with a good sense of humor. Scott had always thought Quint and Ellen made a nice couple. Chelsey attached herself to Scott's leg as soon as he came in the door, and he was soon rough-housing with her on the den floor while Vivian got acquainted with Quint.

Evidently, Quint had often visited in California as a boy, and he was asking Vivian about places he remembered, trying to learn how things might have changed.

"I don't think Disneyland ever really changes," Vivian told him, laughing. "There's always Mickey Mouse and Cinderella and the castle – and there's always a multitude of rides, shows, and color. I never get tired of it."

Quint settled back into the sofa comfortably. "I'd like to take Chelsey there when she's older – either to the Disneyland in California or the one in Orlando. Ellen's been to the Orlando Disney once."

Ellen looked over from the kitchen where she was working on dinner. "I liked Sea World better when my family visited Orlando. But I'd like Chelsey to see all the Disney characters she's read about and seen in the movies. That was fun for me, and I was nearly grown when I went down to Disney."

"You know, Dollywood opens up this month," Scott put in. "We don't have to go far at all to get to Dollywood for a day of fun. Did you guys buy your season passes yet? They're discounted now, you know."

"Renewed mine in January." Quint grinned. "We're all ready to go."

"What's Dollywood?" Vivian asked.

They all laughed and joked then about Vivian being so unfamiliar with one of the area's major tourist attractions.

"It's a local theme park on the order of Disneyland," Quint explained to her. "Not as big as Disney, but unique and colorful. It used to have another name a long time ago, Silver Dollar City or something, but Dolly Parton, our resident country music star, came in and bought the park and has been updating and improving it ever since. You'll have to get to Dollywood while you're here in the area. It's memorable."

"I can take care of that," Scott said. "I always get a bunch of complimentary tickets every year through my old advertising buddies. Vivian can have one. The International Festival is in full swing now. We'll make a day of it and all go together."

They all visited easily and talked about Dollywood and local tourist sites for a while, and then Scott left Vivian with Ellen to go outdoors to help Quint grill the ribs. Out in the back yard, he and Quint argued, as usual, about barbeque recipes and sports and had a generally great time.

In fact, dinner and the whole evening turned out to be a good one, despite Scott's earlier misgivings. Vivian was congenial company and fitted into their group like she had always known them. By the time they finished their meal and the dishes were done, Vivian even had Chelsey artfully charmed. She now sat on the floor with Chelsey, drawing pictures with her, while Chelsey argued unsuccessfully for a later bed time.

The little five-year-old offered Vivian one of her engaging grins. "Vivian, will you come read me a bedtime story before I go to bed? Please? Please?"

Ellen frowned at her. "Chelsey, Vivian doesn't have to do story time with you, so quit pestering her. She's our special company tonight."

"No, I'd love to do it." Vivian looked up with a smile. "Besides, I've already promised Chelsey one of my fairytale stories. I have a big repertoire of those from all my folklore research. This will give me the perfect chance to see if I can still remember one of them all the way through."

Ellen grinned at her. "Well, okay, but you're a glutton for punishment. Chelsey will have you reading as long as she can talk you into 'just one more.' So set some limits when you start and stick to your guns. I'll go up and stuff her into her pajamas for you and show you where everything is upstairs. You haven't had the tour up there anyway. I'll show you around."

"You can see my room and all my dolls!" Chelsey hopped up and down with excitement.

"Yes, and those *two* baby dolls and *two* baby beds I heard about," Vivian reminded her, smiling.

Scott and Quint settled down on the den sofa, and Quint flipped to a ballgame that was playing on television.

"You two can have that set for fifteen minutes," Ellen warned. "But then I'm coming down for my show. You know it's Thursday and *The Foster Girls* is coming on. And Quint, don't you dare moan and groan like it's only a chick show. You know you watch it every Thursday night with me. Plus, we have to find out tonight what's going to happen with Veronica and her cousin."

"Oh, I can hardly wait," Scott said in a high falsetto voice.

Ellen glared at him. "Don't you say another word, Scott Jamison. You know you watch this show, too. I've heard you talking about it often enough."

Scott grinned in defeat and looked at Vivian. "Are you a *Foster Girls* fan, too?"

"I don't watch much television," Vivian confessed. "But I have read the books the series is based on and watched a few of the shows."

Ellen picked up Chelsey to carry her upstairs. "You know, the library here has every one of the books, and they're almost always checked out. I've read all the books, but I really like seeing them come to life in the television series. They've done a pretty accurate job with portrayal, don't you think?"

Ellen and Vivian disappeared up the stairs, their voices drifting away as they reached the upstairs hall.

"Well, that's a rare woman that isn't glued to the television on Thursdays to watch *The Foster Girls,*" Quint commented when they were out of earshot.

Scott was tempted to say that Vivian was not an ordinary woman in any way, but he bit his tongue on the words. He knew it might make him sound too interested.

Quint propped his feet up on an ottoman. "Nice girl. Plus Ellen really likes her."

"Vivian is easy to like," Scott said noncommittally.

Quint raised his eyebrows. "Made any passes yet? She's a pretty good-looking woman. Nice legs, too." Quint knew Scott was a leg man.

"Quint, I think I'm going to leave Miss Delaney off limits since she's renting at my Gramma's Jamison's house and living right next door." Scott smiled casually at his friend. "But I'll certainly enjoy watching her while she's here."

"What happened to that little Jeannie girl you brought over here with you a few months ago?"

"She got too serious, so I introduced her to a banker friend of mine who had the *'itch to get hitched.'*" Scott laughed. "They hit it off and are getting married next month, I think."

"You're good at matchmaking your old girlfriends off among your friends," Quint said.

Scott grinned and settled back into the sofa. "I believe in sharing the wealth."

"No, you believe in getting out before it's time for any serious commitment," Quint countered. "However, to be quite honest, Ellen and I would have been a little disappointed if you'd actually hooked up with any of that string of girls we've met over the last year or so."

"Why's that?" Scott asked.

"Nice to look at, but nothing much up here." Quint tapped his head. "Plus some of them were a little ditsy, if you don't mind me saying so. We never quite figured out what you saw in them."

Scott raised his eyebrows in a telling look.

"Oh, well, that," Quint said, a little embarrassed at the subject. "I was never much of a playboy type myself. It was a lucky day when I met Ellen at the hospital where I was interning. There was just always something there with Ellen from the beginning that was different. Maybe someone will come along for you like that some day."

"Funny how you married guys are always trying to get us unmarried guys hitched up." Scott grinned and gave Quint a punch on the arm.

"Yeah, yeah," Quint said back. "I used to think that, too. But it's really great when you find the right person, Scott."

"I'm not knocking it." Scott lifted one shoulder. "It just hasn't been my time. Besides, I think I'm one of those guys who could always be a happy single."

Ellen came back then, and the three of them soon got involved watching *The Foster Girls*.

"You said there were books this series was based on," Scott commented to Ellen on a commercial. "Who's the writer?"

"Her name is Viva Leeds," Ellen answered. "But she's one of those very secretive writers. There's not a lot out about her. The press are always trying to find her, chasing around any leads on her like the paparazzi, saying she has another life – all that kind of thing."

"A mystery woman?" Scott asked.

Quint threw in a remark. "Might be a mystery man. I read an article just the other day about these guys who take female pseudonyms to write romance novels. They say women wouldn't trust a romance written by a man so they use a fake name."

Ellen frowned at him. "I don't think any man wrote *The Foster Girl* books or the scripts for the series. They tap into the heart and minds of four young women too clearly, and they're too sensitive for a man to have written."

"See?" said Quint. "I've made my point."

They were still arguing over this later when Vivian came back into the room.

"Who do you think wrote the *Foster* scripts, Vivian, a man or a woman?" asked Quint.

Vivian sat down beside Ellen. "There's a woman's name in the credits for the scripts – Roz Devlin."

Quint looked away from the television screen. "Who reads the credits after a television show?"

"Oh, shut up, Quint," Ellen put in. "You're just mad because your theory is blown. And because Vivian has proved there's a woman script writer."

Not wanting to give up the argument, Quint added another point. "Roz could be a pseudonym for a man."

"Yeah, and George Washington might have been a woman in disguise," Ellen quipped.

They all laughed.

"Shhhh. Shhhh," Ellen admonished. "It's back on. And this is the last fifteen minutes."

"I thought you didn't watch television much," Scott whispered to Vivian as the sitcom resumed. "So how come you know the credits on this?"

Vivian shrugged. "I notice odd things sometimes. And odd names like you see in credits. The name Roz is unusual; I noticed it and remembered it."

Her actions seemed to prove her out in a minute, as she got up during the last ten minutes of the show to go get a coke in the kitchen, leaving the drama behind her without a backward glance.

"You missed the big kiss scene," Ellen told her when she came back in the room. "Veronica kissed her own cousin. That can only go nowhere, her getting mixed up with her cousin Cliff."

"He isn't her first cousin; he's her second cousin," Quint put in, flipping off the TV now that the show was over. "So, it's not a big deal."

"But he's still her cousin," Ellen insisted. "I just knew something was fizzling between those two last week. Now what's that poor girl supposed to do after that great kiss? You saw her crying later. Obviously, she's fallen in love with her own cousin. What a bummer."

"It's a television show, not real life," Scott reminded her, grinning. "What happened in the book, Ellen? Maybe that will put you out of your suspense to know."

Ellen frowned at him. "Oh, pooh, that shows what you know about it, Scott Jamison. The publishers hold the books now until after the series airs. That's one reason they're always after the elusive book writer, trying to find out what's going to happen next to leak it out in the press ahead of time."

"And to find out if it's a man writer," said Quint, purposely goading her.

Ellen tossed a pillow at him.

"They both know I like this show, and they always give me a hard time about it," Ellen complained to Vivian.

Ellen smiled and stood up. "Let's have dessert before you guys have to go. Vivian and I will go out to the kitchen and make some coffee to go with the pie. I'll get a sympathetic ear from Vivian there about the new problems on *The Foster Girls*."

An hour later, Scott and Vivian started their walk back on the darkened road from the Greene's house. This time Scott did have a flashlight, although the full moon above made enough light for them to see well enough to get home.

"I've lived in the city for so long, I've forgotten what it's like to be in a place with no street lights or building lights," Vivian said.

Scott pointed to their right. "Through the trees there are the lights from Aunt Mary's. And just beyond, are the lights from Nancy's place. This isn't total wilderness here, Vivian. But there are places you can camp up in the Smokies that truly are. I thought you'd been a Campfire Girl?"

"Well, I'm not that much of a Campfire girl." Vivian laughed that deep throaty laugh of hers. "This kind of quiet and peacefulness right here is more than enough for me. I don't think I'd care to sleep out in the mountains anymore."

Scott sent a teasing look her way. "I can't believe you knew the script writer from the credits of *The Foster Girls*."

"I can't believe you didn't know that the series was based on books." Vivian punched his arm, smiling at him. "That series has been running for over two years now, and articles about it have been in all the popular magazines."

Scott shrugged. "Well, I guess a California woman like you would know all of that. How did this series get started? Have you read anything about that?"

Vivian looked thoughtful. "Some books about four foster girls got rather popular and then the idea was picked up for a midyear TV series to replace a show that had flopped. The network had been getting some pressure about not having enough family shows, and they were looking around for something wholesome. I think there had just been a lot of press about the *Foster Girl* book series and it caught one of the network director's attention. I suppose the rest is history. People have liked the show just like people liked the books."

"Do you think anything serious will happen with Veronica and her cousin?" Scott asked teasingly.

"Who can say?" Vivian shrugged. "As Quint said, they're not first cousins. And as you said, it's just a TV show. Anything could happen."

They were back at the door of the farmhouse now, and Vivian turned to offer a hand to Scott before she went inside.

"Thanks for walking me over with you tonight," she said. "I had a nice time."

"We all had a good time." He held on to her hand longer than he should have, rubbing his thumb over the top of it. "Usually Thursday night is our weekly time together if all our schedules work out. I'm sure you'll get an invitation again. We could use a fourth for some of the card games we like to play together."

"That would be fun." Vivian offered him one of her soft little smiles.

"Do you want a kiss goodnight, friend Vivian?" Scott moved up on the porch beside her, feeling the currents start to stir as he got closer to her. "It might be the friendly way to end the evening."

"No, I think we'll do with a friendly handshake." She stepped back a few paces. "We get along better with a little distance between us."

With that she let herself into the front door, giving him a little wave with her fingertips before she shut it.

As he walked back home, Scott couldn't decide whether to congratulate himself because his plans to put his relationship with Vivian on a new level had gone so well or to curse himself for thinking up the idea at all. On his Gramma's porch in the moonlight, being just friends with Vivian had suddenly not been what Scott wanted at all. He doubted now that he would sleep well with all the titillating thoughts roaming around in his mind.

Chapter 16

A FEW WEEKS PASSED, AND Vivian settled into a good routine at the farmhouse in the Wear's Valley. She was getting a lot of work done, editing for Betsy and meeting her own writing deadlines. It was nice, in a way, to have the day hours free. Always before, she had to do her writing around the hectic full-time schedule of a college professor. Sometimes that meant staying up until one or two in the morning to get any writing done at all.

If she missed anything now, it was that feeling of knowing she influenced and changed lives through her teaching. That was the one aspect of her former academic life that had been the most meaningful to her. However, Vivian knew she impacted lives through her writings now. That knowledge helped. And no one gave her any flack here about her work. She liked that. She had hated the condescension of her colleagues at Armitage over her little novels. Here, she could write, enjoy her writing, and stay unknown.

Vivian had touched base with Betsy and Tad this morning, and she knew she was ahead of schedule with her work. The spring day was sunny and beckoning, and Vivian looked outside with wistfulness. Feeling restless, she wished she could get out and do something. She pulled out some tourist brochures to look through while she had a second cup of coffee at the kitchen table. Maybe she'd go exploring somewhere.

Her thoughts wandered then, as they often did, to Scott. They had spent a lot of time together in the last weeks. He'd made good on adopting her as a new friend, and had taken her on a lot of sightseeing trips around the area. They went to Dollywood with the Greenes, to the Aquarium in Gatlinburg, and to Tuckaleechee Caverns in Townsend. However, the tension still sparked between them. Or at least it did for her. She had hoped it would diminish with time, but it hadn't. Even last night, when they'd gone to the Greene's for their Thursday night get-together, Vivian felt the pull of Scott at every moment.

As if in response to her thoughts, Scott walked in through the kitchen door. He often stopped by in the mornings now before his workday. Vivian had given up asking him why he never knocked.

"Got any coffee left?" he asked her.

She gestured to the coffeemaker in the kitchen, and he helped himself.

He came over to the table with his coffee and settled easily into a chair. "I need to go check the trail up to Slippery Rock Falls today, walk on to the Cascades, and police some of the side trails the campers use in that area. Want to come with me? It's a great day to get out, and some early wildflowers are already starting to bloom. I'll give you a science lesson, professor. Also, if we need to clear some brush off the trail, maybe I'll let you help me."

Vivian grinned at him. "Asking me for free labor might not be the best inducement to get me to go."

"Just being honest." His eyes flashed mischievously. "Besides, there are a lot of benefits to this deal. The girls over at the kitchen said they would pack us a free lunch to carry. They're all over at the camp today starting to cook for the church retreat group that's coming in for the weekend. You'll get to see a stupendous falls while enjoying my congenial company as a bonus."

Vivian looked across the table at him and shook her head. "One thing I can say for you, Scott Jamison, is that you have no personal problems with self esteem issues. Has everything in your life always come easy for you?"

"You make that sound like a vice instead of a virtue, Vivian, to feel good about yourself and to be happy with your life. Maybe the real issue here is that you're just plain jealous."

His response nettled her and she snapped back with a sarcastic reply. "That's exactly it, Scott. Everyday I wake up and wish I was you."

"Smart ass," Scott countered. "Go put your hiking boots on, and let's get started. I can see you were looking at tourist brochures, so, obviously, you were planning to take some time off from your writing today anyway. By the way, how's the new book coming?"

She got up to put her dishes in the kitchen sink. "I've almost finished it. My editor is thrilled with me for being ahead of schedule this time."

"Does that mean you're ready to tell me the name of this upcoming book and your rich and famous identity?" he asked teasingly.

"No." Her reply was firm. "I like just being Vivian Delaney, a regular person again." Vivian looked over to see Scott's hazel eyes studying her thoughtfully.

He frowned at her. "You still don't think I'll act the same with you if I know all about who you are. I wish I knew why you had all these trust issues, Vivian. People are really much more honorable and reliable than you give them credit for being."

"Only in your world."

"You have too many secrets." He scowled. "That's what causes you to be tense and not fully relaxed with people. I've always told you that being open and honest is the best way to live your life."

"Yes, I've heard that lecture from you a few times before." Vivian forced her voice to stay casual. "But you don't have any secrets you want to hide, Scott. So it's easy for you to say that. I bet you've known very little pain in your life. Pain and betrayal make people more cautious, Scott. Less apt to trust readily."

He studied her for a minute, trying to read her thoughts.

She raised her chin. "Stop trying to figure me out and let's go."

A faint smile played over Scott's lips. "I like trying to figure you out, Vivian Delaney. You're my current mystery challenge."

About twenty minutes later, Vivian had dressed for hiking, thrown some necessities into a waist pack, and walked over to the camp dining hall with Scott to pick up their lunch. Edith Harper, one of the main cooks at Buckeye, was in the kitchen baking desserts that made Vivian's mouth water. The McFee girls, Loreen and Betty Jo, helped their mother Doris with jellos and salads that could be made ahead to lessen the work for the weekend.

Scott had to go back to Mary Nell Rayburn's office - Buckeye's other head cook and kitchen manager - to look at some food orders for a few minutes, so Vivian hung out in the kitchen watching the women cook.

Mary Nell Rayburn was a tall, almost skinny, no-nonsense looking woman, in interesting contrast to the rounded, middle-aged, and rosy-cheeked figure of Edith Harper. Doris McFee, a fading blonde with a neat perm, had that sturdy, healthy look of a woman who spent a lot of time outside on the farm, and her two daughters were beginning to look remarkably like her in appearance. The McFee women worked part-time at Buckeye around their schedules at home and the activities of their farm.

"What's that great smell?" Vivian asked Edith, sniffing the air with pleasure.

"Spice cake," Edith replied.

"And we made brownies earlier," Loreen put in. "Mary Nell wanted us over here last night to help some in the kitchen, too, but we couldn't miss *The Foster Girls* on TV."

The usual *Foster Girls* discussion ensued then. Loreen was soon lamenting over the character Veronica's ongoing concerns with her love life.

"No matter how much Veronica is trying to stay away from that handsome Cliff, she's obviously head over heels in love with him, even if he is her own cousin." Loreen shook her head. " I don't know what in the world she's going to do about it."

Betty Jo looked up from chopping celery. "If they get married, their kids will be inbred. Those Farnsworth kids over near Townsend are inbred from marrying in with their cousins, and they don't have a lick of sense."

Loreen turned to Vivian to include her in the conversation.

"Who's your favorite character in the *Fosters*?" she asked Vivian.

Vivian shrugged. "Maybe Isabel, she's so feisty." She leaned over to run her finger around the empty icing bowl to get a sample.

Loreen nodded. "Isabel's so cute. But I like Veronica best. She's the nice one and the oldest, too, and I just hate it that she finally has found herself a man and that he's the wrong one."

"I like Marybeth," Betty Jo interrupted. "She has all the boys running after her. And she's just so beautiful with that long blond hair."

"She's a little spendthrift, too," put in the girls' mother, slapping a pie crust down on the counter. "She's gotten those girls all into a fine pickle or two with her overspending. Let that be a lesson to both of you. It's important to live within your means. Now, myself, I like that little Rachel, nice and sweet, careful with her money and good with children. I like her even if she is foreign and a little dark in her coloring."

Betty Jo gave her mother an irritated look. "Rachel's Jamaican, Mama, not foreign. Jamaica is just down in the Caribbean below America. Besides, Veronica's British and Isabel's Irish in background. Only Marybeth is really just all American. That's what makes the show so fun; all the girls have different cultural backgrounds and look different."

"So what do you think, Vivian; do you think Veronica will actually get married to her own cousin?" Loreen asked, changing the subject again.

Vivian smiled. "Well, looking back and remembering what that first kiss between Cliff and her was like, I'd be thinking yes. It was really a sizzler."

"Oh, I about died when that happened," Loreen said wistfully. "That night was one of my favorite episodes. But what about them being cousins, Vivian?"

"Well, maybe they'll find out they're more distant cousins than they think," Vivian suggested. "Maybe they'll find there is an adoption link in their bloodlines and that they're not so directly related as they thought."

Betty Jo grinned widely. "Oh my gosh, wouldn't that be great! You ought to send that idea into the show writers."

"It wouldn't matter if she did," Loreen said practically. "I read in *Star* magazine that the scripts are written up way in advance based on those books the author has written. I remember back when the show first started, you could go to the library and get the next book so you could cheat and find out what was going to happen next. But the directors of the show and the book publisher got into cahoots and now they're holding the books 'til after the show episodes air. The next book that's coming out is called *Kissing Cousins*. What's going to happen next is probably right there in that book if we could just get our hands on it."

"Oh, well, I guess we'll just have to hang in suspense for a few more weeks to see." Betty Jo dumped the chopped celery into a big bowl and sighed.

"Isn't part of the fun of watching *The Foster Girls* not knowing?" Vivian asked with a smile. "Anticipating and wondering what might occur?"

Loreen considered this. "Most of the time, yes. But sometimes it just seems real hard to wait."

Vivian laughed.

"Listen, you girls need to get busy cutting up the rest of that celery for these salads and stop daydreaming about the *Foster Girl* series," their mother admonished. "That's just a TV series, you know. This getting ready for a crowd of hungry men tonight is real life."

"Oh, Mama," Betty Jo complained. "You gotta have some fun in life, too."

Loreen looked up and sighed wistfully. "Well, I can tell you it would be a thrill for me to me to meet the person that writes all the *Foster Girl* books. I can't believe she can think up all those things to write down."

"Well, maybe you'll meet her some day," Scott said from the doorway.

Vivian turned to find him lounging comfortably in the door frame.

"How long have you been standing there listening in?" Vivian asked, flushing slightly.

"Not long." He was watching her in that way he did sometimes that always made Vivian nervous. "Ready to go?"

"I have been for a while." She sent him a matter-of-fact look. "And I've packed the sandwiches Edith and Doris made into our packs."

"We put in some of those brownies, too." Loreen giggled, tweening and flirting a little around Scott. "We know you like them a lot."

Scott gave her an impish smile. "Chocolate is one of life's great pleasures."

"What I can't figure is why you can eat so much of it and still stay so thin," Betty Jo complained. She looked down at her plump figure. "Me, I just look at chocolate and gain three pounds. It's not fair."

"There's just more of you to love," Scott teased, getting a smile out of her.

"Go on off and clean up those trails and quit flattering these girls here," Doris said. "They've got work to do."

Scott laughed and then whisked Vivian out the back door before another conversation could get started to delay them.

"Putting on the charm again," Vivian observed as they started off through the back of the camp, jumping the rocks to cross Laurel Prong as a shortcut.

He shrugged. "Why not, if it makes a woman feel good." He gave Vivian a hand as they clambered up the bank on the other side of the stream.

"By the way." He looked down at her thoughtfully. "How come you had so much to say about that kiss episode on *The Foster Girls*? Seems to me I remember you leaving the den that night when that scene came on so you could go out to the kitchen for a cola."

Vivian gained her footing and then started down the path ahead. "Scott, they show reruns all the time of the choice scenes in those sitcoms to get people to watch the next episodes. It's hard to miss them."

"That's probably true," Scott conceded. "But it seems to me you're the one that said you hardly ever watch television either."

She reached over to pick up a pinecone on the ground. "I don't much. But I watch some. And they repeat a lot on those shows. It's called a teaser to suck the viewer in, two acts or so to entertain, and a tag, or catchy closing scene, to make people want to tune in next week to see what will happen next."

Scott adjusted his waistpack. "You learn all that teaching literature classes?"

"No, I learned all that living in California where most television series and movies are made and where everybody talks about the process all the time."

"Good answer," he acknowledged.

"What's that supposed to mean?" Vivian glared at him.

"Nothing." Scott grinned at her and spread his hands. "Quit being so touchy, Vivian. I was just making conversation."

They hiked a little over a mile through the camp to Slippery Rock Falls. Vivian had been meaning to hike to the falls ever since she moved into the farmhouse, but she just hadn't made it up yet. When they climbed over the last little ridge to find the waterfall, Vivian let out an exclamation of delight. The stream dropped down over a high series of rock ledges in a froth of white cascades.

"Oh, Scott, look how the water tumbles down the rocks like it's falling down a set of stairs. It's beautiful!" Vivian's enthusiasm rushed into her voice as she took in the scene before her.

Scott smiled. "You can see why the campers like to hike to the falls. They also like to hike on up to the Cascades, where we're going next. It's only a half mile farther. Two major streams converge at Deep Hollow Cascades as they tumble down from two directions off Cove Mountain. There's a spectacular series of cascades at that spot with a good swimming hole below. We'll hike there next for our lunch stop."

"Does one of the streams from the cascades branch off down here to create this falls area?" Vivian looked around curiously.

"That's right," he answered. "The Laurel Prong stream converges with Deep Hollow Creek at the cascades; then it veers right to roll down the mountain and drop over these ledges here on its way. Below the falls, the Prong winds its way on down through Buckeye Camp and then, eventually, out into the valley to pour into Cove Creek. The Deep Hollow Creek angles left after the cascades, and then it runs on down the mountain between the farmhouse and Leo and Mary's place. It's the larger stream that sings to you beside the house."

"I know, I love listening to it in the quiet of the night with the windows open. Wonder what formed these rock stair ledges that the water cascades over?" Vivian studied the neat layers of rock that the falls plunged across. "They're so unusual. They look almost manmade, you know, but I know they can't be."

"Walker Bailey, our resident forest ranger who lives nearby on Falls Road, says it's all due to geological changes that happened here in these mountains thousands of years ago. They shifted rock in certain ways, and then, later, stream changes sent water over them, creating falls and cascades all through these mountains."

Vivian smiled at him. "Those water stair-steps make you want to get out and walk on them. But I bet they would be slippery and dangerous."

"You've got that one right." Scott nodded in agreement. "That's why we have to be careful when we bring our campers up this way. We have to keep them out of the water here. There's a good reason for the name Slippery Rock Falls, and I'm not willing to take a chance with my campers' safety by letting them play on the rocks in this area. They can come look, but there's no wading allowed."

Vivian looked out over the splashing falls with pleasure. "Well, it's nice enough just to look at. And I love this great bench you've made here out of an old log. It makes a good spot for a rest."

She sat down for a minute to try it out, while Scott puttered around the area looking for fallen limbs and moving them out of the pathways. A short time later, they hiked on up to the Deep Hollow Cascades where Deep Hollow and Laurel Prong collided in a series of rushing falls and spills over a tumble of giant boulders. Scott and Vivian ate lunch there by the side of the cascades on an old throw that Scott had brought along for them in his backpack.

"The sounds of the water here make you want to take a nap," Vivian said lazily after she and Scott had polished off the last of the brownies.

"It's probably because you ate more food than you usually do at lunch," Scott teased.

"But everything always tastes so good up here in the mountains." She grinned. "And Edith Harper's brownies are really hard to say no to."

Scott stood up then. "Well, lounge around here and enjoy the cascades for a little while. I'm going to explore along a couple of these little side trails and make sure no fallen trees or problems need to be reported. We're inside the National Park now. Slippery Rock Falls, behind us, is almost at the park boundary. Up here in this section of the park, I'm officially a trail volunteer for an area Smokies hiking club. I hike up here once a month to check the trails and look for any trouble to report."

"That's nice. You go look for trouble," said Vivian sleepily. "I'm going to lie down here for a minute to rest and just enjoy listening to the cascades."

Chapter 17

$\mathcal{S}$COTT CAME BACK FROM HIS hike to find Vivian asleep, curled up on the blanket with her arm wrapped under her head like a pillow. He sat down beside her quietly to just watch her for a minute.

She was so beautiful, with such a regal elegance and presence about her, even when she was asleep. Her long hair was tied up in a ponytail, but little tendrils had escaped to curl around her ears and over the nape of her neck. Her long legs were pulled up under her so that he could see the soft skin of her upper legs peeping out from beneath her shorts. Scott sucked in his breath softly.

He sat there and just studied her, enjoying being able to indulge his passions about her freely without her being able to see his face and guess his feelings. He'd worked hard these last weeks to keep their relationship on a friendship level. And he'd watched Vivian relax in his company, and begin to talk to him more easily, now that she knew he wasn't likely to jump her at every turn. Not that he still didn't want to do that. Scott grinned at the thought. And not that the electricity didn't still flow like hot voltage between them whenever they got too close to each other.

It was amazing, that. He'd never known another woman who had made him feel the way Vivian had. Lusty but protective and tender, too. Like right now. He wanted to just touch her face, run his hands over her, explore the wonder of touching her, getting close to her. He hadn't even given a thought to another woman since the night he met Vivian. That knowledge really made him nervous. Scott liked women, and he always noticed women. But lately ...

Vivian moved slightly, and sighed in her sleep. Then she rolled over a little more onto her back, exposing the tops of her breasts to him where the button had come undone. Scott might have avoided temptation even then, if she hadn't licked her lips a little in her sleep, almost in invitation.

With a groan of pent up sexual frustration, he dropped down over her, gathering her up in his arms and burying his face in her neck. However, she didn't curl sleepily into his embrace, as he had hoped. She screamed - not with surprise, but with sheer terror.

"Joe, no!" she screamed, moaning pitifully and beginning to try to coil her body up into a ball away from him. "Please no. Oh, Joe, please no. Don't hurt me."

He realized she was dreaming then, and he shook her awake harshly.

"Vivian," he said sharply. "Vivian, wake up. It's a dream. It's only a dream. Vivian, wake up. It's Scott, not Joe."

She woke up, with another scream just starting in her throat. Then seeing his face, Vivian threw her arms around him and started sobbing.

He held her and crooned soft words to her, just like he would to one of the children at the camp who had a bad scare. Anguished tears streamed down her face, and she shook and shuddered in his arms as she fought to escape her memories. Scott found that he was shaking, too.

At last, the crying and hiccupping sobs subsided, and Vivian began to calm. Scott rolled her around then to curl her up on his lap, propping his back against a tree.

"It's all right," he told her over and over. "No one's going to hurt you."

Her eyes grew wide then as she came fully awake and realized her situation.

"Oh, Scott, I'm sorry," she murmured, trying to wipe off her tears and pull herself off his lap at the same time.

"No, stay here." Scott held her gently in place. "Relax a minute. Everything's all right. I'm a master comforter of bad dreams, Vivian.

Don't be embarrassed; just relax here a minute."

Surprisingly, she minded him, leaning against him, letting her shaking gradually subside and her breathing calm down. Her head was tucked up against his shoulder and her legs were still curled up, almost in a fetal position.

"Tell me." He dropped his voice in a comforting tone. "Tell me what happened."

She shook her head. "It was just a bad dream."

"No," Scott said firmly. "This was a bad memory. Tell me, Vivian. If you'll get it out, the dream will be less likely to occur again. Surely, as an academic woman you should know that. This is some bottled up memory you've kept inside yourself. Let's get it out today so you can leave it behind."

She shook her head against his chest. "I don't want to tell," she said in a small voice. "It's too embarrassing."

"It doesn't matter. Just tell, Vivian." He smoothed her hair back gently from her face. "We're friends. You can trust me. I know how to keep a confidence."

She looked up at him, weighing the idea.

"All right," she said in a quiet voice, moving herself off his lap to lean against the tree beside him now. "You know my mother died when I was nine."

"Yes, I remember," he answered, tucking an arm around her shoulder in encouragement.

Vivian sighed heavily. "Well, I didn't go straight to the Meros then. They put me in foster homes. First I went to the Clayburn's farm - an older couple that kept a lot of kids. They were good to me. I was in a lot of pain after losing my mother, and the farm was a healing place that summer. I wanted to stay there, but they moved me. When you're a foster child, you don't get any choices. Other people decide about you. Other people shape your life. They don't even ask you what you want."

She stopped to cry a little then.

"They sent me to the Kemper's next. They thought it would be better for me. The Kemper's were rich, and their daughter, Amanda, wanted to have a little sister. She thought I was fun at first, and then she tired of me, like someone would of a new toy. I was nicer than Amanda, who wasn't always kind. Her friends soon started liking me better than her. Her parents liked me, too. Amanda wasn't always nice to her parents, either. But pretty soon, she convinced them to send me away. So they moved me again."

She sniffed and cried some more, leaning into Scott with a painful sigh that nearly broke his heart.

"I went to the Patterson's then. It wasn't a nice home like the others. It was shabby. A large group of foster children lived there; many of them were boys and they were older. They looked at the girls and said things that I didn't understand, but it scared the girls and it scared me. The Patterson's son Joe was a bad person, too. He would come and peep at the girls in the bathroom or in their rooms at night. I would see him sometimes, and he would smile at me like we had some secret. Then one night, while I was asleep, he was suddenly there. He lay on top of me, groping me. And he didn't have any clothes on. I was only ten, Scott, and frightened. I didn't know anything, but I knew to fight. I'm sure Joe would have raped me if he hadn't heard his parents come in the door, calling for him. He whispered that he would be back later."

Vivian started to sob then.

"Finish it, Vivian. What happened," he said quietly, his own heart beating, the anger churning up inside him that boys like Joe even existed to take advantage of innocent little girls like Vivian.

She took a ragged breath. "I dressed and put my things in a backpack. I slipped into the Patterson's room next door and stole some money. I knew where Mrs. Patterson kept her emergency cash. I'd heard her talking about it. Then I climbed out the window and ran. I ran all the way to the old Greyhound station downtown. There, I heard this old black lady say she was taking the bus to Mendocino. I took a chance, told her what happened, and begged her to help me get to a friend's home in Mendocino. She believed me. Thank God. I don't know what I would have done if she hadn't.

"I remember she hugged me and said: 'Girls have to deal with painful things in this world, honey, before it's all done. But you be strong, girl. The Lord will help you through.'" She helped me buy my ticket and told everyone she was a family friend and that she was traveling with me out to my uncle's place in Mendocino. I was so scared, Scott. I couldn't even sleep on the bus. I was terrified they would come after me and take me back."

Vivian stopped to cry again before she could continue. "That dear lady cared for me. When we got to Mendocino, her daughter picked her up, and she took me straight over to Henri Bernard's house. I still remembered the way to his place. Henri had the wine store right next to my mother's old bookstore. He was a sweet middle-aged gay man who had always been kind to my mother and I. I fell into his arms sobbing when he opened his door early that morning, and he took me in."

Vivian sighed. "Henri hid me for awhile, and he sent back the money I'd taken from the Patterson's to protect me from any possibility of a theft charge. He sent it anonymously as a money order with a note that said that I'd gone to stay with relatives and that they shouldn't try to find me or the authorities would be notified about Joe's actions. So I was a fugitive for a while. Henri said he didn't trust the social services department to do the right thing by me after all I'd been through. But he knew they'd never let him have me."

"How did you get to the Mero's?" Scott asked.

"Dorothy Mero was Henri's sister. He told them about me, about my mother, about how smart I was. He was my advocate. He found me a good foster home and then got social services to approve it. I got to grow up with his sister and her husband. And I stayed close to Henri, too, until he died. I'll never forget him, Scott, what he did for me. What his family did for me. They saved me."

"It was a terrible experience, Vivian. I'm so sorry it happened to you." He pressed a kiss against her forehead.

"I know it could have been worse," she whispered.

"But it wasn't," he reminded her. "And like the black lady said, you've been strong and the Lord has helped you through."

Vivian cried again, and Scott wrapped her up tightly in his arms once more. He kissed her without thinking, and his heart was pained and full at the same time.

Vivian looked up into his face. "You know I've had trouble being close with anyone ever since that time, except with you. But with you, it's been different, Scott."

Her heart was in her eyes. And a side of Scott knew he could make love to her right then if he wanted to. She was vulnerable. She had opened her heart to him, and he had been kind and not judged her, which was what she had always been afraid of. He had helped her to open up and get an old pain lanced out.

But he kissed her on the nose instead and then kissed her again softly on the mouth. He made no effort to go further. Probably because it was in that moment he realized he loved her. It scared him to know it and to realize it. He had been waiting, he guessed, to see that trust in her eyes, to realize that she needed him. To know that she wasn't totally self-sufficient without him. That she had weaknesses and soft areas that he could fill.

He thought of telling her about his feelings then, but somehow it didn't seem the right time. He was afraid she would just think he was only saying the words because he felt sorry for her. No, he'd find another time. For now, it would keep.

As a tenderness slipped its fingers around Scott's heart that he'd never experienced before, he wrapped Vivian tighter into his arms, and let the lightning of their contact forge through him. He knew at that moment, too, without a shadow of a doubt, that he'd found the woman he wanted to spend his life with. He just had to find a way to make her know it, too. He would do that, he thought fiercely. If there was one thing Scott Jamison was good at, it was getting what he wanted. And he didn't mind to work hard to get it.

He smoothed Vivian's hair back from her face and kissed her softly again. "Everything's going to be alright, Vivian. Old secrets are out now, and you'll start to heal."

"I do feel better somehow," she told him, sniffling. "I didn't think I would. I thought it would be better to keep this all to myself. Only Henri and the Meros know."

"Some things aren't the kind of story you want to tell everyone, Vivian, but there should always be people you feel safe to share yourself with. To trust."

"I guess," she admitted. "I haven't very been good at trusting."

He smiled at her. "Well, you've started now. Who knows what layers we'll peel off before you're done. You might get to be an open book sort of person just like me."

"Oh, I'd say you have your share of secrets, too," she returned, more saucily now, and beginning to sound more like her old self again.

"Probably I do," he told her, grinning. "And one is that I just love to throw gorgeous girls into mountain streams."

He picked her up then, pretending he was going to toss her out into the water. She shrieked and struggled, of course. It helped to break the intensity of the moment, and to get Vivian's dander back up. He knew how to deal with an argumentative and angry Vivian better that this gentler, tender Vivian he'd uncovered. Besides, he sensed that getting her provoked with him in their old teasing way was just the thing she needed at the moment. He also understood better for the first time why she had been so reticent to share herself with him.

Vivian was right when she had told Scott that he didn't understand anything about real pain and betrayal. He didn't have sorrows in his past like Vivian had known, and he found himself deeply thankful for that. When he got home that night, he called his family. It was good just to hear the love of their voices. To know that he had them in his life.

Chapter 18

Vivian knew, over the weeks to come, that something had changed in her relationship with Scott. A subtle difference existed in how Scott related to her, how he treated her, how he looked at her. He treated her more gently, and in some ways she liked that, and in other ways she didn't. She knew the changes occurred after she confessed what happened with Joe when she was ten. Scott knew she had been passed around in foster homes for a year after her mother had died now. Did he feel sorry for her? Was that it? Did he not want to get involved with someone who had so many past problems? Who had been a foster child? Or had their friendship just moved into a different, more comfortable zone? Vivian couldn't tell.

Tad suggested, "Honey, you just need to jump him. Let him know how you feel."

But a part of Vivian didn't want to take their relationship back to that old level. She didn't really want to be backed up against walls and counters with Scott trying to push their relationship into a purely sexual encounter.

"I want more," she admitted to herself softly. "I've fallen in love with him, and I don't want just an affair. Plus I couldn't stand it if that was all I ended up with. It's hard enough now, loving him and not having any idea how he feels about me."

She sighed and looked out the window from her desk in the upstairs sitting room. She'd been writing all morning, then editing, and now she was ready to call it quits for the day.

A flit of yellow among the maple trees caught her attention. It didn't fit into the normal landscape of the yard she was so used to viewing. She looked more carefully and saw it again.

"Now what was that?" she asked herself. It looked like a fairy running in and out among the shrubbery, a fairy with yellow wings.

Just then, the shape slipped out from behind the old snowball bush, and Vivian could see that it was a little child and not a fairy. A small girl in a fluffy yellow tutu with matching yellow fairy wings. She was pretending to fly, lifting her arms up and down, and flitting in and out among the shrubs and trees. Vivian smiled to herself.

"Wonder who she is?"

Well, it was certain she'd need to find out. There weren't many families around here with children, and Vivian had met most of them already. This little girl didn't look familiar at all. She might be lost. Maybe she was visiting over at the camp and had wandered away from her family.

Vivian slipped her feet into her shoes below the desk and started down the stairs for the front door. When she got outside – with Fritzi happy to tag along beside her - she couldn't see the child at first. Then she saw the edge of her behind some trees beyond the swing.

Vivian went over to sit down on the swing and said calmly, "You know, Fritzi, I think I saw a little fairy behind that tree over there. I hope she's a friendly fairy and that she'll come out and talk to us."

A small head looked around the corner of the snowball bush. She had dark red hair, a smattering of freckles across her nose, and a sweet, impish grin. She looked to be about five or six years old, probably the same age as Chelsey. There was something oddly familiar about the child, but Vivian couldn't place it.

"Hi," Vivian said. "What's your name?"

"Ophelia Odelia, queen of all the yellow flowers," she announced in a regal voice.

Vivian smiled. "And where does Ophelia live?"

"Sometimes she makes herself small and lives inside a daffodil. She can do that, and she can fly, too."

"I see," Vivian observed.

The child came out from behind the bush and cocked her head to one side impishly.

"Ophelia really likes to live inside an old tree trunk, the kind with a big hole in the front, but she hasn't found one today."

"You know, I saw one of those on my hike up past Slippery Rock Falls a few weeks ago. It had a wonderful big hole in it, and, at the time, I thought that it would be a fine tree for fairies to live in."

The child came closer now, her blue eyes big with wonder. "Is that tree far from here?"

The girl looked a little less like a fairy up close. There were shorts and a t-shirt under her fairy clothes and tennis shoes on her feet. But around her head was a garland of yellow artificial flowers with streamers down the back. Goodness, she was cute.

Vivian smiled at her again. "Too far for you to go alone. But maybe if you tell me where Ophelia lives when she turns herself into a little girl, I might take that little girl there some day. Although it's a long walk up the mountain."

She pointed up toward Buckeye Knob and watched the child's eyes follow the direction of her hand.

"I'm strong, and I can walk far," she informed Vivian. "My mother and I used to go walking together a lot up in the big mountains there." She pointed up toward the misty Smokies' ranges in the distance.

Her face fell dejectedly. "But then she died," the child said very quietly, looking down at her feet and scuffing her shoe in the dirt.

Vivian's heart wrenched. "I'm sorry." Vivian spoke the words softly and reached out to put a hand on the little girl's shoulder. "My mommy died, too, when I was small. I remember how much it hurt to lose her."

"You're nice." The child moved a little closer toward Vivian and leaned up against her leg. "What's your name?"

"Do you mean my real name or my fairy name?"

The little girl giggled. "Both, maybe." She turned her head to grin at Vivian then. "Do you really have a fairy name?"

"Of course. My favorite fairy name was always Princess Willowdeen Willowette. I remember Princess Willowdeen had a long silky green dress with silver trim and a real tiara with a jewel in the front. Her favorite home was under the low hidden branches

157

of a weeping willow tree in my back yard. But when Willowdeen went home to her own bed at night her other real name was always Vivian Leah Delaney." She looked at the child then. "What's your other name, Ophelia?"

"Sarah Louise Taylor." She recited her name in a sing-song voice. "And right now I'm staying over at the Greene's with Ellen, Quint, and Chelsey."

She hung her head and scuffed her shoe along the ground again. "I'm a foster child," she said quietly. "And the Greenes are keeping me for a while until somebody might want me to live with them."

Vivian felt an old pain streak through her heart that she had almost forgotten. "I was a foster child, too, once long ago, Sarah Louise."

"Did you find a nice family?" Sarah lowered her voice. "Someone that wanted you?"

"That I did." Vivian smiled at Sarah. "A very nice man and lady who raised me just like their own little girl and who still love me a lot, even now that I'm grown up."

Sarah's eyes widened. "Didn't you miss your mother?"

"Oh, yes," Vivian assured her. "And I still do. My mother will have a very special space in my heart forever. You should never forget your mother either, and it is all right to miss her and even to cry sometimes. But a heart is big enough to be able to have love for other people in it. Yours will love again, too, after some of the sadness goes away."

"Maybe." Sarah considered this idea while watching Vivian swaying back and forth in the old tree swing.

"Will you swing me in your swing?" she asked, in the way of children who can handle only so much analytical talk before shifting their thoughts in another direction.

"For a few minutes." Vivian paused. "If you'll let me walk you back over to Ellen's house afterwards. She might be worried about you, Sarah. Did you tell her you were coming over here?"

Sarah hung her head again. "No. Ophelia just got to flying and before we knew it we were over here. Did I come far?"

"Not very far. But I'll walk you back after we swing, just in case Ophelia can't remember the way she flew."

"Okay," Sarah said.

A short time later, Vivian walked Sarah back over to the Greene's place. She left Sarah at the house with Quint and Chelsey, and then went down to the barn to find Ellen. It was Thursday and one of Ellen's regular soap-making days.

"Lord, I thought that child was in the house with Chelsey and Quint all this time," Ellen said, after Vivian told her why she'd come over. "Quint was home this morning, and he said he would watch both the girls while I did my soap. I don't like the children out here playing when I'm doing soap. Because of the lye mix. It's so caustic."

Vivian laughed. "Well, Quint had fallen asleep on the sofa with Chelsey after reading both of them to sleep over a pile of picture books." She peered into the vat where Vivian's soap mixture was bubbling. "But they're up now, and Sarah is playing with Chelsey outside in the front yard while Quint is trimming some shrubs. No harm was done, Ellen."

"Maybe, but we should have been watching her more closely than that. I promised Alice I would look after Sarah carefully for her." Ellen stirred her mixture while she talked.

"Vivian, hand me that bottle of peppermint oil," she directed, pointing out a brown bottle sitting on a side shelf. "The soap is tracing now and it's almost ready to pour out. See?" She demonstrated, pulling the stirrer out so Vivian could see the soap stringing down from it in long, sticky strands like hot pizza cheese.

Ellen added the peppermint oil and some herbs and continued her stirring. "In a few minutes I can pour this batch out in those wooden molds over there and then I can sit down to take a break and talk with you."

Vivian leaned against the barn wall, watching Ellen work. "Quint said Sarah was a foster child."

"Yes. Alice Graham is a real good friend of Quint's, and mine, and a social worker with the Wayside Agency. She needed a temporary place for Sarah until she could find her a permanent foster home. Every now and then we help Alice out when she gets in a bind about a child."

"Tell me about Sarah. She seems like a nice little child."

"Oh, she's a delight. And Chelsey's enjoying having her. Sarah's mother died a few months ago. I actually knew her. She had a little shop at the west end of Gatlinburg, sold wind chimes and whimsical items and bought some of my soaps, too, for the store. She was a charming woman. Died of an aneurism or something. Real sudden and unexpected, Quint said. There wasn't any family to step in."

Ellen stopped stirring and began to dip out the soap mixture, pouring it into the wooden molds.

"Gosh, that smells wonderful," Vivian sniffed appreciatively as the odor of the soap mixture permeated the air.

"Yeah, I always like making peppermint soap. It smells so good." Ellen grinned. "It makes me want homemade peppermint ice cream every time I make it, so Quint and I are making some up for our Thursday night dinner. This will get you in the mood."

"Ummmm. What a great idea. I haven't had homemade ice cream in years."

The Greene's Thursday night gatherings had become a weekly ritual for Ellen, Quint, Scott, and Vivian. They were always fun.

"What about Sarah's father?" Vivian asked, returning to their former conversation again.

"He's not in the picture." Ellen found a new set of molds and started to dip out soap again. "Alice told us Sarah's mother Eleanor never married him or even told him about Sarah at all. It's always been just the two of them – Eleanor and Sarah. Alice said Eleanor never even recorded the father's name on the birth records. So he can't be tracked down."

"Aren't there any other family members to step in?"

"Evidently not," Ellen confided. "After Eleanor died, Sarah stayed with an older couple who own a shop near Eleanor's, but they had to take off to help one of their grown children who had a new baby coming in. And they can't take Sarah permanently. So Quint and I said we'd fill in for a little while - especially because we knew Eleanor and because we'd met Sarah. She's a really bright and good child. I'm sure Alice can find her a nice family."

"Most people want babies and not children Sarah's age." Vivian frowned.

"Sarah's only just turned five," Ellen responded. "She's still young. She hasn't even started school yet. But she can already read and do numbers. In fact, she's teaching Chelsey and getting her more psyched up for kindergarten this fall, which is a good thing. Sarah also has this huge imagination and loves to play pretend games."

"Like fairies?" Vivian smiled. "She was dressed up like a fairy when I found her over at the farmhouse."

"Oh, yeah. That's her favorite, playing fairies of some sort and creating all sorts of stories about them. We had to go out and buy fairy wings for Chelsey after Sarah arrived with hers. You know, I remember Eleanor used to sell fairy wings, garlands, wands, and all sorts of fairy figurines and chimes at that store of hers. I guess that's what kicked Sarah off on the fairy jag."

Ellen paused to ladle out the last of the soap mixture into the molds. "Actually, it has been really good for Chelsey having Sarah here." She pushed a loose strand of hair back behind her ear. "It has given Chelsey someone to play with. All the other children around here are really too old for her. I sort of hope Sarah will get to stay for at least part of the summer with us. But Alice is hoping to get her settled with a new family before fall so she won't have to change schools."

Finished with pouring the soap now, Ellen wiped off her hands and gestured to Vivian to follow her out to a couple of lawn chairs by the barn door. Both were set up in a shady spot out of the sun.

"Want a cola?" Ellen asked Vivian. "I keep some in the cooler out here."

She pulled two out and then plopped down in one of the chairs with a sigh.

"Don't worry too much about Sarah." Ellen leaned over to tie a loose shoe string. "Alice is wonderful in finding just the right families for her kids."

She smiled. "You know, she'd probably have taken Sarah herself for a while. Alice does that sometimes. Except that she's fostering six children right now that just lost their parents in an accident. It's really hard to place six kids in one family, Alice says, and she doesn't want to break the family up. So she's helping out with them right now. She has her hands full."

"She sounds remarkable." Vivian was impressed.

"Oh, Alice is great, real smart and a dynamo of energy." Ellen took a long drink of her cola. "You'd never know it to look at her though. She's one of those petite, pretty, fragile little blonds. Looks like the type you'd want to shelter and protect."

Ellen laughed. "But no one had better try that with Alice. She'll put them in their place real quick." She smiled at Vivian. "I'll introduce you to Alice when she comes over the next time. You'll like her."

"I like her already for what she's doing for Sarah and those other kids," Vivian said. "You know, I was a foster child myself for a time - just after my mother died when I was nine. I know how much it means to have someone that cares helping you find a new home when yours is lost. It's a devastating time for a child."

"I'd forgotten that you had that experience." Ellen propped her feet up on a stump.

Vivian told Ellen briefly about moving around in a few foster homes before she found her way to the Mero's home. However, Vivian decided against telling Ellen about the experience with Joe at the Patterson's. There didn't seem to be any point in it. She just told Ellen she hated it there and that she had run away once.

After their visit, Vivian went back to the farmhouse. There she made potato salad and cookies - her contributions toward the Thursday night dinner. The four of them always chipped in together now to come up with their weekly meals. The men usually grilled some type of meat outdoors, if the weather permitted, or they bought a ham or barbeque. Ellen and Vivian took care of vegetables and desserts.

Tonight, Quint and Scott were grilling hamburgers. Scott was bringing the meat and helping with the sides. Ellen was making baked beans, and Quint was making the homemade peppermint ice cream, a specialty of his. Also, they were eating outside on the patio tonight, since the days were getting longer.

As Vivian worked preparing the potato salad for dinner, her mind kept returning to thoughts of Sarah Taylor. She knew so well the sorrow in the little child's heart right now and about the brave front she put up for everyone.

"I'm going to be a special friend to her," she promised herself. "I know what it's like to be alone as a child."

In fact, Vivian decided to go on over to the Greene's early so that she could entertain the girls while Ellen got ready for their dinner. She called and left Scott a message just to meet her there.

Chapter 19

As MAY SETTLED IN, SCOTT'S days at the camp grew longer and busier. Returning from town, Scott stopped by the camp mailbox and rolled his eyes at the huge stack of mail he found. Applications still swamped Buckeye's mailbox everyday, despite the fact that most of the camp sessions were already full.

"Morning, Nancy." Scott dropped the fistful of envelopes on Nancy's desk as he walked into the camp office.

Nancy groaned as she added them to the towering stack of mail in her in-box. "I think this is the most applications we've ever received for the camp, Scott."

"Better too many than not enough." Scott grinned at her, dropping down into the chair across from her desk.

Nancy pushed a neat stack of papers his way in reply. "Here are the last of the signed contracts from the camp counselors for you to look over. On the top is that agenda you wanted me to type up for the counselor-training week the first of June. Check that over, too, and if it's all right I'll start running copies for the training staff and counselors." She paused. "And don't you dare take off again before you look over that list of camp supplies that has been ordered so far. It's on your desk in your office."

Scott glanced over the training schedule Nancy had typed, drumming his fingers on the table and whistling under his breath.

Nancy put a hand on her hip. "Honestly, Scott Jamison. You're not stressed at all, are you? Look at you, relaxed and whistling. You're just in your element now that camp is ready to gear up."

"That I am." He reached over to tweak her cheek. "I'm a man who loves his job."

"Well, I suppose I shouldn't complain about working with someone who is always so cheerful." She paused and gave him a teasing look. "Anything else contributing to this radiant happiness lately? Or should I say anyone?"

Scott smiled at her smugly as he got up to carry his papers back to his office. "You know I'm always happy when I've got a woman in my life, Nancy."

"Smarty-pants." She flipped a hand at him in exasperation and then gave him a thoughtful look. "You know, Scott, I really like Vivian Delaney. Be nice to her."

"I am being nice to Vivian," Scott said in response, as he snagged a cup of coffee to carry back to his office.

He closed the door to insulate himself from more probing questions from his cousin and settled easily into his desk chair. After taking a few sips of his coffee, he pulled a small photo of Vivian out of his desk to study it. It had been taken over at the lake when he'd been helping her brush up on her canoeing skills. She was laughing and the sun was in her hair.

"I am being nice to you, don't you think, Vivian?" he said softly. "We're more comfortable with each other; we're getting to know each other better. Our relationship is strengthening nicely. I'm working hard to be a good boy."

Scott smiled at his own thoughts. After he had realized the depth of his feelings for Vivian at the cascades in April, he changed in his approach to her. He stopped pressing her for further intimacy, for one thing. Not that he didn't want that. But he knew Vivian was 'the one' now, and that made everything different somehow.

He tapped her picture with his thumb. "You're really testing me, Vivian Delaney. Being nice doesn't come easy for me. There are times when I think I'll go crazy with the desire to touch you, to teach you how sweet loving can be. Especially now that I understand why you guarded yourself so carefully from intimate contact before. But I'm trying to be patient and wait."

Wait for what, he wondered? The thought gave Scott a shiver. He knew he was thinking seriously about the big M word now. That's what he and his brothers had always called marriage. Scott knew this was a huge life step.

He frowned at the photo in his hand. "I'd probably take the big plunge if I didn't think you were still keeping secrets from me, Vivian. It's the one factor that makes me uncomfortable in this relationship and the main reason I've held back from really sharing all my feelings. I want you to trust me, to not keep secrets from me."

Laying the photo on his desk, Scott frowned and leaned back in his chair. "Irritating woman. I can't figure out why you're so ashamed of your writing identity, anyway. Or why some college would be so upset about your books that they'd want you to give them up. Are they syrupy romances or bloody mysteries? Or something trashy and tasteless? Maybe you write silly fairy stories like you tell to Chelsey and Sarah. After the Andrew Lang dissertation I could see how that might tick your department off."

Scott shrugged. He had no idea what sort of books academia would dislike that much, but Vivian's work must be something really frivolous or inappropriate for them to have gotten so upset over it.

"Maybe we'll talk this over again as we walk over to Quint and Ellen's tonight. Maybe you just need another little nudge to start to share." Scott shook his head in annoyance. He had tried to be patient about this whole thing, but the truth was, he often wanted to wring Vivian's neck over it. In addition, it took all the discipline he possessed not to make some calls to find out more about Vivian's past on his own. He knew he could track down the truth easily enough if he just got to the right person at her college.

Back at his house later in the day, Scott found a message from Vivian on his answering machine saying she was going over to the Greene's early. "Guess we'll have to have that talk later," he said.

Even though he wasn't meeting Vivian, Scott stopped by the farmhouse as he headed out to the Greene's. He had gotten some more pet food for the animals and wanted to drop it off. As he opened the back door of the farmhouse, arms loaded with bags and Fritzi weaving excitedly around his legs, he saw Dearie suddenly streak past him.

"Terrific. She's got something in her mouth," he observed in annoyance. "She's caught something and brought it into the house. Dang cat."

He dropped the pet food on the counter and took off after the cat. Naturally, when Dearie heard him in pursuit, she streaked up the stairs with her prey. It looked like it was a bird, a finch from the size and color of it.

That proved to be the case, as Dearie dropped it on the floor for a minute and the little bird took flight. Scott took off to chase the bird now, with Dearie after it at the same time. Eventually, he trapped the bird in the upstairs sitting room that Vivian used for an office. After shutting Dearie outside the door, yowling in protest, Scott managed to catch the finch in a towel. He opened the sitting room window, pushed out the screen, and let the bird go free. Amazingly, it seemed unharmed. Lucky break for the bird, Scott thought.

He dropped on the couch to catch his breath just as Vivian's office phone rang. After the third ring, a message for Vivian came in on the answering machine.

He heard a man's voice, deep and honeyed. "Viv, darling. It's Tad. The sales numbers on the new book, *Kissing Cousins,* are starting to come in. You marvelous woman, it's a smash, as always. And this new twist in the Foster series of having Isabel get this financial legacy is just thrilling the television fans to death. They're all wondering if the letter Izzy got about an inheritance from a long lost uncle is even genuine and, if it is, how much money it will be for Isabel, and what the girls will do with it. Yadda, yadda. The idea was just brilliant, Viv. And, of course, by the time the follow-up book, *The Legacy,* comes out, all the fans will have to have that one, too. I just want you to know we're all so proud out here of all your success."

There was a warm laugh then. "And of course you know I'm proud of my success as the show's director. It has enhanced my credentials out here tremendously, darling. I've been approached about doing another network show if I can make the time, and I bless the day that Betsy Picardi came to me with your little books and suggested we make them into a pilot. It was just the perfect time for a good family series like *The Foster Girls.*"

A rustling of papers came through then. "You hear that, Viv? That's the sound of new scripts for the upcoming episode. Roz wants me to fax them to you so you can look them over, be sure all the dialogue she's written is consistent with the girls. You know the drill. I'm sending them through by fax, so look them over tomorrow and give us a heads up if everything is okay. And call me, darling. I want to know every little thing that has been going on there in farmsville."

There were some kissing sounds. "Kiss, kiss to you, my pretty woman. You be careful that you don't give your heart away to anyone else but me. Especially to one of those local boys. You know you're the only woman I love."

There was a laugh then, and the phone clicked out. The sound of the fax soon followed, and the script papers began to come through.

Scott leaned back on the couch, stunned. Incredulous.

"Vivian is Viva Leeds," he said out loud to the empty room. "She's the writer of *The Foster girl* books, the genius behind the award-winning *Foster Girl* television series."

He got up then, to let the still yowling Dearie into the room.

"Your bird's been sprung, Dearie," he said to her, watching her go around the room looking for her catch. "He escaped this time. But it looks like I've been snared in a big mess myself."

Scott picked up one of the fax sheets, saw the lines of script across them. And tried to absorb the reality of what he had just learned.

He sat back down on the couch, his thoughts still reeling. Yes, Vivian had told him she was well-known in her field. But he had not expected this.

"She's Viva Leeds." He said it again, shaking his head, trying to take it all in.

His mind now replayed all the times Vivian snapped her computer shut when he came over and found her writing or the times she made excuses to keep him out of her upstairs office. He also remembered how little interest she showed in the television show every Thursday night while the rest of America was enthralled with it. Yet, she always seemed to know what was going on in the series.

Scott hit his hand against his forehead as a stream of past memories flooded in.

"No wonder she guessed that Cliff wouldn't really be Veronica's full cousin," he said to himself, recalling her suppositions to the Mc-Fee girls in the camp kitchen one day. "She wrote the story. She knew where it was going while the rest of us were only guessing.

She was writing the stuff right here."

He paced around the room looking for more evidence and spotted a group of books tucked into his Gramma's bookshelf. Copies of all *The Foster Girl* books, neatly arranged in the alphabetical order they were famous for –from A for *Almost Home* right up to K and the newest publication, *Kissing Cousins*. Also, on a shelf beside Vivian's computer sat four small dolls. Scott had read in a tabloid, which the McFee girls had left lying around at the camp, that Viva Leeds had built her whole book series around some childhood dolls she'd had since she was small. There were actually a series of purchasable *Foster Girl* dolls on the market now, but these little well-worn dolls were probably the real things. The real, original *Foster Girl* dolls. A good thief could probably make a million dollars just from hocking these little dolls.

Scott laughed at the thought, and then became offended as a new set of emotions flooded over him.

Why hadn't she told him? This wasn't something to be ashamed of. These books were highly acclaimed and the series was wholesome family entertainment.

"And who the heck is this Tad, besides being her show director?" He paced the room in irritation. "Calling her *darling* and *pretty woman*. Saying she's *the only woman he loves*. Does Vivian have someone else out in Hollywood? A secret man with her secret life? Have I just been some kind of interlude?"

He found himself getting really angry then. Angry at all the secrets, angry that he was fancying himself in love and thinking about marriage with a woman that had a huge second life he obviously knew nothing about. He spouted out a few expletives as he pushed his way out the door of the sitting room and started down the stairs. He wanted out of that room and out right now.

And he wanted answers. Tonight, after they got back from this deal at the Greene's, he would get some. They would talk this out. Between then and now, somehow he would get through the evening. If she could play games, he could, too.

Scott took the long route to the Greene's, trying to walk off some of his anger, trying to get himself back in control. He didn't want a confrontation in front of his friends, so he worked hard to collect himself before he arrived at Quint and Ellen's.

"You're late," Quint said throwing Scott one of their Grill Man aprons Ellen had bought for them as he walked into the Greene's backyard.

"It's the busy season at the camp now." Scott shot a grin his way and started patting the hamburger meat he'd brought into burger patties. He whistled while he worked, purposed to put on a jovial front.

From the side lawn nearby, Vivian and Ellen waved at him. They were playing croquet with Chelsey and another little girl.

"Who's the extra kid?" Scott asked.

"Another of Alice's foster kids we're keeping for awhile." Quint poked at the charcoal in the grill and started putting the burgers on. "Remember those two we kept last year for a little while, those two little boys?"

"Yeah. Cute little guys. I took them over to the camp with me a few times. And Nancy's boys really enjoyed having them around. Nice kids." He paused thoughtfully. "Aren't they the ones that the Kincaids over in Kodak adopted?"

"That's right." Quint spritzed the charcoal in the grill as the grease from the meat whipped the flames up. "And you and your mother helped Alice with that placement, knowing that Bart and Diedre couldn't have kids and wanted to adopt."

"I see that family every now and then." Scott finished the burgers, wiped his hands, and sat down on a patio bench. "Bart and Diedre love those boys. It's been a happy match." He shifted a glance over at Vivian when Quint wasn't looking, trying not to glare at her.

"Well, maybe you can help with this one, too." Quint raised a brow suggestively. "That little girl there – name's Sarah Louise Taylor – just lost her mother. Has no other family. She needs a home, too. You may have met the mother; she ran one of those craft stores in Gatlinburg that Ellen sells her soaps to. Little place back in the corner of Mountain Laurel Village. Pretty woman, too. Single and on her own with just the child."

"Must have missed that one," Scott commented, with a grin to Quint. "But I know where the village stores are in Gatlinburg. Is there no father in the picture?"

"None that anyone knows about." Quint flipped the burgers as they cooked. "Woman came here and bought the shop, single and with a small child. Never married. Past a bit of a mystery. She obviously had some money from somewhere. But never told anyone anything that could be tracked down about the father or about any family. Always said her parents had passed on. Alice said she figured that was where she got the money to relocate and buy the store. Guess no one will ever know now."

"Tough break for the kid," Scott said, thinking about the stories Vivian had told him about being a foster child when she was younger. "She's lucky that it's Alice that's working with her. She's one terrific lady."

"Well, Sarah's a great kid, too." Quint smiled, glad he'd gotten Scott interested. "Smart and creative. Well-behaved. Better manners than Chelsey actually." He laughed at that. "We're hoping some of that will rub off on the Chessie Cat while Sarah is here."

"Aw, Chelsey's fine," Scott said, defending her. "But it was good of you and Ellen to take Sarah in for awhile. I'll start putting my feelers out about potential homes. She's still just a little thing. They'll be someone that will want to adopt her, I'll bet."

"Well, I know Alice will appreciate any help you can give," Quint replied.

The new child helped to provide Scott with a needed distraction. Scott really loved kids. He made a big effort to entertain Chelsey and Sarah that evening. Quint set up a small tent for the girls in the backyard, and Scott played 'attack bear' with them, bringing on shrieks and giggles from both the girls. Then, they all played several games of croquet. With a vast amount of satisfaction, Scott knocked Vivian's ball almost down to the creek.

Later, after dinner, Vivian volunteered, as usual, to go up to read with the girls while everyone else settled down to watch *The Foster Girls* on television. But, this time, Scott had done a little priming with the girls ahead of time, promising to tell them true camping stories, so they begged for him to go up with them instead.

"I'll go and help you," Vivian said graciously, smiling. "Maybe I'll like your stories, too."

"No, you watch the television show, Vivian. Perhaps actually watching the show for once will help you better predict to the McFee girls how the series is going to develop." He gave her a pointed glance. "You're so good at that."

He enjoyed seeing a slow blush steal over her face at his remark.

"You know it is uncanny how Vivian seems to know what's going to happen on these shows when she watches them so seldom," Ellen observed.

"Yes, isn't it just." Scott's reply had a nasty edge to it, and he saw Vivian's look of question and surprise at his tone.

He stalked upstairs to tell the girls bedtime stories, glad of yet another space of time in which he wouldn't have to keep acting pleasant and personable around Vivian, Ellen, and Quint. His layer of contrived congeniality was growing thinner as the evening wore on.

Chapter 20

$\mathcal{A}$s VIVIAN AND SCOTT STARTED their walk home from the Greene's, Vivian felt nervous and uncomfortable. Scott was upset about something. Vivian was certain of it. He had been acting peculiar all evening, almost as if he was carefully controlling some inner irritation or anger. Perhaps he'd had a bad day earlier at the camp but didn't want to inflict his problems on all of them.

Vivian chewed on her lip as she watched him. Scott strode along a few paces ahead of her, scowling and not speaking. He hadn't said a word since they left the Greene's and they were almost back to the farmhouse porch now. Tension radiated from him. Even in the dark, Vivian could see that Scott's face looked edgy and drawn. This just wasn't like Scott at all. He must be really upset about something.

Vivian reached over instinctively to touch his arm and tried to take his hand. But he jerked away from her.

"What's wrong, Scott?" She tried to read his face. "You haven't been yourself all night."

He glared at her. "And so when are you ever yourself, Vivian Delaney. And how do you even keep all your many selves straight?"

The little porch light showed Vivian the raw anger on Scott's face now.

"I think we'd better sit down so you can tell me what's going on." Vivian gestured to the porch chairs.

Scott shrugged off the offer, pacing in restless random patterns instead. When Vivian sat down on the porch steps, Scott turned to confront her.

"You're Viva Leeds," he announced in a steely voice, seeming to dare her to deny it. "You're the writer of all those *Foster Girl* books and the writer behind the television series. Why didn't you tell me, Vivian? What is there to be ashamed of in writing material like that? The books are bestsellers; the series is on a family network and well-respected. It's practically like another Walton's series, it's so clean. Why would you not want people to know you are behind something fine and wholesome like that? It's not like you write bodice ripper romances or bloody crime thrillers you might not want your name associated with."

Vivian glared back angrily, tears starting in her eyes.

"You promised you wouldn't look into my background, Scott," she accused resentfully. "You broke your word."

"Oh, don't start that teary eyes and broken promises crap," he snapped back. "I found out inadvertently. I didn't go snooping into your ever-so private life."

"How did you find out then?" Vivian wanted to know.

"I don't really owe you an explanation, Vivian, but I'll give you one, anyway. I came by to bring some more pet food to the farmhouse on my way over to the Greene's." He gestured toward the house behind them. "Dearie came racing in under my legs with a bird in her mouth and started off through the house with it. Geeze. I started chasing her down and, then, when she let the bird loose in the house, I had to chase the bird down. I finally trapped it in the sitting room upstairs, with the dang cat yowling outside the door in protest."

"Oh, how awful. Was the bird dead?"

"No, incredibly, it wasn't. It was still flying around all over the room banging into the walls and windows. I finally caught it in a towel and let it loose out the window after I pushed the screen out. It flew off as if it was all right."

"Thank goodness for that." Vivian wrapped her arms around her knees.

"Yeah, well your phone started ringing about the time I let the bird out the window. I flopped down on the couch to catch my breath just when your Hollywood boyfriend called. He left you quite a message. He spilled the beans on you, Vivian. I didn't have to go snooping." He scowled angrily at her.

"What boyfriend?" Vivian asked, confused.

"The one who calls you *darling* and *pretty woman*." Scott's voice was laced with sarcasm. "The one who says he loves you and that you're *the only woman in his life*. Some Tad guy."

"Oh, Tad," Vivian said, starting to giggle then.

"Don't laugh about this, Vivian." Scott leaned over her with a furious look, his tone dangerous. "It's bad enough you've kept this whole Viva Leeds thing from me. But I don't like it that you've kept a secret love relationship from me, too. You have someone else in your life, someone else who's in love with you and that you're obviously involved with."

Vivian was still laughing and couldn't seem to stop herself.

Scott tossed out an unexpected expletive and yanked Vivian to her feet.

"I've never hit a woman in my life, Vivian Delaney or whoever you are. But you're pushing me very close to the edge here." He gripped her arms and looked into her eyes with a fury that had Vivian's senses reeling in alarm.

"I'm sorry I laughed, but Tad Wainwright is not my boyfriend in the sense that you mean. He is the director of my show and he is avowedly gay," Vivian told him, in her firm and authoritative professional voice, trying to defuse the situation. "And I want you to let go of my arms right now, Scott. You're hurting me."

Scott loosened his grip on her arms a little.

"What did you say?" he asked, trying to calm down now.

"One of these days that impulsive streak of yours is going to get you into some real trouble, Scott Jamison," she told him quietly. "It's always been the thing I've found least attractive in you."

Scott pushed away from her then, sitting down on the steps to try to channel his anger back under control. Vivian sat down beside him, rubbing her arms and watching him struggle with himself. He was actually shaking.

"I won't apologize." He muttered his reply, breathing heavily. "I've been through hell tonight."

"Mostly of your own making." Vivian knew her tone was snappish and unsympathetic but she didn't care.

"That man on that phone said he loved you and called you darling." Scott frowned at her, his anger flaring up again. "Said for you not to fall for any guys from over here in farmsville. How do you think that made me feel, Vivian? Especially after just learning you were *The Foster Girls* author - and probably a millionaire off that television series. I felt like an absolute fool."

"I told you I didn't want you to know because it would change things." Vivian dropped her eyes, not wanting to keep looking at Scott's angry face.

"The only thing that's changed is that I'm pissed at you for keeping this from me. And I'm hurt that you didn't think I was important enough for you to talk to about this. That you still don't think of me as someone you can trust." Scott propped a foot up on the porch beside her. "I've waited patiently these months for you to come to know me well enough that you would want to tell me about yourself. But you never have. This is not the way I wanted to learn about you, Vivian. So it's no wonder I thought the worst. Whose fault is that, Vivian? I ask you?"

"Dearie's?" she suggested with a grin, trying to get a little smile out of Scott.

"No, Vivian, it's yours," Scott returned, refusing to soften. "Now this is D-Day. And I want you to talk to me. Why have you kept all this from me?"

Vivian sighed. What could she tell him? She wasn't even sure she knew the answers herself.

"I'm kind of a private person," she told him, trying to offer him some answer. "I've had a lot of losses and betrayals. I was close to my mother, but my relationship with the Meros was more formal, I guess. It wasn't as rich and intimate as with my own mother. I always had a big imagination, a whole private life of ongoing dramas in my head. My mother understood. We imagined together. But when I shared with people after mother was gone, they thought I was odd. Peculiar. Over time, I just found it easier to keep myself to myself. To be more what people seemed to want. I guess it became a pattern with me."

She stopped to think, and Scott stayed quiet, listening. Watching her again.

"When I started writing, it was my secret thing. A way I got release. It was private." She looked up at him then, hoping she could find a way to make him understand. "I never told anyone about it until somehow it came up in conversation with Betsy Picardi in my college years. Over the years before that, I'd been polishing my little *Foster Girl* stories into better and better dramas as I studied English and learned more about language and writing. I knew they were nice little books, but I knew they weren't the type of books English professors would see as good literature. They were just cute. Warm stories about four girls coming of age who were foster kids without parents. It was something I understood. When I was growing up as a foster child, I never really had anyone special, another sister or close foster sibling, but these girls had each other. I created that for them. I lived the life I dreamed of living through them, I guess. It felt exposing for anyone to know I'd written those books. It was my private side. I wanted it kept there."

"Why is that person, Viva Leeds, that writes *The Foster Girls* so different from Vivian Mero and Vivian Delaney?" Scott caught her eyes.

"I don't know." Vivian's reply was quiet. "Maybe because Viva's books reveal the lost child in me. I based them on the little dolls my mother gave to me."

A few tears ran down Vivian's cheeks, and she clenched her hands in her lap. "My mother gave me those small character dolls every birthday from five to eight. First Veronica, then Marybeth, then Rachel, and then Isabel. Mother and I named them and created stories about them, made them come alive. They had different nationalities; they were a part of an Around the World doll series. Each one came in a special box with a booklet about the country and a wardrobe of little clothes."

Vivian looked up at Scott again. "After mother died, I took them with me to every foster home. They would fit in my suitcase. I wasn't allowed to carry much with me, to keep much from my home or my life with my mother. Just two little suitcases. That's what my life got reduced to. So I lived all the pieces of my missing life through the dolls. I kept them growing up. I had them become foster girls, just like me, in my imagination. I wrote little stories about them in my mind, and when I could, I wrote them down on paper. But sometimes other people found them and made fun of them. And they made fun of me for writing them. Even at the Mero's, I kept my stories and my writing secret. It became my special thing that kept me in touch with my mother. It was private, Scott. I haven't wanted to share it."

"But you shared your books with Betsy." Scott's words held accusation.

"That was an impulsive thing," she admitted. "Betsy and I had such a harmony. We still do. Her mind and her way of thinking mirrored mine. We related. I didn't feel threatened or criticized with Betsy. I felt valued, especially when she convinced me other people would like to read and share in my foster girls' adventures and lives."

Scott eyed her silently for a minute. "Shouldn't the fact that people have liked your stories make you feel better about your work and who you are as a writer now, Vivian?"

"It should." She admitted that honestly. "But that scared little girl is still in there, I guess. I loved it when I could have both lives - Vivian's more normal life that everyone approved of plus Viva's secret writer's life. Both were important to me. And when everything blew up at Armitage, I almost fell apart. I couldn't choose between the lives. I couldn't give up writing to just teach, but I didn't want to be a famous Hollywood person, either. I hated that environment. I didn't fit in."

Vivian smiled in thought. "Tad loves that life style, you know. He and his partner, Boone, just thrive on that Hollywood world. But I don't, Scott. It locks me up. I can't think; I can't write. I can't produce. When everything became public at Armitage, I shut down. I felt nervous and conspicuous all the time and my stomach hurt. Reporters followed me around. People called and wanted me to be on radio and television shows, to come to events and parties. I didn't know these people and suddenly they wanted to know me just because of my work."

"Vivian, most people would find that flattering." Scott smiled and shook his head indulgently.

"I don't know why they would." She puzzled the idea in her mind. "Sometimes these were people who never even noticed me or gave me the time of day before. Who didn't even like me. Not the real me. Don't you see?"

Scott sat quietly for a minute considering what she'd told him.

"Here's what I see," he replied, calmer now and reaching down beside the porch to pick one of the flowers that grew there.

He held out the flower on his palm to Vivian. "What is this?"

"It's just a little purple violet," she told him, wondering at this turn of thought.

"That's right." His voice was kind now. "And, look, it has these five petals or parts – kind of like you do."

Scott picked off one of the petals and put it in Vivian's hand. "Here's Vivian Delaney, the child, her mother's daughter, the one that lived in that little bookstore in Mendocino and played fairies like Sarah and Chelsey."

Vivian smiled in the dark.

"And here's Vivian the foster child," he said, picking off a second petal to put it in her hand, also. "She had some bad experiences, and then some good ones. She grew up with some pretty nice folks, the Meros, from what I hear. That led to this next person."

He picked off another petal. "This is Vivian the professor, a smart woman, a good teacher, someone who cared about her students."

"Here's yet another Vivian." He put a fourth petal in Vivian's hand. "This is Vivian the creator, the writer, with a brilliant imagination and an incredible story-telling gift. Becoming rather well-known, this Vivian." He chuckled at that.

"And here, this last petal, is just Vivian the woman." He took the last petal off and held it in his fingers for a moment before laying it in Vivian's hand, too. "Full of promise to be someone's love, someone's wife, someone's mother, maybe someone's grandmother some day."

"All those fragmented pieces." Vivian looked down sadly at the petals scattered in her hand.

"No, you miss the point, Vivian," Scott admonished gently, reaching down to pick another violet from beside the porch. "There's just one violet here with many parts. With any part gone, the violet isn't whole. It is all the parts together that make it beautiful, that make it whole, that give it its full identity."

He took her hand then, and reassembled the petals he had pulled away back into a whole flower shape in her palm. "You're not just one part, Vivian. You're not supposed to be. No one is. And you're not meant to keep the parts separate or secret. They're all you. They're all worth celebrating. They're all worth knowing."

"Maybe." She studied the violet petals in her hand.

Scott waited while she thought about it. He always seemed to know when she needed time to be quiet and just think.

"What about you?" Vivian asked him then, reaching down to pick another violet. "If it's true, what are your parts?"

Vivian knew by the quick frown on his face that he hadn't expected that response from her.

"All right, Vivian," he said, humoring her and giving her a quirky smile. Such a contrast to the Scott who had been so angry before.

He stretched out his tanned legs, took the violet she'd picked from out of her hand, and pulled off a petal. "Here's Scott the kid who grew up with two brothers and enjoyed great times on the lake and here in the mountains."

"And here's Scott the fox." He smiled that smooth and easy smile of his. "A boy who began to have his own identity, his own dreams - who went to college to become a businessman, who was fascinated with marketing and liked the challenges of pursuit."

He pulled off another petal then. "Then, here's Scott the successful young marketing graduate, out in the business world, on his own, finding his way. And doing a dang good job of it most of the time, if I remember right."

Vivian smiled at him. "And then Scott the camp director?" she asked, looking down at the flower in his hand.

"Yeah, I guess that's certainly another dimension. And, then maybe this last petal is just Scott the man. A man that has fallen in love with this crazy woman with multiple personalities and multiple lives."

"Is that me?" Vivian asked with a touch of wonder.

"Yeah, and if she could ever realize that all of her is good – that all of her identities are okay and of worth and value – and that no part of her needs to be kept secret, we just might have something." He stopped and looked at the petals they had torn off, still loose in her open palm.

"Vivian, I don't want just a petal or two." He looked at her intensely. "I want the whole flower or nothing at all. I want to offer you my whole self and, believe me, it's your whole self I want in return. I don't want to live with part of a person that is always holding things back and keeping parts of herself private and secret from me or from anyone else, either. I'm an open and straightforward guy. I'm not good at playing games. I've told you that from the start."

He stood up then, dusted off his shorts, and turned to look down at Vivian.

"When you can give all of yourself to me – and to the world, too, Vivian, – without hiding little aspects of yourself like they're shameful rather than beautiful, then you let me know. We might just make a go of it. We might just have a shot at something like my Gramma and Poppy Jamison had, like my folks have."

"You think about it, Vivian." His eyes narrowed. "I don't want just some piece or two you decide you might want to give me. I want the whole thing. I want all of you, united, no secrets. I want to meet this Tad guy, Betsy Picardi, and the Meros; I want to go see California and the places you've lived. I want to take you to my parents' house, to meet my brothers and their wives, and all of my friends. I want to be able to tell them about you, about every aspect of you and not just a part or two. It's all or nothing with me, Vivian. I don't want any more secrets. And I certainly don't want any more surprises like tonight."

Vivian looked up at him and watched the face that had been so angry before soften in the gathering darkness. He touched her cheek and turned to head home.

"I don't want just a kiss goodnight anymore, either, Vivian," he added from the shadows as he started away from the farmhouse. "I want a ring on your finger and a place in your life and every night in your bed. No pieces, Vivian. No single petals. You think about it."

And he walked off back toward the camp.

Vivian sat there a minute trying to digest all that happened, all that he had said.

He knew who she was now. He'd been so angry about finding out. He'd been so angry about Tad. She almost laughed over that again. There was nothing to be jealous about with Tad.

Vivian opened her fist and looked at the violet petals she held crushed in her hand. He wanted her whole, he'd said. He valued all of her. She studied the petal pieces again. He said he liked all of her, all the Vivians, all the parts of her.

She sat up in surprise as another piece of Scott's conversation penetrated into her consciousness. He'd said he loved her, that he'd fallen in love with her. How had she missed that? And he'd said something else. What was it? That he didn't want just a kiss good-night anymore. That he wanted all of her and to be in her bed. And, oh my Lord, that he wanted a ring on her finger. He actually said he wanted to marry her.

Was he proposing and had she missed it? Vivian's heart started to beat almost out of her chest. He loved her and wanted to marry her and she'd been so mad at him and so confused over everything that she'd missed it.

She looked down the path to see if she could still see him. But he was gone.

Vivian got up and started running after him.

"Scott!" she called out into the night after him. "Scott, stop. Please stop. I'll put it in the newspaper. I'll be on the local news station. I'll do a television special from the camp. I'll quit hiding anything, I promise. You can have all of me, all the petals."

She ran on into the woods into the dark, wishing she had a flashlight, hoping she wouldn't trip. And then she did trip and fell straight into the big solid wall of Scott in her pathway.

"I didn't see you," she whispered up against his chest now.

"I figured that." His reply was soft and sultry.

She started to pull away, but he held on to her.

"What was that I heard you screaming through the woods just now?"

"I wasn't screaming," she argued in a muffled voice against his chest. "I was just calling out, trying to get your attention."

"Well, you've got it." His answer was soft again and Vivian began to be conscious of how Scott's hands had slid around to find a place up under her shirt.

"I thought about what you said," she told him, finding it harder to speak now that he was so near. "I want to be there for you, whole like you asked."

"No petals?" His voice was husky.

"No petals. I'll call the media tomorrow if you want, Scott." She let her fingers drift over his back. "I'll let them know I'm here. I'll do interviews. I'll go on television. I can do a special at the camp; it will probably be good publicity. Oh, Scott, I've never wanted to be totally genuine with anyone like I want to be totally real with you.

Do you believe me?"

"I might." He tilted her face up so that he could look down at her in the dark. "Do you love me, Vivian?"

"I have for a long time," she confessed softly. "Did you mean that about the ring on my finger?"

"Yes." He traced a finger down her face. "And that part about you being in my bed, too. I'm especially looking forward to that one."

He slipped his hands into the back of her shorts and right down inside her panties then, cupping her bare bottom in his hands. Vivian caught her breath, feeling her legs and all her defenses grow weak at their close contact.

"Isn't this nice?" he murmured, pulling her up against him and holding her tightly there. "It's going to be great between us, Vivian." As the lightning flashed between them as it always did, Vivian leaned against him more in wonder than in outrage, her heart beating madly up against his.

He ran his lips softly over hers. "It's okay to touch a little when you're practically engaged," he informed her softly, allowing his hands to roam around inside her clothing in a way that had her breath coming in little ragged gasps.

He chuckled in the darkness and then moved his hands up under her shirt again.

"Scott." Her voice was barely a whisper. "Will there always be this magic when we're together? Do you think it will always be this good between us?"

"Vivian, honey, we haven't even begun to tap into good yet," he whispered back, moving his lips to hers and starting to run his tongue gently over hers. "We're just enjoying the surface. You just wait, sweet girl. You just wait."

They were caught in the moment for a long time there in the woods between the old Jamison farmhouse and Buckeye camp. And for a while there was nothing but sensation and new joys. Then, all too soon, Scott walked Vivian back to the farmhouse.

"You won't forget about that ring, will you?" Vivian said into the darkness as Scott started back toward his house and the camp.

"Not a chance. End of summer when camp's out. Start making your plans, Vivian."

He laughed then. "Lord, Aunt Mary and Mother are going to

have a fit with another wedding to plan, aren't they?"

"Especially when they find out who I really am." Vivian giggled. "The press will turn out for Viva Leed's wedding, Scott. I hope you're ready for this."

"We'll handle it together, Vivian." Scott stopped for a moment and blew her a kiss before he walked on back home. "We'll handle it together."

And somehow, for the first time, Vivian knew they would. She hugged herself at the thought. Life didn't get much better than this.

Chapter 21

SCOTT'S OLD CONGENIAL TEMPERAMENT RETURNED as soon as he had fully committed to Vivian. She had changed toward him, too, now that there was a new understanding between them and no secrets keeping them apart. In fact, it seemed as if the floodgates had opened with her. She was more confiding and natural. And she laughed more. He liked that, especially.

They spent more time together these days, enjoying activities, sharing their lives, staying up late talking. Yesterday they had explored the Tremont area of the Smokies near Cades Cove. Vivian hiked an eight-mile roundtrip trek up the Middle Prong Trail to Indian Flat Falls and back without a feminine whine or complaint. They picnicked on a big rock in front of the falls, enjoying the peace and beauty of the scene. This boded well for their future, as Scott knew he wouldn't be very happy with a prissy sort of woman who didn't love the outdoors.

It was Sunday now and they sat together at the morning worship service at the Wildwood Church. Reverend James was doing the morning announcements.

"Does anyone have any special prayer requests or announcements?" he asked.

Ruth Hart asked for prayer for a hospitalized member, and then Scott raised his hand.

"I have an announcement." He stood up and grinned at Vivian. He hadn't told her he was going to do this.

"Vivian and I are engaged." He enjoyed hearing the collective gasp from the congregation. " I guess we'll be having a wedding here at the end of summer after my camp sessions are finished. We wanted all of you to know."

Seeing Vivian's mouth gaping open in surprise, Scott pulled her to her feet to join him. Whispers of congratulations and good wishes traveled through the congregation while everyone applauded.

"Vivian's been asking me about a ring ever since we first talked about this." Scott grinned at the laughter this remark brought. "So I thought it would be nice if I gave her that ring right here, with all of you as witnesses." He pulled a small square box out of his pocket and offered it to Vivian. It had been a push to get into town, get the ring on Friday, and keep it hidden as a surprise until now.

Vivian opened the box with tears in her eyes, pulling out a shimmering oval diamond set on a slim, gold band.

She smiled around the room while muttering at him under her breath. "I can't believe you've done this right here in front of everybody."

"I told you I was an out in the open kind of guy," he whispered back in her ear while he gave her a kiss on the cheek.

The church service was entirely disrupted now as everyone came over to see Vivian's ring, to shake Scott's hand, and to give Vivian hugs.

Even Ellen cried, and she wasn't ever the weepy type. She hugged Scott and then Vivian. "Thank you, Scott Jamison. Now I'll get to keep my best friend here."

Eventually, Reverend James brought the well-wishing to a close. "Let's settle down now and all take our seats again."

Scott dropped into the pew and then realized Vivian was still standing. He tugged on her hand to pull her down, but she remained upright.

"I have a little announcement to make, too," she stated.

Scott heard her take a deep breath and wondered what she was up to.

"Because I'm going to be living among you and because you will all be close to me as my new church family, I want to entrust a new aspect of myself to you today."

Startled, Scott hissed up at her, "You don't have to do this, Vivian."

"I know," she whispered back, before she gathered another breath to go on.

She looked around her. "Most of you know that I do some writing. But what most of you don't know is what kind of books I write. Many of you have asked, and I'm sure you remembered I was evasive. That's because what I write is rather well-known and because I actually came here to the valley to escape the hounding of the press and all the reporters about my work."

A speculative murmur trickled through the church members then.

Vivian paused. "Now, don't get unduly upset," she admonished them. "I don't think I write a type of literature you will disapprove of. At least I hope not. I write *The Foster Girls* books and collaborate with the FBR network on the scripts for *The Foster Girls* television series."

There was a collective gasp now around the room. And everyone heard Mrs. McFee say out loud without thinking, "Well, I'll be switched!"

Vivian giggled at that. "My writer's name is Viva Leeds, but my birth name really is Vivian Leah Delaney as you all know me. My father's people lived around here in this Smoky Mountain area, and one reason I chose to come here was hopefully to find some of my family, if I could."

She smiled around the room. "I've come to love every one of you already, and I am happy that I am going to be able to stay here among you and make my life. But I can't keep my writer's identity a secret forever and I wanted to be the one to tell you about myself before some persistent journalist tracks me down and exposes me." She sighed. "It's bound to happen. It has before."

Scott watched Vivian look around at the stunned faces. His, admittedly, was one of them. This was a really brave thing for her to do when she so valued her privacy.

A small silence fell.

"Would you sign a copy of one of my *Foster Girl* books for me?" asked one of the McFee girls, breaking the quiet and bringing a needed laugh to all.

Clyde Harper, a quiet man of few words, stood up to speak then, further surprising them. "Miss Vivian, you can be sure we'll help keep your secret right here in the valley so you can keep writing in peace and quiet. We take care of our own here, and you can be sure we'll help protect you from nosy outsiders."

A murmur of agreement moved around among the congregation. Scott saw tears gather in Vivian's eyes at their concern and protectiveness.

He stood up and took her hand. "Thank you everyone. Your support for Vivian is really appreciated."

Somehow the service moved on and finally ended.

Well-wishers bombarded Vivian and Scott at the end of the service. Plus many questions were directed to Vivian about her writing life.

Reverend James laughed as he shook hands with Scott and Vivian at the front door. "I doubt anyone will remember the topic of my sermon after your joint announcements this morning."

He gave them an affectionate smile. "I'll expect you both in for marriage counseling sessions soon. And we'll look at the calendar for a good wedding date."

Scott led Vivian out into the May sunshine.

"Are these all of your surprises for today?" Vivian asked Scott as they got into his truck.

"Nope." He flashed her one of his quick grins. "Now, we're going out to my parents to have Sunday lunch and meet all the family."

Vivian groaned.

He leaned over to kiss her on the cheek. "Come on, you know you want to show off the ring," he teased.

They chatted happily about friends and family all the way out to Scott's parents' house. Scott's family home was outside of Sevierville on a hillside above Douglas Lake - a sprawling, rustic two-storied house with a broad back porch looking down the hillside toward the water's edge. A rock pathway wound down the hill to a lakeside patio and pavilion beside a covered boat dock on the water. The Jamisons had always been a boating family, and Scott had grown up on the lake skiing and swimming. Every month or two the family all gathered to eat, boat, and enjoy each other's company by the lake. They were lunching out on the pavilion by the lakeside today, and Vivian was soon enveloped into the warmth of Scott's family.

"VIVIAN AND I ARE ENGAGED," SCOTT told them right away, pulling Vivian protectively to his side as he announced it. He knew his mother and his Aunt Mary would spot the ring in the first hand-shakes, so he figured he'd better just get one step ahead of them or he'd have no chance to be the one to tell his own news.

"Oh, I just couldn't be happier!" bubbled Aunt Mary. "Now I'll have an excuse to plan another wedding. What date have you set?"

Vivian's smile was bright. "Not until the end of summer after Scott's camp sessions are over. Scott will be too busy before then. And we both need some time to plan."

Aunt Mary, Nancy, Scott's mother, and his two sisters-in-law soon had Vivian off to the side talking about weddings, so Scott went over to join his brothers, his father, and his Uncle Leo around the grill. Pork loin was smoking over the coals along with foil-wrapped ears of corn. Bowls of green beans, slaw, macaroni salad, sliced tomatoes, and an army of desserts stood on a side table near by.

"Smells great." Scott sniffed the air with pleasure before settling down in an outdoor chair to prop his feet up on the boat railing. He smiled contentedly, watching his niece and nephews and Nancy's boys paddling on floats in the lake.

"You look smug and content for someone who's getting ready to take the plunge into the big M world," Scott's brother Raley drawled. He and Kyle were sitting by Scott, keeping an eye on the kids while their father and Uncle Leo supervised the grill.

Scott grinned lazily. "Don't razz me, brothers. I'm a happy man, and I've found a good woman to spend my life with."

A call to lunch interrupted any further conversation and the brothers got busy hauling kids out of the water and toweling them down so they could eat.

Scott's second surprise for Vivian showed up just as the women were setting out plates and glassware on the tables. He smiled and nodded at his mother before pulling Vivian away from the women and toward a blue van that was just pulling up.

"You're being rude." Vivian chided him under her breath as he dragged her away.

"No I'm not, and, besides, they understand. There's someone here I want you to meet." He kept her arm in his. "Some extra company."

Out of the van came two couples, an older and a younger, and two children.

"Are these some more relatives of yours you want me to meet?" Vivian looked at him with a question in her eyes.

"No, actually, I believe these are relatives of yours." He enjoyed the shocked expression that crossed her face.

Scott watched Vivian's eyes come back to his with confusion and question.

He put his arm around her waist. "See that van there, Vivian? It says Delaney's Florist on the side. I saw it stop for a delivery when I was in town one day, and I got to wondering if it might be a link to your family tree. I remembered you telling me your father, Will Delaney, was in the military, but had a side passion for the garden and flowers. So I just had to ask. Turns out the lady driving the delivery truck was your daddy's sister, Patti."

Scott gestured to a tall, sandy-haired woman, probably in her late thirties, walking up to meet them.

"Patti Delaney Hale," Scott said. "This is Vivian Delaney Mero."

Patti reached out to take Vivian's hand in hers, tears welling in her eyes. "I'm so pleased to meet you. Your father, Will, was my older brother. Vivian. I idolized him and followed him around everywhere when we were kids. I named my son after him."

She kept Vivian's hand in hers. "When Scott approached me that day in Sevierville, I thought there was a very good chance that you might be Will's daughter. Once Scott gave us some information about you, we were able to do some further checking through the military records and birth records in California to confirm our suspicions. We just got all the verification back a few days ago."

She smiled and gestured to the group behind her. "We're your Delaney family, Vivian. These are your grandparents, Everett and Vi Delaney, and this is my husband, Gordon Hale and our two children, Will and Melanie".

The older man came forward then. "I'm your grandfather, dear." He held out his hand with tears in his eyes. "I guess this has all been a big shock for you. Maybe Scott should have talked to you about us before we came over today, but he said he wanted it to be a surprise."

He hung his head a little then. "I regret we didn't even know you existed, child. You see, Will went through a wild stage before he took off and joined the military. We had a lot of family rows then. For a long time, we didn't hear from Will. Finally, a few years after he left, we got a letter from him. He said he was in the Army and stationed in Ft. Irwin, California. We also learned he'd met a nice girl and gotten married – said he wanted to bring her home to meet us someday. Your grandmother and I were eager to make peace. We even started planning a trip to California but learned Will had been sent overseas to the Middle East in military intelligence. We hoped for more word from him after that, but the next news we got was that he'd been killed.

"We never met your mother," Everett Delaney told Vivian with a sad shake of his head. "And she never got in touch with us after Will's death. We just assumed she went back to live with her own people."

Vivian looked at Scott with questioning eyes.

"Is all this true?" she asked.

He nodded. "The pictures they have of their son Will look like the ones you have of your father, Vivian. All the facts we investigated match up."

Everett Delaney held out two photos to Vivian and watched as she examined them. "That top photo there is the military picture Will sent us in his letter."

Vivian studied the first picture quietly and then turned to the second one underneath.

"That next photo is of Will and his wife. Your mother. Will wrote us that her name was Charlotte. She looks a lot like you."

That's when Vivian started to cry.

"I have this same picture," she whispered.

Scott felt like a real heel then, but he watched as Vivian's grandmother, Mrs. Delaney, came forward in a purely instinctive way and gathered Vivian into her arms for a strong hug.

She patted Vivian and made soothing sounds. "There, there, dear. It must have been a terrible shock to lose your father when you were just a mite and then your mother at such a young age. And to have no family you knew of to go to. We're just real sorry that we didn't know about you. We'd have come right away. But here we are now, and maybe we can all be a comfort to each other even now."

She smoothed back Vivian's hair gently. "Did you know my first name is Vivian, too?" She smiled. "Will and his wife must have named you for me. That just makes you even more precious to me, child. It's like getting a bit of my boy back to have you."

They both cried then, and Patti came up and threw her arms around them and cried as well. The men shuffled around in discomfort.

Patti's son Will interrupted the scene at last. "Mama, are you all going to cry all day? You're getting Melanie upset. She doesn't understand what you're crying about."

Patti pulled away from Vivian and gestured for the little girl to come over, giving her a brief hug. "It's okay, Melanie," she assured her. "We're just crying because we're all so happy to meet your Aunt Vivian."

Everett Delaney offered Vivian a somewhat awkward but fond hug then. "We're real glad to welcome you into the family, Vivian. We have a little florist shop over at Dandridge. Usually we don't deliver over in Sevierville, but we'd made an exception for a friend the day Scott saw our van. Your father grew up in Dandridge, Tennessee, which is not far from here, and someday, if you'll come to visit with us, we'll take you around and show you all the places he knew. There are a few aunts and uncles you might want to meet, as well."

He brushed away one of Vivian's tears as if she was one of his own children. " If you came to Tennessee looking for family, Vivian, I think you'll find you have a right strong group of kinfolks here."

"I don't know what to say." Vivian looked around at her new family in wonder, her face lit up in pleasure.

Scott noticed his mother waving at him from the patio and interrupted the ongoing reunion. "Well, the Jamison family is getting hungry and dinner is ready. Let's all go down to the patio to eat and we'll get more acquainted over lunch."

"How about a piggy back ride down the hill?" he asked Melanie. "I've got a niece about six years old that looks to be just about your size. And she'll be real glad to see you with all the boys in our family."

He tossed the little girl up on his shoulder and took Vivian's hand in his as they started off down the hill.

"You're not mad at me, are you, Vivian?" He said this quietly so no one else could hear.

"I'm absolutely furious," she answered him in a hiss. "But I love you for this, too, Scott Jamison. I can't believe you saw that van and tracked all this down for me."

Scott shrugged. "Well, I didn't know when I started up my conversation with Patti that day that I'd gotten so lucky. I figured I might have found a remote Delaney link for you to start working on with your genealogy research, but I didn't expect to have found the mother lode right off."

Vivian took off her sunglasses to give Scott a direct look. "Well, today is a day I'll never forget – getting officially engaged, receiving my ring, and getting acquainted with two new families at the same time. And with no notice that I would be doing any of it! You really are something else, Scott Jamison."

"Want to give the ring back and call it quits?" Scott asked teasingly.

"Not a chance." Vivian tucked her ring finger under her arm with a possessive gesture. "You've gotten us in too deep now – announcing all this at church, bringing me out here to your family's home, and getting your mother and Aunt Mary started on wedding plans. Plus, now you've brought in a whole Delaney family as witness. No sir, buster, you have sunk both our ships now. There's no going back for us. We're in this for the count."

"That's just what I wanted to hear." Scott smiled and then adjusted Melanie on his back so he could lean over to give Vivian a quick kiss. "Let's go join our families, Ms. Delaney-Mero-Leeds and soon to be Mrs. Jamison."

Vivian kicked out at him playfully for that, but Scott avoided a hit by taking off at a trot down the hillside, Melanie laughing merrily at her unexpectedly bumpy ride.

Chapter 22

THREE MONTHS LATER ON AN early August morning, Vivian sat on the front porch writing. It had rained the night before and cooled things down from the steamy summer days.

All three of Vivian's regular companions kept her company today. Dearie, the cat, was curled up on a cushion on an old rocker nearby, Fritzi, the little collie, lay napping under the porch swing, and Sarah Louise Taylor sat cross-legged on the wooden porch floor, not far from Vivian's feet, drawing and coloring pictures in a children's sketchbook. Vivian stopped for a moment to watch her. Sarah had her tongue in the corner of her mouth in fierce concentration, trying to make the picture she worked on one of her best. Vivian knew this was a distinctive characteristic of Sarah's after watching her over the summer. She gave so much serious effort and concentration to everything she did. Plus she was always quiet while Vivian wrote, respecting the silence needed to produce a good story.

Yesterday, when Ellen announced Chelsey had a doctor's appointment today, Vivian volunteered to keep Sarah. Having Sarah around the farmhouse most every day was more the norm than a novelty now. She and Sarah had grown close.

Vivian's life had settled into a warm, comfortable pattern over the summer. She felt a sense of home she had not known since she was very small. Scott was occupied full-time with the camp during the days now and sometimes at night. But Vivian, comfortable on her own, didn't need to be entertained to be content. She had her own work and was well into another *Foster Girls* sequel in which Marybeth and Isabel were opening a little retail boutique. It was fun to work on.

Ellen and Vivian, and the girls, Chelsey and Sarah, had become a happy foursome over the long summer months. They spent part of many of their days together. Ellen and Vivian took the girls swimming, shopping, on hikes and picnics, and to events at the camp, and Vivian kept the girls on Ellen's soap-making days.

One day when they all stopped by the camp kitchen to visit the staff, Mrs. McFee had commented, "Lord, Vivian, that child Sarah looks almost like the spittin' image of yourself with that dark red hair and blue eyes."

Sarah had spoken up primly at that. "Scott says our hair is chestnut, Mrs. McFee, and not red. And Scott says I look just like Vivian did when she was a little girl. Vivian has a picture of herself when she was six in her bedroom. I've seen it, and I really do look like her."

Mrs. McFee winked at Vivian. "Well, I'm sure that's so Sarah Taylor. Didn't I just say it myself, after all?"

Later, back at the farmhouse, Vivian and Sarah examined that young photo of Vivian that Scott had been talking about.

"Well, Sarah. I guess you do look a bit like I did when I was small – including having those freckles!" Vivian tapped the scattering of freckles across Sarah's nose, making Sarah giggle.

"You know what?" Sarah asked Vivian, leaning up against her leg as she'd done since the first day they'd met.

"What, Ophelia Odelia?" Vivian smiled and wrapped an arm around Sarah's shoulder automatically.

"You look like my mother," the child said softly, looking up at Vivian with her heart in her eyes. "Mother's name was Eleanor, and she looked a lot like you. She had chestnut hair like us and she had blue eyes, too."

Vivian's response was gentle and she stroked the child's hair. "Well, that's a sweet thing for you to say, Sarah. Because I've seen some pictures of your mother, and she was very beautiful."

"So are you," Sarah assured her vehemently. And then she whispered, "I wish you were my mother."

That wish went down deep into Vivian's heart, and she often heard the words replayed in her quiet moments. Perhaps because of that thought, Vivian had started to spend even more time with Sarah. Also, she started offering to take Sarah and Chelsey on outings when she went out with Scott.

Scott had offered a good-natured complaint about it one day. "Lord, woman. As if I don't have enough children to deal with all day long at the camp. I want time just with you."

"Please, Scott? Just this once?" She gave him a pleading look. "We'll be together later, you know. And Ellen and Quint need some time alone sometimes, too."

Scott conceded then, as he usually did, and helped her to show the girls a wonderful time. His energy and imagination never stopped, and his charisma and ease made him a natural with children. Sarah Louise now idolized him as much as Chelsey did. He could hardly get into the door of the Greene's on their Thursday night get-togethers before both girls launched themselves on him for hugs and piggy-back rides and then a tussle on the floor. And Scott was always game.

"Are you having a break time in your book?" Sarah asked Vivian, noticing that she had stopped writing for a while.

"Yes, I'm thinking things over between scenes."

Sarah nodded, as though that seemed perfectly sensible to her.

Vivian smiled. "What are you drawing, Sarah?"

"I'm trying to draw the flower I've picked," she said, pointing to a somewhat wilted sunflower lying on the porch in front of her. "I want to have a sunflower fairy sitting on the top of it in my picture." She made a frown at her paper. "But I can't get the fairy's legs to look right."

Vivian looked over Sarah's shoulder. The child really had a fine artistic gift for her young age. "Why don't you just draw a long skirt over her legs? Maybe a flowing yellow skirt? You haven't colored your drawing in yet, so it would be easy to add a skirt right now. Then you can erase her legs underneath and just not worry about drawing them."

"I could do that," Sarah said. "But someday I need to learn how to draw good legs." She studied her drawing thoughtfully. "Legs are hard."

"So are hands." Vivian agreed. "I always had trouble with hands, too. But you will get better with both the more that you draw. Everything gets better with practice."

Sarah looked up with interest. "Like writing? Did you get better and better at writing with more practice?"

"Yes, I did. And I started my first stories when I was not much older than you."

"I see stories in my mind." Sarah bit her lip thoughtfully as she confessed this. "I wish I could write so that I could try to put them down."

"What kinds of stories do you see?" Vivian was genuinely interested in this new aspect of Sarah Taylor.

"Lots of kinds." Sarah shrugged. "But today I'm seeing a story about a fairy who lives in this sunflower."

She pointed to her drawing. "My fairy's name is Susanella, and she got lost from all the other sunflower fairies in Sunflower Field." Her young voice was animated as she told her story. "You see, Susanella was carried off in the night time by an owl who flew her far away and then dropped her accidentally down into a deep forest. Susanella flew and flew, but she couldn't find her way home. Then she found this one sunflower to live in for a while, but she still needs to find her way back home to Sunflower Field."

Sarah paused to frown and think. "I'm trying to think how she can get back to her field. It doesn't seem likely that the owl will fly her back. He had planned to eat her, you know."

Vivian tried to remain serious and not giggle. "What if another kind of bird flew her back, perhaps in return for a favor?"

"What kind of favor?"

"Well, let's think. What can your Sunflower Fairy do well?"

"She sings most beautifully," answered Sarah right away.

"Well, perhaps Susanella could sing a mother bluebird's babies to sleep and give the mother bird a nice break. Then the mother bluebird will gladly fly her back to her field as a thank you."

Sarah's face lit up with a smile then. "That's a good idea!"

"I'm glad I could help you," Vivian said.

"You should write some fairy books for children to read, Vivian." Sarah picked her crayon back up and started to color on her fairy drawing. "You always tell me and Chelsey the bestest fairy stories ever. And I know lots of your stories you make up right in your own head all by yourself."

"Well, I'll consider your suggestion, Sarah. And thanks for your confidence in me."

Actually, Sarah's idea was not a bad one to consider, Vivian thought. She certainly had enough background in the field.

The sound of a car interrupted their talk, and Vivian looked up to see Alice Graham from the Wayside Agency pulling into a parking spot near the front of the house. She was Sarah's social worker.

Vivian waved a warm greeting, but Sarah got up quickly and hid behind Vivian's chair.

"I don't want her to take me away," she whispered to Vivian.

Seeing Sarah hide behind Vivian, Alice called out to her in reassurance. "I've just come for a visit, Sarah. It isn't time for a change yet. But I'm working on finding a nice family for you."

Vivian watched Sarah frown while Alice made her way up to join them on the front porch.

Alice smiled at both of them as she pulled up a chair and sat down. "I was out in the area and decided to drop by and see how Sarah was getting along. I called Ellen on her cell phone, and she told me that Sarah was over here visiting with you."

Vivian could still feel Sarah's discomfort.

"You know what, Sarah?" Vivian proposed. "That new doll we bought for the dollhouse was feeling lonely this morning. You know how it is to be new." She paused. "Maybe you could go up and check on her, maybe play with her for a little while? I'm sure Alice wouldn't mind."

Sarah brightened and she looked to Alice for an okay.

"I think that's a good idea," Alice said.

And Sarah made her escape.

Alice settled back into her chair and crossed her legs to relax. "It's part of my job that the children are either glad or sad to see me come." She shook her head. "Actually, it's better if they're sad to see me show up. That generally means the foster placement is a good one and that the child is happy. When I see too much eager hope when I arrive, I worry things are not going well for the child, that they are hoping to leave."

"I wish I'd had someone as thoughtful as you checking on me

when I was a foster child. " Vivian's reply was wistful.

"It's hard to be alone without your own family," Alice replied.

Vivian remembered her manners. "Want a cold drink? I keep a cooler out here with drinks in it." She flipped open the top. "Take your pick."

Alice looked into the cooler and pointed. "I'll take that diet lemon-lime one."

Vivian fished it out, and got a bottle of water out for herself.

They two women sat for a minute, enjoying the day, listening to the hum of bees around the flowers and the sounds of children's voices floating over from the camp.

"It's nice here," Alice observed. "Will you and Scott stay here when you get married?"

"Yes." Vivian smiled. "We both love it here. It's a great house. Scott will keep the director's house, too, but he'll probably let his assistant directors use it during summer camp sessions. The camp is growing, and some more directors are needed. Having the house free will give Scott space for them. Plus, it will sweeten the employment pot, as he says. Help him get the best people."

"You know, I think I may have a prospective placement for Sarah," Alice said, changing the subject. "I've wanted to get her settled by fall so she wouldn't have to change schools. Besides, it worries me how attached she's getting to the Greenes and to you, Vivian."

"I haven't meant to make it harder for her." Vivian felt a rush of anguish around her heart to think she had made anything more difficult for Sarah.

"Will you get to place her somewhere around this area?" she asked Alice. "So I can see her sometime?"

Alice took a grateful sip of her cold drink. "The family is over near Cosby. A nice couple that has one child but couldn't have another. They thought Sarah might complete their family."

"What are they like?" Vivian swallowed uneasily. "Do you think they'll understand that Sarah is special, really bright ... that she has gifts that need to be encouraged? Look at this picture she's been working on, Alice. Very few six year olds can draw like that or think the way Sarah does. She told me an entire story about the fairy, Susanella, she's been drawing this morning. She's so creative ...."

Vivian found tears welling up around her eyes to think of Sarah leaving at all.

"You're fond of her." Alice interrupted Vivian's words, studying Vivian thoughtfully. "In fact, you're more than fond of her, Vivian. You've grown to love her. Why don't you foster Sarah yourself? You could. I'd have no trouble approving that. And if you want, you could adopt her yourself, as well. With your education and financial situation, there would be no roadblocks to you having her. I don't want to move a child like Sarah around any more than I have to. You know what that's like."

Several weeks ago, Vivian had told Alice some of her past as a foster child as the two had started to develop a friendship.

"Do you really think I could?" Vivian knew her voice was eager. "Do you think I could foster Sarah and maybe adopt her? I don't think Scott would mind. He's crazy about Sarah and Chelsey both, and he's wonderful with children."

"Well, I'd do some serious talking with him before we even hint to Sarah that staying with you might be a possibility. She's already told me she wants to be with you ... in fact begged me to let her stay with the Greenes so she can be near you. She says you remind her of her mother."

"She's told me that, too." Vivian smiled at the memory.

"It's nice to be loved by a child," Alice observed. "But it's hard on children when they have to leave people they love, go to a new place and new people they may or may not have as much affection and affinity for."

Alice took Vivian's hand then. "If you're not going to think about keeping Sarah, I think it would be a good idea if you begin to step back from spending so much time with her, Vivian. Help prepare her for her new home and family. I'll let you go visit the Perrys so you can tell Sarah that you know them, so you can tell her how nice they are. She needs that from you, Vivian, if she can't stay here. This is one time I know a move will be hard on a child. There will be heart pain because of how attached she has become to you."

Vivian put her hands up to her eyes to scrub away the tears that were flowing freely now. "Oh, Alice, I didn't mean to make things harder for Sarah."

"I know." Alice squeezed her hand affectionately. "You've just let your heart rule without thinking. I've been in the same situation."

"What did you do?"

Alice hesitated. "A few times I had to work hard to prepare a child to go on, to leave me. It was hard, but, in time, it worked out well. Another time, I found I couldn't say goodbye."

"And did you foster or adopt that child?"

"Actually I decided to foster all six of them." Alice laughed. "I don't know if I'll be able to adopt them, but I am definitely keeping them. They've become my family. I've bought a farm, sort of like yours, except bigger, over near Greenbrier. The kids and I have been settling in all summer. Before that I had them all packed into my tiny little stone house in two converted attic bedrooms. Believe me, we are glad to spread out."

"If you could take six, surely I could take one," Vivian reasoned.

"Listen, Vivian. The reason to take one or six children to foster is only partly due to *their* need. It has to be the right thing for you, too. And for Scott. You're getting ready to be married, Vivian. Scott may like Sarah well enough in her position as a foster child staying at the Greene's, but it may be another thing for him to want to raise her as his own child. Don't assume too much about how Scott feels. You may have to let Sarah go on to the Perrys. They're a very fine family."

"I don't think I can." Vivian's voice came out in an anxious whisper. "She's gotten into my heart, Alice. I don't think I can bear to let her go. Surely Scott will understand?"

Vivian turned to look at Alice appealingly then. "Perhaps you can talk to him about it, Alice? Help him to understand how I feel?"

"Nothing doing." Alice lightened up the situation now with a laugh. "That's your department, Vivian. Mine is just to find the best homes for children in need that I can and, then, to follow up and see to it that every one of them is well loved and well-cared for in that home. Interfering between couples is not in my job description, Vivian. You're on your own with that one."

Vivian sighed.

"No matter what happens, Vivian. You can be sure that I will see that no harm comes to Sarah. Her experience will never be like yours. I don't want your past to influence your decision here."

Alice stood up then, putting her drink bottle down on the table. "Think and pray about this, Vivian," she suggested kindly. "It's a serious commitment to consider fostering a child. And it's a lot different from babysitting Sarah on a day when Ellen has gone to the doctor. A child is a twenty-four hour commitment through cross and cranky days as well as sunny ones, through sickness and health, in good times and bad. It is very important that you think this through very carefully before we even consider suggesting the idea to Sarah. She loves you already, you know. There is no question as to what her response will be."

Vivian watched Alice look back toward the house, thinking about Sarah upstairs playing with the dollhouse. She knew she was remembering Sarah's reluctance to see her drive up for a visit.

Alice looked at Vivian and shook her head. "It will be hard enough as it is when I have to move Sarah. I don't want to keep her here much longer because of that. I hope you understand."

"I do," said Vivian on a sigh, getting up to tell Alice goodbye.

"Here's my card." Alice handed her a business card from out of her suit pocket. "You let me know how you feel after you think all of this over. And please don't feel guilty to say no, Vivian. You are a busy career woman. And Sarah will be fine with the Perrys. You can keep ties with her and visit her there. I have no objection to that. You can stay loving friends. Remember that."

But as Vivian sat down and watched Alice's car go down the driveway, Vivian knew that wasn't possible for her.

She spoke to herself thoughtfully as she stood watching Alice's car disappear from sight. "I've fallen in love with Sarah. As much so in one way as I've fallen in love with Scott in another. Sarah and I have a connection. I think I've known it from the very first day we met." She smiled to herself remembering Sarah flying in and out of the shrubbery in her yellow fairy wings.

"Ophelia Odelia will just have to be mine," Vivian acknowledged. "It's our destiny as two past fairy princesses."

Chapter 23

$\mathcal{S}$COTT SAT CROSS-LEGGED IN Buckeye Knob's Tuesday night closing circle down by the lakeside. Songs of the campers drifted around him but his thoughts were on Vivian. They were having a late dinner as soon as circle ended and his last announcements were done. Dinner together had become a tradition for them now, and, admittedly, Scott looked forward to it every day. He had never thought that any one woman could keep him interested over any great length of time, but Vivian was the exception. The more time he spent time with her, the more he wanted to be with her. It amazed him continually. She had really gotten into his blood.

Their wedding date was set for early September. His mother and Aunt Mary were joyously working out all the details, and Vivian seemed glad to let them do it. For a honeymoon, he and Vivian planned a trip to Hawaii with a stopover to see familiar sites in California on the way back. Vivian thought she might use the material she gained in Hawaii and their travels for a book later on. Scott laughed to himself. Everything to Vivian was potentially book material, but Scott hoped he could provide some honeymoon entertainment that would take her mind off her writing for a while. He certainly planned more interesting things for himself than thinking about camp during those weeks. He'd fantasized about it all summer.

Later, Scott walked over to the farmhouse with a jaunty step, whistling a campfire song into the evening darkness. He slipped into the back kitchen door and found Vivian stirring something on the stove.

He came up behind her and wrapped his arms around her. "How domestic - the little woman at the stove."

"If you consider comments like that romantic to me, you know you're way off base." Vivian's reply was snappish and she struggled to get out of the grip he had on her. "You know I hate sexist comments."

He laughed. "And you know I'm only saying them to get a rise out of you." He nuzzled her neck, enjoying the floral scent of her cologne and some subtle undertone essence of one of Ellen's soaps still lingering on her skin.

Scott took the big, wooden spoon out of Vivian's hand and turned her around to kiss him. He loved to tease-kiss her - moving his lips lightly over hers, touching his tongue over her lips and teasing at her mouth, until their breaths heated up. Then the jolt would hit, the sizzle that always happened between them, and she would fall into him and begin to grow soft under his touch. That punch never failed to happen. Yet, it always amazed Scott and took his breath away when it did.

He deepened his kiss with Vivian now, loving her quickened breath and response, excited by the feel of her heart racing under his. Sexist or not, Scott loved the sense of power he felt in knowing he could move Vivian's emotions, make her respond to him. He loved taking his time with her and drawing out her passions. Scott had always been a slow and competent lover, but he especially enjoyed prolonging his loving with Vivian. He had started learning all the special ways she liked to be kissed and touched over the summer. And he reveled in the knowledge that she wouldn't be able to resist him when he finally took their loving to a deeper level. He looked forward to pleasing and amazing her.

"If you don't stop this, I'll burn our dinner," she murmured against his neck.

"I like having dessert first." He slipped his hands teasingly under her shirt to draw a little gasp from her.

She looked toward her cooking with concern, her mind diverted. "Was your day good?"

"It was." Realizing she needed to finish their dinner, he loosened his hold on her and let her turn back to her pot on the stove.

"I've made a homemade soup for tonight." She gave him a bright smile. "It's Ruth Hart's recipe. I know the weather is a little warm for soup, but it's really wonderful. I hope it turns out all right."

He took the spoon from her for a taste. "Ummm. Tastes good. Is it vegetable?"

"A vegetable beef – and thick, too - almost like a stew; so it's hearty." She passed him a smug look then. "I think I am getting rather domestic for a professor who seldom had time for more than TV dinners before."

"I think so, too." He lounged against the counter where he could watch her work. "But you know you don't have to do a lot of cooking for me."

"I know that. But it hurt my ego that you could cook better than me, Scott, so I've been working on it." She wrinkled her nose at him mischievously.

"I hope that doesn't mean that you won't let me cook after we're married." He gave her a wounded look. "You know how I like to get in the kitchen."

"We'll trade out," she promised him. "I've warned you that sometimes I get lost in my writing and forget the time. On those days, especially, you'd better get in here and cook or you probably won't eat at all." She laughed at that.

"I love the idea of being married to a famous writer." He leaned over to kiss her neck again. "I'll get to have my picture in the tabloids."

She turned on him then, her eyes heated. "I hope you're teasing about that, Scott Jamison. You'd really hate that."

"Oh, I don't know." He purposely made his response sound casual, enjoying goading her. "It might be fun. I've never experienced being one of the rich and famous pursued by the press. It might be a novelty."

"Well, Mr. Celebrity Seeker, eventually some journalist will track me down here." Vivian flashed him an annoyed glance. "We'll see how much you like having your life invaded and lies told about you then. They doctor their pictures, you know, and give you quotes you've never said. It can really be humiliating, Scott. They put a horrid photo in one of their magazines of me walking across campus with one of my students and suggested he was my lover. It was terrible."

"I'm sure your Armitage colleagues loved that one," he drawled.

Vivian heaved a sigh, getting upset just remembering it. "Fortunately, they never saw it. Tad told me about it, though. I went to the grocery stores in the area and bought every magazine I could find that had printed that story and trashed them all. I was so mad and so humiliated."

"And couldn't write for a week afterwards?" Scott couldn't resist teasing her.

"Don't make jokes," she snapped back. "I was really upset, Scott."

"You need to be less thin-skinned." He heaved himself up to sit on the counter. "Not care so much what people say or think. It makes life easier, Vivian. Besides, stuff like that passes over quickly. People whisper and talk for a few days, and then they are off on some new seven-day wonder. I've seen it happen often in my own life."

She passed him a disapproving look. "Yes, I've heard about some of the scandals you and your brothers got involved in when you were growing up. I guess you got used to notoriety with some of the tales I've heard."

"Well maybe it's a good thing you didn't hear all those tales before we got engaged and started planning a wedding." Scott reached over to pat her bottom. "Wanna give the ring back?"

Vivian gave him a shove. "No. But maybe I should put one in your nose."

She looked at him more seriously then. "Scott, you won't ever fool around on me after we're married, will you? I know you have a big past with women, but I don't think I could stand it if you started philandering, like Nancy's husband did."

"Nancy's husband was an ass," Scott said with a scowl. "Jamison men may sow their wild oats before marriage, but they are very faithful afterwards. Ask around."

Scott noticed Vivian's face still looked troubled.

"There is no one for me but you, Vivian." He dropped down off the counter, gathered her up in his arms, and kissed her forehead tenderly. "And there had better be no one for you but me, either.

I'm a one-woman guy now."

She sighed in his arms then, comforted.

"You know," she murmured against his neck, nibbling on his ear in a tantalizing way that started his blood racing again. "I'm starting to really look forward to our wedding night now."

"Is that right? Well, if you don't stop nibbling on my ear like that, I'm probably going to skip ahead to that time prematurely." He pulled her against him and slid his hands down over her hips. As he did, that zing sizzled in the air between them.

She pulled back from him with a slow little smile and turned back reluctantly to the stove. "I never thought I was a very passionate woman before I met you, Scott," she told him, while stirring her soup. "But you've made me have some of the most incredible and embarrassing dreams and fantasies."

Scott grinned delightfully. "No kidding. Tell me a few."

She kept her back to him, partly in embarrassment, he knew. "Well, let's see. I've dreamed of us swimming together and bathing together and stuff like that."

"Water fantasies." He smirked and leaned back against the counter again. "I like that. I've had a few of those myself. I promise you we'll try a few of those ideas out later on. What else have you fantasized?" He was intrigued.

"Woods dreams." She turned her head to look at him, a blush stealing up her cheeks. "And you know I'm not as eager as you to sleep in a tent or under a tree, so I can't figure out where those dreams are coming from."

He came up behind her and ran his hands softly down her body. "I've had those, too. Those woods dreams make great bedfellows, don't they, Vivian?"

"Is it normal to think about things like that, Scott?"

"More than normal," he assured her with a chuckle. "It's also normal to do them all as well."

Scott heard her suppress a little gasp and loved it. He decided it was going to be wonderful to be married to an imaginative woman. There was no telling what her mind would come up with that would be absolutely delightful to try.

"I like a fertile imagination in a woman." He said this in a whisper against her ear, running his tongue over her earlobe at the same time.

"Well, you're in luck." Her voice came out in a husky whisper. "Because I'm certainly an imaginative sort of person."

They quit snuggling and teasing after a little while, and sat down to try Vivian's soup. As they ate, they talked and visited comfortably and caught up on events and news of their day.

Later, they took iced tea out on the porch so they could watch the late summer fireflies flashing in the woods and around the lawn. Here in the dark they bared their hearts and talked about the deep things of life.

"Alice Graham came by to check on Sarah today," Vivian told him, pushing the glider back and forth with one foot. "She stopped by over here since I was keeping Sarah for Ellen. She told me she thought she might have found a home for Sarah."

"Well, that's good." Scott lounged back into an old porch rocking chair and propped his feet up on the rail. "She's a good kid and deserves a really nice place. I'll miss her."

"Me, too." Vivian gave him an engaging smile. "In fact, I realized as we talked that I didn't want to let Sarah go. I talked to Alice about fostering her myself."

Scott sat up straight in the rocker, dropping his feet from the rail and turning his full attention on Vivian.

He knew his voice was testy. "I think that's the sort of thing we're both supposed to talk about together now, Vivian. And not the kind of decision you just make on your own."

"Well, that's why I'm talking about it now." She smiled at him again. "I told Alice I was sure you wouldn't mind, that you were very fond of Sarah and good with kids."

"You're talking about this in the same way you might discuss getting a new puppy or something, Vivian," he countered, his irritation rising. "Of course I'm fond of Sarah, but deciding to foster a child is a serious matter. You, of all people, should know that. Sarah deserves to go to a family that will think about not only fostering her but adopting and raising her as well. Like the experience you had with the Meros. I don't think fostering Sarah for a little while longer would be the right thing for her."

Vivian pushed the glider back and forth casually. "Well, I told Alice that after we were married that we could adopt Sarah. I'd want stability for Sarah, too."

Scott was stunned. "And you were discussing all this and making all these decisions without even talking with me about it first?" He fidgeted in annoyance, having trouble sitting still in his chair. "That's not the way married people do things, Vivian."

She looked at him in surprise. "Well, we're not married yet, Scott. And you weren't here when Alice came by anyway. We got to talking and one thing led to another."

"And you jumped in and offered to foster Sarah Taylor without even asking me how I feel about it," Scott accused.

"I don't know why you're so upset, Scott. I'm talking to you about it now. And I'm asking you about it now."

"Well, fine." Scott got up to pace in exasperation across the porch. "And now that you're asking me I'm telling you that I *don't* think it's such a good idea."

"Why?" Vivian asked in that quiet, wounded voice Scott knew always meant trouble for him.

He struggled to control his anger and talk reasonably. "Because we're just getting ready to be married, to go on a honeymoon, to start our lives together, to have time together as a newly married couple. It's a special time in a marriage, a time to really come to know each other before a family is started. I want that."

"But you want children, too, don't you?" Vivian asked in a hurt voice.

"You know I do." Scott sat down in the glider beside Vivian and put his hand over hers. "I have fantasies about you holding our babies, about the two of us laughing down into their faces together, about us walking along holding their little hands in ours. I'm a sentimental guy, Vivian."

"But we could make room in our hearts for Sarah, too." Vivian put her other hand over his and gave him a wistful look. "We could love her and still have children of our own."

Scott studied her then. She was getting that serious set to her face that indicated she wasn't going to give in easily to argument.

"Listen, Vivian," he offered. "It's one thing when you wheedle me into taking Sarah and Chelsey to Dollywood for the day when I'd rather just be with you, but it's entirely another thing for you to try to wheedle me into adopting a child when I'm not even married yet. This is simply not some place I want to go, Vivian."

He got up to pace again, stopping to lean against the porch railing to look down at her on the glider.

"I know you've gotten attached to Sarah, Vivian. I've seen it." He kept his voice casual. "With the girls not in school, and with you and Ellen doing so many things together with the girls, it was bound to happen. With your past, it would be easy for your heart to get overly involved in this matter. You know that."

He turned to sit down beside her and take her hand.

"I love you, Vivian," he said with sincerity. "And I want above all things to make you happy. But I don't think this idea is right for us now. We're just starting out as a couple. We can have our own children. Probably the family that is wanting Sarah can't have children at all. They probably really need her."

"Alice says they have one child. They just can't have another." Vivian dropped her eyes. "They think Sarah will round out their family."

"Well, you see? She's needed there." He patted her hand. "They've been married a while, Vivian. They're already into children and that stage of their lives. She'll be loved there. I'm sure Alice wouldn't have decided on any family that wouldn't be right for Sarah."

"But I love Sarah, Scott. And she loves me," Vivian pleaded. "Don't you understand? Haven't you seen it? We have a connection. We're meant to be together. And Sarah loves you, too, Scott. She worships you. She wants to stay here. She loves Ellen and Quint and Chelsey, too. She needs to stay here with us."

"Look, Vivian." Scott tried a reasonable approach. "At the end of every camp session, half of my kids bawl and squawl that they don't want to go home. They want to stay with the camp and their counselors forever. They weep over the friends they've made, they cry over parting from the staff. Then they go on home, readjust, and everything's fine. Every summer, I want to keep about half those kids. And every summer, I always fall in love with some special child at the camp. Some kid always really gets in my heart. But at summer's end, I say goodbye. And we all move on. When Sarah goes to her new family, we'll all move on, too. You'll see."

"It's not the same." Vivian started to cry then. "I can't let her go, Scott. I can't. Can't you see that this is something I need?"

Getting irritated now, Scott opted for honesty. "Can't you see that this is *not* something I need or want? I matter in this, too, Vivian. This is both of our lives we're talking about here. I like Sarah. I really do. I'm genuinely fond of her. But I don't want to become a father right now. I've just gotten my mind settled that I want to become a husband."

"And what if I decide that I will foster Sarah anyway?" Vivian insisted, a little testily now. "I'm not married yet, Scott. I don't have to do what you say. Alice says that with my education and my financial situation I'd have no trouble becoming a foster parent to Sarah."

Scott looked into Vivian's eyes, noting the challenge there. Anger flared in him along with hurt.

"You're right, Vivian," he announced flatly. "We're not married yet. You can still do whatever you want and the heck with me if I don't agree or see things as you do. That's a choice you can make. In fact, that's the kind of choice couples make every day that often hurts and breaks up their relationships and their marriages. Couples have to work out their differences together to have a successful relationship. They have to compromise."

"And your idea of working this out is for me to do all the compromising and give up Sarah and break my heart?" she demanded, her own anger flaring up now.

"You're turning this into a purely emotional matter, Vivian, and trying to turn me into the enemy because I don't want to adopt another person's child just as I'm getting married for the first time." Scott tried to stay reasonable and calm.

He came over to sit down by Vivian again and put his hand gently on her face. "Stop and think this through, Vivian. The one thing we both want here is the best solution for Sarah. Maybe the best answer is for her to go into a family where both the mother and the father are eager and ready to have her. Into a family where the couple has been married for a long time already. Where there is another child."

"And maybe the best thing is for her to stay with me," said Vivian stubbornly.

She looked up at Scott then with a tear-streaked face. "Don't make me choose, Scott. I love you both too much."

Stunned, Scott stared into her eyes. "You'd choose fostering this child over marrying me?" He found the idea even difficult to put into words.

"You're bringing it to that for me." Vivian lifted her chin defiantly.

"No," Scott said, standing up now, almost shaking. "You're bringing this to that point yourself, Vivian. You committed to me months ago. Took my heart. Took my ring. Gave me your promises and pledges before God. And now you're adding new conditions to that commitment. Wanting to add amendments." He paused to take a breath. "Well, listen clearly, Vivian. I proposed marriage and meant it with all my heart. I didn't propose fatherhood. I want some time before I'm ready for that. I don't want to start my married life with both a wife and child. If that sounds harsh to you, I'm sorry for that. But this wasn't in our original agreement."

"I didn't know I would fall in love with Sarah, too, along the way," Vivian protested. "It just happened. Won't you think about changing your heart about this?"

She was weeping profusely now, but Scott found his heart wasn't moved.

"I only want to be with you right now, Vivian." He looked down at her. "And I believe it's best for us and for Sarah that she go on to this other family. We can go meet this couple Alice has found if it will make you feel better. We can have Sarah come to us for visits. Surely, Alice would let us do that."

"She said she would," Vivian admitted, sniffing. "But I want more. I don't want to let Sarah go. I can't, Scott. I just can't. I believe it was destiny that she came when she did, met me and you and all of us when she did. Don't you remember? The first time I met her she was even wearing fairy wings. It was meant to be."

"It's a pretty story you're weaving, Vivian. You're always persuasive with words. But the ending you're weaving isn't right for me. And I honestly don't think it's right for Sarah."

He started off the porch then.

"I'm going home now, Vivian. I don't want to talk about this any more tonight. If you feel you've got to make some kind of dramatic life choice and pick a foster child over a husband, then so be it. I'll get over it in time, I'm sure. You haven't given me much choice or thought in all of this, anyway."

"Scott, please," Vivian started.

"No, Vivian." Scott turned back toward her coldly now. "Don't start. Taking on a child is a serious commitment. And I'm not ready. So don't ask me anymore. I want our own children some day, but not a child right now. You've asked me, and I've told you as honestly as I can. I'm sorry you don't like my choice or respect my feelings. But I can't change them. And I don't want to. I think it's wrong of you to ask me to. I don't know what else to say to you."

As he walked home through the dark, Scott's anger simmered and grew. He couldn't believe Vivian would pick a child she'd just come to know over him. That she'd threaten not to marry him if he wouldn't agree to foster and adopt Sarah Taylor. For God's sake. What sort of woman was she? And what new side of herself had she hit him with now? The way he was hurting at the moment, he wished he'd never even met her.

Chapter 24

*T*HURSDAY MORNING, A WEEK LATER, Vivian wandered restlessly around the Greene's barn while Ellen made soap. Finished with the early critical mixing stages, Ellen now worked on the lengthier stirring phase to thicken the soap mixture. She was making lavender soap today, and a nice hint of lavender fragrance hung in the air. Vivian found herself toying moodily with the lavender buds on the workbench that Ellen used for texture. She had dried hibiscus petals laid out, too, which she used to give the soap a purplish color.

Ellen looked up at Vivian with a frank stare. "You want to quit pacing around my shop and tell me what's going on with you and Scott?"

Vivian turned around from the workbench to stare at Ellen in surprise.

"Oh, come on, Vivian." Ellen frowned. "It doesn't take a rocket scientist to see that the two of you have had some kind of spat. One, you've been moping around for over a week, being overly quiet, even for you. Two, Scott has nearly snapped my head off every time I've seen him. And, three, both of you came up with a bunch of lame excuses last week to avoid our Thursday night dinner."

"I told you I had a script deadline to meet." Vivian turned away to toy with the herbs on Ellen's workbench again, avoiding Ellen's perceptive eyes at the same time. "You know I'm flying out to California early tomorrow morning to have meetings about the show, and there are a lot of things I have to do before I leave."

"Right," Ellen said, sarcastically. "And I'm sure that explains why after you caught the bridal bouquet at Norma Jean and Trolley Harper's wedding on Sunday afternoon that you sneaked into the church bathroom and burst into tears."

Startled, Vivian put her hand to her heart and turned to search Ellen's face. "How did you know that, Ellen?" Vivian almost whispered.

"I followed you." Ellen announced this calmly with a shrug. "I could tell something was wrong at the time, Vivian. You should have been excited about catching that bouquet. And you should have been laughing along with everyone else when the McFee girls wailed that it wasn't fair you caught the bouquet when you were already engaged."

As if remembering the day herself, Ellen smiled. "It was a great wedding, you know, Vivian. Not that you hardly noticed."

She paused to check her soap mixture to see if it was tracing yet, and then continued. "When I heard you boo-hooing in the bathroom stall, I decided I would just wait and talk to you about everything later. And now it's later."

Ellen was always very matter-of-fact like this. Usually, Vivian appreciated her candor, but now she studied her thoughtfully, deciding what she wanted to tell her.

"I'm your best friend now, Vivian," Ellen prompted, seeming to read her mind. "I think I can be trusted with your confidences, don't you?"

She blew a strand of hair out of her eyes and grinned sideways at Vivian. "Besides, if you don't tell me I'm going to send that horrid picture Quint took of the two of us off to the tabloids. The one where we fell in the creek running away from that snake we saw in the water."

Vivian laughed then, in spite of herself. "That was a truly awful picture, Ellen. We were both wet and shrieking, and we looked absolutely ridiculous."

"Yeah, it's a great blackmail opportunity. So sit down and talk, Vivian." Ellen gestured to a chair. "All couples have spats. It can't be all that bad."

"It's worse than bad." Vivian dropped down into the old folding chair. "I don't think Scott and I will be getting married at all now, Ellen. We've had two terrible fights."

Just admitting this much started Vivian's tears again.

"You'd think I wouldn't even have any tears left after all the ones I've cried this last week," she complained, sniffling.

Ellen tossed her a tissue tucked in her back pocket. "My grandmother always said that love brings more mixed joy and sorrow than any other event in life, Vivian."

"Well, it's mostly sorrow right now." Vivian wiped her eyes and blew her nose.

"So, talk and tell me what happened, would you?" Ellen prompted impatiently. "Just start at the beginning and give me the facts."

"Okay." Vivian gave in reluctantly. "You remember last Tuesday, I kept Sarah while you took Chelsey to the doctor?"

Ellen nodded.

"Well, Alice came by to check on Sarah and visited for a while that day."

"Alice called me and said she might stop by over at your place to see Sarah." Ellen stirred her soap while she listened. "So?"

"So Alice told me that she might have a home for Sarah."

"She told me that, too," Ellen paused in her stirring. "The Perrys – Harvey and Blanche, I think their names are. I met them over at Cosby once. They own rental cabins and a log house out in the country. It's a nice family. They have one boy about ten and they want a little girl. It's not a bad situation for Sarah. What does that have to do with you and Scott?"

"I told Alice I wanted to foster Sarah myself," Vivian explained. "We've bonded, Sarah and I. I realized when Alice started talking about taking Sarah away that I couldn't bear it if she did, Ellen. I want to adopt Sarah, too, if I can."

Ellen looked at Vivian thoughtfully then. "That doesn't really surprise me in some ways, Vivian. Anyone can see you and Sarah are crazy about each other. Sarah even tells stories about you. I thought it might be a wrench for both of you when she had to move on in time. I assume that Scott wasn't as enthusiastic."

"I thought he'd love the idea," Vivian said, sighing. "He's so fond of Sarah and Chelsey both. I thought he'd be happy about us keeping her, adopting her, raising her. But he wasn't at all."

"What did he say?" Ellen tested her soap and started stirring again.

"He said he liked Sarah but that he didn't want to foster or adopt her." Vivian's words came out in a rush. "He said he wanted it to be just the two of us when we got married. That he wanted us to have some years together before having children. That he wanted us to have our own children. He was adamant that he didn't want me to foster Sarah. He said if I did that our marriage was off."

"That doesn't sound like Scott, making ultimatums." Ellen studied Vivian's face. "Are you sure that it wasn't you that made that ultimatum?"

"Well, it doesn't matter how it happened." Vivian scuffed her foot along the ground. "The result was the same. I want Sarah and Scott doesn't."

"And then you said?" Ellen raised her eyebrows inquiringly.

Vivian lifted her chin. "I said what Alice told me. That my education and my financial situation would make it possible for me to have Sarah even if he didn't want her. And that I was going to foster Sarah, even by myself, if I had to." She stopped and looked up appealingly at Ellen then. "I can't let her go, Ellen. I've come to love her."

"And what about loving Scott?" Ellen asked softly.

"Well, I love Scott, too." Vivian twisted her hands and started to weep again. "I love them both. That's why this is so hard. This whole thing is just tearing me apart, Ellen. I tried to go over to talk to Scott again this week, to get him to see how important this is to me. And he just won't bend at all, Ellen. He thinks Sarah should go on to the Perry's. Do you think you could talk to him, Ellen?"

"No way." Ellen shook her head. "I'm not taking sides in this. I'm staying the neutral party here. This isn't like arguing over what color of bride's maids dresses to have. This is about a child's life. And this is about both of your lives and your futures. You have to find a way to be in agreement over this."

Ellen stopped to check her soap. It was tracing now and beginning to look like liquid honey in its consistency.

"Start handing me those oils and herbs over there on the workbench," she directed Vivian. "My soap is starting to trace."

Ellen worked for a little while, adding color, scent, and herbs to her thickened soap mixture, and then stirring it well. The rich scent of lavender filled the air.

"I don't know what I'm going to do," Vivian told her dejectedly.

"So what options have you been thinking about, Vivian?" Ellen turned to look at Vivian sympathetically before starting to dip her soap out into the molds. "I know you've been considering options. People do."

"I really only have two." Vivian stood up to help Ellen pour the soap. "Give up Sarah and marry Scott - if he'll still have me, that is. Or foster Sarah and give up Scott. That's basically it, Ellen, and both choices are going to break my heart."

"And which decision are you planning to make?"

"I just can't bring myself to give Sarah up," Vivian confided. "Even if it means losing Scott. In fact, I'm thinking about asking Alice if Sarah and I can go back to California. I don't think I could stay here in the area where I would see Scott all the time. I think it would just gradually destroy me."

The tears came again then. "While I'm in California, I thought I might look at property around Mendocino where I grew up. I think Sarah would like it there. I was happy there when I was her age. It's on the coast."

"Well, that's hardly an answer I'm happy with." Ellen looked up with annoyance. "I'd lose you from the area, and Chelsey would lose Sarah, too. Cosby is at least close enough for the girls to remain friends. But California is a long way from here."

"I know," Vivian said, her voice breaking. "But I don't know what else to do!"

"Couldn't you consider Scott's feelings for a while?" Ellen got out another mold for the soap. "This must be tearing him up, too, being caught in the middle. It's not totally unreasonable of him to want to start off a new marriage without a ready-made family."

"I know, but I can't help what has happened between Sarah and myself, Ellen. It's a strong love, too. I believe it's meant to be. Sarah is meant to belong to me. I'm totally sure of that."

"And Scott?" Ellen looked up at her with surprise. "Don't you think your love with him is meant to be any more? That you belong with him?"

"How can you even ask me that, Ellen?" Vivian paced around in agitation. " I love him so much I ache inside. Even not seeing him this week has made me almost sick. I can't sleep. I've had trouble working. It's just the worst time ever. But I don't know what else I can do. I love Scott desperately, but I love Sarah, too."

Ellen shook her head. "You've got a real problem," she conceded. "But only you and Scott can work it through and decide what to do."

Ellen, finished with the soap, wiped her hands on a rag, and came over to wrap her arms around Vivian. "Lord, I'll miss you if you go. We all will. And I worry what this break-up will do to both you and Scott. And what it will do to Sarah if she figures out that she came between the two of you."

"Don't tell her!" Vivian backed away, upset at this set of new worries.

"Do I look stupid?" Ellen frowned and went back over to check the soap a last time. "The child has just started to get over her first grief of losing her mother this summer. I worry that you and Scott might inadvertently bring her more sorrow through this fight over her."

"That's one of the reasons I'm thinking about going back to California." Vivian sat down on the folding chair again. "It would be a new start for us both."

"It sounds like running away to me," Ellen put in. "And it might not work. I could run to Timbuktu and still not get Quint Greene out of my heart and mind. I hope you know what you're doing, Vivian. I really believe you and Scott are right for each other. It's a big loss you're considering."

On the plane to California the next morning, Vivian kept hearing those last words over and over again. "I hope you know what you're doing. ... It's a big loss. It's a big loss ...."

"But what else can I do?" she whispered to herself. "I can't let Sarah go to someone else. Maybe someone wrong for her. I need her, and she needs me."

She looked out the window into the clouds.

"But I need Scott, too. How can I never see him again? Hold him again?" She buried her face in her hands.

"Oh, God," she prayed. "What am I going to do?"

Chapter 25

SCOTT WALKED AROUND THE CAMP doing his morning rounds. Breakfast was over and the camp units were dispersed out over the campground in scheduled activities. Scott strolled around randomly, checking to see how the different camp activities were working out and interacting with the staff and the kids. Being a cheerful and positive camp director had not been easy this last week. There were days when Scott felt his smile was plastic. When just focusing on his work was an effort. He could not recall a more difficult week in his life than this last one had been.

He stopped to stand by the lake to watch the canoeing lessons. A few of the younger campers still struggled to get the rhythm of the oars but, overall, they were doing well now that their camp session was nearing a close. Scott had one final two-week camp block coming to Buckeye in mid August, and then the camp was finished for another year. He tried to keep a pleasant look on his face as he watched the kids. A little girl looked up to wave at him, and he found himself frowning at her before he realized it. She looked almost like Sarah Taylor in an older version.

Scott caught himself scowling and quickly sent a smile toward the child and waved at her. He hated it when he allowed his personal emotions to color his work. It was unprofessional. And it was unlike him. He realized this was one of the reasons he had never allowed himself to get emotionally involved with women. They were irrational creatures. They tore you apart. Wasn't he seeing that happening right now?

He stalked back to the office, mulling over all that had happened this week. Scott found he was still stunned that Vivian would hold fast to this notion of fostering a child above her commitment to marriage. Scott liked kids. Wasn't he a camp director because of that love for kids? Didn't he participate in all sorts of philanthropic and civic activities related to kids? He just wasn't ready for his own family yet.

It wasn't right for Vivian to pressure him in this area, either. He kicked open the screened door of the camp office, letting it slam behind him as he walked in.

"Well, I gather you haven't made up with Vivian yet," Nancy remarked from her desk across the room.

"And what would you know about that?" Scott snapped at her, without thinking.

"More than I care to, since you and Vivian had your last spat right outside on the front porch where I couldn't help but hear every word," Nancy countered back.

Scott slumped into a chair and heaved a sigh. "Sorry, Nancy. This has been a bad week for me. And I regret you had to be a witness to my problems."

"I'm not sorry. It's helped me to know why you've been so moody and short-tempered this last week."

Nancy paused and looked at Scott with a smile then. "Want to talk, cousin?" she asked him.

Scott shrugged. "You know the deal, Nancy. Vivian's got this notion she wants to foster and adopt Sarah Taylor, whether I want it or not. She's basically given me an ultimatum, her and the kid or I don't get her at all. It's like the old movie theme – love me, love my dog."

"Sarah's hardly a dog." Nancy scowled.

Scott smarted back. "No kidding. I'd have given in to a dog. You can put them outside when they get on your nerves or when you want some privacy."

Scott flipped a pile of brochures off the table in annoyance.

Nancy watched him. "I've been thinking about this a lot, Scott.

And I believe that what you're really worried about here is sharing Vivian's love."

"I don't think that's it at all, Nancy," he started to argue, but she held up a hand and interrupted.

"Just listen a minute," she insisted. "And don't be so quick to get mad. You may not know it, but I've been seeing a lot of Walker Bailey, the park ranger that lives up on Falls Road behind the camp."

"I didn't know that." Scott lifted a brow, momentarily distracted. "When have you been out with him?"

"Well, that's just it," Nancy explained. "We aren't officially going out yet. But I know he likes me. He's been coming by the office more and more on different excuses. We're comfortable together. But there's more than that going on, too – a little flirtation. You know." She smiled and flushed. "Plus Walker is great with kids. He does all those talks for you at the camp and to kids at the visitors' center. And my boys like him."

"Yeah, Walker's a good guy." Scott gave Nancy a puzzled look. "But what does that have to do with Vivian and I?"

"I have baggage, too, Scott." Nancy dropped her eyes. "I have two little boys that come with me from my first marriage. I know it makes a man think twice."

"Yeah, but Martin and Jordan are both great kids," Scott put in defensively. "Any guy would be blessed to have those kids. Maybe I need to have a talk with Walker ..."

Nancy shook her head at him. "Scott, you're missing the point here. Sarah's a great kid, too. And you're having a problem thinking about taking her with Vivian in almost the same way."

"It's not the same thing at all." Scott stood up in irritation, frowning at Nancy. "You were married before. It's not like you have a choice in being a mother."

"From what I heard Vivian tell you, she doesn't feel like she has a choice either." Nancy caught Scott's eyes with hers. "I've seen Vivian with Sarah, Scott. I've listened to her talk about Sarah. I've watched their faces when they look at each other. There is love, devotion, and commitment there between them. I think it would just about tear them apart not to be together."

"Well, what about me?" Scott complained, kicking at the pile of brochures still on the floor.

"Did you hear your voice and attitude, Scott?" Nancy's voice had a chiding tone. "That sounds like pure jealousy to me. I think maybe you need to analyze more closely what you're really feeling about Sarah. Maybe you're experiencing some rivalry about Vivian and Sarah's love for each other. Maybe you just want to be the only love in Vivian's life."

"So, what's so wrong with that?" He paced the room in annoyance. "That's what a man is supposed to feel before he gets married."

"I don't think loving Sarah will change Vivian's love for you, Scott. She has a big heart. And so do you," Nancy confided. "Before this problem came up between you and Vivian, I observed that the three of you made a very happy, loving team. Sarah adores you as much as Vivian does, Scott. Maybe you haven't stopped to realize that. I've seen real warmth and affection in your eyes when you're with Sarah, too. Are you sure you couldn't make room for her in your heart? Loving Sarah won't mean that Vivian and you will love each other less."

Scott leaned over to pick up the brochures he'd dumped on the floor.

Nancy got up to help him and put a hand on Scott's arm. "I'm starting to fall for Walker," she confided to him. "I wouldn't have told you if it wasn't for this situation. But I wanted you to see the similarities. I see Walker struggling with the idea of taking on not only me, but also my boys. I know he would have made a move on me already if I wasn't a mother, if I didn't have the boys. But he holds himself back because of it."

"Maybe I should talk to him." Scott studied Nancy's serious face. "Help move things along."

"And maybe you shouldn't," Nancy challenged. "Seeing as how you seem to feel the same way about taking on Sarah along with Vivian. It might not help my case."

Scott looked at Nancy with hurt eyes. "You know I only want your happiness, Nancy."

"And I want yours, Scott. What would you think of Walker if he confessed his love for me but shared with me his reluctance to take on the boys?"

"He hasn't said that to you, has he?" Scott clinched a fist at the thought.

"No, and I hope he never does," Nancy assured him. " But what I want you to think about here are the similarities in our situations. Vivian didn't mean to fall in love with Sarah, Scott. She didn't do it to hurt you. But now she loves you both and she's torn in two with it."

"And you think I'm not?" Scott kicked at a trash can and started to pace angrily around the office again. "You think I've had a good week with all this crap going on in my life. Do you know she's threatening to take Sarah off to California with her? She's out there now looking into options while she's meeting with her producers and her editor. How do you think that makes me feel, Nancy? It's ripping my heart out!"

He turned back to her with a scowl. "I really thought you'd be on my side in this, Nancy."

She sat back down at her desk wearily. "There aren't sides here, Scott. Just different ways of thinking about the situation. I was trying to get you to look at things in another way."

"Yeah, Vivian's way," he scoffed. "You talk about this just like Vivian does. You're not seeing the logic at all from my side. You're going with emotions."

Nancy shook her head. "Scott, love is emotions. It isn't logical."

"You can say that again." He looked at his watch, his anger just barely in check. "I've got to get back out to camp."

He headed out the door, hearing Nancy sigh heavily as he walked off down the steps.

"Women," he muttered to himself, as he started up the loop road toward the dining hall and the center of the camp. "They're all the same."

He'd just gotten to the steps of Spruce Hall, ready to go in and check the lunchroom before the campers started lunch, when he saw Ellen hurrying up the drive behind him.

Expecting another lecture, Scott considered whether he could duck around the building and avoid her. But she had already seen him.

"Scott!" she cried out. "Wait! I've been looking for you!"

Resigned now, Scott turned around to greet her with a smile.

"Well, now you've found me." He made an effort to respond cheerfully. "What can I do for you, Ellen?"

"It's Sarah," she said, sitting down on the steps, out of breath.

"She's missing."

"What do you mean, she's missing?" Scott felt a thread of alarm.

"Well, we're beginning to think she's run away." Ellen took a deep breath, putting a hand to her heart. "I wasn't that worried this morning, but now we're getting frantic. Quint is coming home as soon as he can get away from his patient load. He's already called Sheriff Fields, and he's coming over from Sevierville now. He's been in court. Quint also called the ranger, Walker Bailey, and he's putting a search team together. And your Uncle Leo is gathering a group of locals to start looking for Sarah, too. Scott, I'm really getting upset."

"Where's Chelsey?" Scott asked anxiously. "Is she with Sarah?"

"No, she's fine. Mary's keeping her while I'm looking." Ellen dropped her face into her hands wearily. "I came over to see if you could get some people to search the camp, Scott. Maybe she came over here, mixed in with the kids or is hiding out somewhere."

Scott had seldom seen Ellen as distraught as this. She usually took life's upsets more in stride. Scott sat down on the porch stairs beside her.

"What's going on here, Ellen?" he asked suspiciously. "You're awfully upset about a kid just wandering off from home. You know Sarah is fantasy prone and that she sometimes flies off on some fairy mission or other. She may turn up a little later, not even realizing she's worried everyone. You know how she is."

"This is different." Ellen dropped her eyes. "I didn't want to worry you with it because of that, but now I have to."

"How is this different?" Scott asked testily. "Tell me what's going on."

Ellen sighed. "Yesterday, Vivian was over at the barn visiting with me while I was doing soap. She told me all about the problems you and she were having."

Scott's face darkened and he scowled at Ellen, despite himself.

"Listen, I pinned her into a corner and made her tell me everything," Ellen explained to him. "She didn't really want to confide in me. But that's not the point here, Scott. Evidently, Sarah came out of the house looking for me and heard us talking. Chelsey said Sarah told her that she hid beside the door and listened once she realized that we were talking about her."

Ellen twisted her shirt nervously. "I swear, Scott, we had no idea the child was there. And we were pretty candid in our discussion. Vivian said a lot of things Sarah didn't need to hear. How she was being put into the position to have to make a choice between you or Sarah. How it was tearing her apart. She cried a lot. She was upset and let her hair down to me. And Sarah heard it all."

Scott said an expletive under his breath.

Ellen ignored it. "I should have realized she might come out there. It should have dawned on me that she might have overheard something. She was really quiet all that night. Said her stomach was hurting. Didn't want to eat much at dinner."

"What else did Chelsey tell you about this?" Scott quizzed.

"Chelsey said Sarah cried a lot last night after they went to bed. And Sarah told Chelsey that she thought she needed to run away." Ellen said these last words with anguished eyes. "That you hated her. That Vivian was sad because of her. That you wouldn't marry Vivian unless she went away."

Scott groaned.

"I'm so sorry, Scott. We didn't even know the child was there."

"Have you called Vivian?"

"No," Ellen told him. "We hated to worry either of you if we could find her first. Quint and I thought we could talk to Sarah. Help her understand. Without getting either of you involved. Without any more unnecessary emotion."

"That poor kid," Scott said. "She didn't really need this right now after losing her mother and not having any real family anymore."

"I know." Ellen lowered her voice. "I just feel terrible. And I can't think where else to look for her, Scott. I've searched every area of the yard, house, and the woods behind us. I've looked over at the farmhouse. Your Uncle Leo let me in and helped me. We searched the grounds there and the barn and the sheds, too. We've called all the neighbors we know, and no one has even seen the child, Scott. I just have no idea where she might have gone."

Scott stopped to think. "What did she take with her?"

"The little school backpack I bought her when we all went school shopping last week." Ellen smiled sadly. "She was so proud of that. A few pieces of her clothes were missing, not much. Her fairy stuff and a picture of her mother. There was a water bottle on her backpack, and I think she may have taken a few snack food items from the kitchen. I'm not sure. She's only five, Scott. She didn't pack like a Girl Scout would."

"Did you check in Gatlinburg where she and her mother lived? Check with their old friends or call the store her mother used to own? Maybe she tried to go back there."

"We've called everyone there that we could think of. Alice has been checking all those ties for us. God, I hated calling and telling Alice about this."

Ellen put her head into her hands again. "I don't know where else to look, Scott. She's so little. I'm scared for her. Anything could happen."

"Well, talking is not helping," Scott said, standing up. "I'll free up some older counselors and CITs and we'll start a search of the camp grounds. There are a lot of places to hide here, and Sarah knows the camp. Go to Nancy's office and tell her to start calling every business up the highway, every neighbor in the area. She has a list, and she knows everybody around here. Tell her to call buses and trolleys in the area, in case she walked or got a ride farther into town. Also tell her to call Mother and Dad and my brothers, too. We need to get people looking farther abroad, just in case. Get outlying authorities involved if the sheriff hasn't already started that. We'll find her, Ellen."

Scott was moving into his action mode now.

"Who's at your house in case Sarah calls or in case anyone finds her?" Scott asked.

"Mary's there." Ellen's voice was weary. "We thought of that. She's there with Chelsey."

"I'll keep checking over at the farmhouse," Scott said. "I know every inch of that house. She might try to come back there, knowing Vivian is gone."

Ellen gave Scott a tortured look then. "Chelsey told us that Sarah didn't want to go to California. She didn't want Vivian to go to California, either. She said Vivian was sad there. And that she had been happy here. Sarah told Chelsey that when she was gone you and Vivian would be happy again."

"Great. That makes me feel like a monumental heel," Scott muttered.

He shook his head as if to free those negative thoughts. "We'll find her, Ellen. She can't have gone far. We'll find her."

"Do you think I should call Vivian?"

"Let's wait a while. Maybe we won't need to." He dreaded the thought. "Sarah is only a little kid. From my experience they don't go far."

"Vivian did once," Ellen remembered, a pained expression on her face.

"Yeah, but she was ten then. Also, I don't think Sarah knows enough about the area to go very far without help."

"That's the part that scares me." Ellen's worried eyes looked up at him. "Without help."

Scott scowled. "There's enough to worry about without borrowing trouble. Go back and search your own property a second time. Talk to Chelsey again, see if she can remember anything else that might help us. A lot of times, little kids don't realize they know important things. Call me on my cell right away if you find out anything."

Ellen got up and started back down the road.

"And don't worry, Ellen," Scott called after her. "We'll find her."

Scott thought of those words again after night had fallen heavily over the valley and there was still no sign of Sarah Taylor. Not a footprint. Or a scrap of clothing. Not a single clue to go on.

He sat on the front steps of the old farmhouse now, trying to think what else to do. The sheriff, the ranger, and the locals had called off their search effort now until dawn tomorrow. They assumed the child would find shelter somewhere for the night and sleep. Tomorrow they would begin to search again.

Scott had called Vivian about an hour ago. He thought she should know at this point that Sarah was missing. He also hoped she might think of some clue that might help them find her. But she only thought of all the places to look they'd already searched not once, but several times.

Vivian had been calmer than Scott had expected, but he could hear the pain underlying her voice. "I'll make arrangements and be on the first flight I can get," she told Scott calmly. "Tad will help me with the travel plans. I don't blame you and Ellen for not calling me sooner, Scott. It is my responsibility that this has happened. Alice and Ellen warned me Sarah could get caught in the middle of this and get hurt. I was naïve. I thought I could keep her from finding out."

Scott hated hearing Vivian take all the blame for this on herself.

"Look, I'm partially to blame for this, too." He needed to say it. "And the rest is just an accident. No one knew Sarah was listening."

"She's very sensitive and intuitive," Vivian said flatly. "I knew that. She'd already been sensing I was upset about something. I should have seen this coming."

Scott heard a despairing sigh over the line.

"I think you were right, Scott," Vivian confessed to him. "Going to be with a seasoned set of parents would be best for Sarah. Look what I've caused with my love and involvement. I must not be ready to take care of a child. All I've brought her is hurt and pain. And I've brought it to you and me as well."

A short silence followed and then sniffling sounds. "I love you so much, Scott. I should have listened to you. It looks like you knew all along what was best for Sarah - more than I did. And now, look what I've caused. I've hurt you and I've hurt Sarah. I feel so wretched, Scott. I haven't slept in days. I think about you all the time. About how you feel and how you smell. About how I feel when you touch me."

She sighed deeply. "And I don't know if you'll ever forgive me now, Scott. Or if Sarah will ever forgive me, either. I've just made a mess of everything."

Scott listened to Vivian start to sob softly now.

"Vivian," he said to her after a moment. "Don't tear yourself apart over this. We'll find the child. And we'll work this out between us. I love you, too. I haven't slept well either. I think about you and want you, too. You come home so I can hold you. So I can be with you. We'll see this through together. That's what people do that love each other."

"Okay." Her voice was soft. "And I'll try to listen to you more in the future. I need you in my life, Scott. I don't want to live without you."

A painful place in Scott's heart healed over a little at those words. And he found himself softening, opening up again.

"I don't want to live without you, either, Vivian," he told her softly, and heard her sigh.

"Call me when you get your travel arrangements made." He

gave her his cell phone number. "I'm over here at the farmhouse. I think someone needs to spend the night at Gramma's place in case Sarah decides to come here. She might do that now that heavy dark has fallen."

"Poor little thing," Vivian muttered. "She's too little to be out at night alone. I'm scared for her. Pray that we find her, Scott."

"I'll be praying," Scott assured her. "And Reverend James has got half the church praying, too. He said to tell you God would watch after her until we could find her."

After he hung up the phone, Scott sat looking out into the dark hoping that was true. A five-year-old didn't know much about staying safe out of doors at night. He looked up at the shadow of the mountain and hoped that Sarah hadn't headed that way. It would be harder to find her in the mountains, and it was more dangerous there.

Despite all this tragedy over Sarah, Scott's heart was soothed at Vivian's words. She'd told him she loved him. And she'd told him she wanted him and needed him. She'd conceded to his way of thinking about Sarah, too, and that was good. Or at least, Scott thought it was. Just now with all this anguish in his heart and mind over the child, Scott didn't know what was right any more. That talk with Nancy just before all this happened hadn't helped much. Scott didn't like the niggling thought Nancy had planted in the back of his mind that he might be jealous of Sarah. She was just a kid, after all. The love Vivian felt for him was bigger and different than what she would feel for a kid like Sarah or for any other child. He knew that.

Scott kicked a rock on the steps in frustration. Fritzi got up from her spot on the porch to come and nuzzle his hand.

"Where is she, girl?" Scott asked the dog. "Why haven't we been able to find that child?" Fritzi looked up at him questioningly.

He looked up toward the shadows of the mountain, shaking his head. "Somewhere out there in the dark is a little child all alone and scared."

Then Scott did the only thing he knew to do. He put his head into his hands and offered up prayers. God knew where Sarah was, even if they didn't, and Scott prayed that she would be kept safe until they could find her.

At the end of his prayer, he added a postscript, "Let me know in some way if I've been wrong about the child, Lord. About what is best for her."

Unable to just sit and wait, even in the dark, Scott started another search around the farmhouse grounds, with Fritzi following along behind.

As he headed out of the barn and back toward one of the sheds, his cell phone rang.

"Scott here," he answered.

"Scott, it's Vivian. Tad has a flight booked for me and we're on the road to the airport now. It will be almost morning before I can get there, but I'll pick up my car at the airport when I arrive and be there as soon as I can. Will you still be at the farm?"

"I will," he replied. "I'm outside going over the grounds again right now. I might walk over and look some more around Ellen and Quint's, too."

"I thought of something," Vivian said then. "You said that Ellen told you that Sarah took her fairy stuff with her. That means she's probably wearing it. She couldn't get those wings and skirt into a backpack. That means she's probably Ophelia Odelia right now. It's probably helping her to cope. I used to do that to escape when I was unhappy."

"So how does knowing that help us?" Scott frowned. "Other than to know she's probably decked out in yellow wings, a yellow tutu, and a tiara."

"She might go to one of Ophelia's places," Vivian explained to him. "Most of them are places around the houses where you've already looked, but one isn't. It scares me to think of it, but she might have gone to Ophelia's tree, the old hollowed out tree off the trail above Slippery Rock Falls. Do you know the one? It has a big hole at the base large enough to climb inside of. When I first met Sarah she had this thing about Ophelia Odelia's real home being inside a hollowed out tree. She had known of one near her old home in Gatlinburg. I told her I knew of one here in the valley, too. And she pestered me until I took her up there one day. You said for me to tell you if I thought of anything that might help."

"That's almost two miles from here, Vivian. Do you really think she'd go up there again alone?" Scott looked up toward the mountain as he considered it.

"One of the places fairies live is in hollowed out trees," Vivian said thoughtfully. "And Sarah said Ophelia Odelia especially liked to live inside an old tree trunk."

"Well, I'll get a big flashlight and check it out." Scott sighed in resignation. "At least it will give me something to do."

Scott had grown up in these mountains, so following a trail up the back of Cove Mountain in the dark didn't spook him as it might some people. He'd camped in these hills many times and hiked this old trail up to the cascades and to Slippery Rock Falls a multitude of times, as well. Scott knew it wasn't likely he'd find Sarah up here. The ranger's search team had gone all over this area earlier in the day, searching and calling for the child. They'd not found a footprint or a trace that she'd been in the area.

Still, it was comforting to Scott to be out of doors and walking. It helped dissipate some of the built-up stress.

It took Scott about an hour to hike up above the falls. He'd enjoyed the sounds of night frogs and crickets, and, now, he could hear a hoot owl out enjoying his nocturnal pleasures. His flashlight picked up the main trail ahead of him easily, and he found himself swinging his light around in an arc, looking for the remains of an old rock wall that would help him know he was close to the cut off trail to the hollowed-out oak.

He found the intersection just past the wall. After a short walk down the less maintained side trail, Scott spotted the big oak. Nearing it, he shone his light down toward its base and caught his breath. There was a clump huddled up inside the tree with a chunk of yellow crinoline skirt sticking out from it.

"Sarah?" he asked in a hushed voice.

A small voice replied. "Sarah is gone. There are only fairies here."

Relief swept through Scott like a storm, making his knees weak. He knelt down closer to the hole in the old tree.

"Well, actually I'm looking for Ophelia Odelia," he said, humoring her.

"Why?" came the little voice again, quieter now. "You hate her and Sarah, too."

Scott's heart turned over in his chest. "No, that's not true," he claimed. "I've been looking for her all day and even now at night when most people would be scared to be out. Aren't you scared up here alone?"

"Yes," came Sarah's whimper. "Especially when I heard the owl. I was afraid he would carry me off or eat me. Owls do that to fairies, you know."

She was plucky, Scott thought.

"Do you think I could take you home?" Scott asked her.

"No. I don't have a home." Sarah answered on a sob. "My mother's dead, and you hate me. And even if Vivian could keep me she'll be sad if she does because you won't like her anymore. So I'm staying here forever and ever."

Scott propped the flashlight against a rock so that it illuminated the inside of the tree a little more and also freed up his hands. He reached into the tree to turn Sarah around so he could see her better. Her soiled and tear-stained face looked out at him, and something ripped inside Scott's heart.

"I could never hate you, Sarah," Scott whispered softly.

"But you don't love me and want me." Sarah's lip formed a sad pout.

"I'm working on it," he told her honestly. "I didn't think before that it would be the best thing, but I think I might be changing my mind now."

"Why didn't you want me before?" Sarah asked him with the open candor characteristic of a child.

"Because I don't know much about being a father." Scott pushed Sarah's hair back from her face tenderly. "I thought I was going to have enough trouble learning to be a husband."

"Vivian thinks you would be a good father." Sarah looked at him with wide, honest eyes, chinking a little more into Scott's heart with her words. "I do, too. But Vivian said you only want your own babies. And not girls who are already five."

She sniffled again. And Scott thought he was about ready to cry himself.

"Sometimes people are wrong about things." Scott stroked her hair. "Maybe I need a little girl, too. And maybe she could help me with the babies later on if there were some."

"Maybe," Sarah said quietly.

She reached out a small hand to wrap it around his. "Maybe if I love you enough you'll start to love me back," she told him softly.

That was when Scott broke and reached into the tree trunk to pull Sarah out and wrap her up in his arms.

"I think that's already happening," he confessed to her, pressing her up against his chest. "I've been worried sick about you, Sarah. I'm so glad to have found you. You could have been hurt out here by yourself. Don't ever run off like this again."

Scott felt a little hand steal up to his face in the dark. "I love you, Scott. Please don't be mad at me. And if you want me to, I'll go to those other people's house to stay. If you will just be happy and not hate me."

Scott felt his own tears sliding down his face then. "I don't think that will be necessary, Sarah. I think you're supposed to stay with Vivian and me. At least we'll try it out and see how it works for all of us. What do you think?"

"I would like that. Do you think Vivian will like that, too? Or will she still be sad? I don't like her to cry, Scott."

"I think Vivian will like it, too," Scott said, hoisting Sarah up into his arms and draping her little backpack over his shoulder. "And I don't think Vivian will be sad anymore, either, Sarah, but she might cry because she's happy. Girls do that sometimes, you know."

"Is that why you're crying?" Sarah asked him, putting her hand on his face.

"Yeah, well, sometimes guys cry when they're happy, too."

"Oh," said Sarah. "All right."

Scott picked up the flashlight, and started his way back down the trail.

"Is Vivian still in California?" Sarah asked.

"No, she's on her way home now." Scott wiped a smudge of dirt off her cheek. "We'll go back, call a few people to tell them you're all right, and then take a nap until she comes in. How does that sound?"

"Good," Sarah agreed, sleepily. "Will the farmhouse be my new home now?"

"Yeah," replied Scott, pulling her more closely into his arms. "Wherever Vivian and I are that's where you'll be, Sarah Louise."

"Even on your honeymoon?"

"No, not there," Scott said firmly. "There are times when newly married people need to be alone and private. That's definitely one of them."

Sarah yawned. "Well, Ophelia and I will stay with Chelsey when you need married times. Ellen won't mind."

Scott grinned at that. "No, I don't suppose she will."

Back at the farmhouse, Scott made a few necessary calls to let everyone know Sarah was safe. Ellen wanted to come and get her right away, but Scott insisted that he wanted Sarah to stay there with him until Vivian came home.

"Vivian will want to see her," Scott explained to Ellen. "Besides, Sarah and I have some family matters to talk over with Vivian."

He paused then at a comment Sarah made in the background. "Oh, by the way," he added to Ellen. "Sarah wants to know if she can stay with you and Quint for a while when Vivian and I go on our honeymoon later on. I explained to her that honeymoons were a grown-up thing only, and it was her idea then that she could stay with you."

"Yeah. Good plan." Ellen answered with a laugh. Scott could almost imagine the conversation she and Quint would have over that one after she hung up.

When he had finished talking to Ellen, Scott got Sarah to drink a glass of milk and eat a snack. Then, somehow, he got her washed up and into a clean shirt and panties from her backpack before she crashed into an exhausted sleep.

"Will you stay with me, Scott?" she whispered, just before she drifted off to sleep on Vivian's bed. "The owl might come back looking for Ophelia."

"I'll keep a watch," he told her, smiling. He lay down beside her on the bed, draped an old quilt over his legs, and soon fell asleep himself.

Vivian found them there at four a.m. when she let herself into the farmhouse and walked back to her room to drop her bags.

She stood there amazed for a moment at the sight of them both on her bed.

"Keep it down or you'll wake Sarah Louise up," Scott whispered into the dark. "And don't turn on the light, either."

"Where did you find her?" Vivian asked softly, coming up to the bed to sit down beside him. She reached a hand out first to touch him and then over to touch Sarah.

"She was in that tree, being Ophelia Odelia just like you said."

Vivian smiled in the dark.

"Lean down here so I can kiss you," he instructed her. "Sarah has herself wrapped around my arm over here, and I don't want to move too much and wake her up."

Vivian leaned over to press her mouth to his. Their light kiss deepened, and Scott pulled Vivian over on top of him, murmuring to her and running his hands over her, loving the feel of her again. She sighed and moved against him as the old familiar magic rolled over them.

"God, I love you," he whispered to her.

"And Scott is working on loving me, too, Vivian," came a sleepy little voice from beside them.

Vivian pulled Sarah over into their embrace. "Oh, Sarah, I'm so glad you're all right. Please don't run away like that ever again. Promise me that. It scares and worries everyone terribly."

"Ophelia and I were worried, too, because there was an owl," Sarah explained to Vivian. "But Scott came and then it was okay. And he says we can be a family so you can be happy and not sad. Scott said he is almost starting to love me and he had tears because he was happy."

The moonlight was drifting through the window enough so that Vivian could study Scott's face then. She saw him grin.

"I changed my mind," he said to Vivian, shrugging. "She got to me."

"She'll do that." Vivian smiled and wrapped her arms around them both.

Sarah piped up again. "Vivian, Scott says I can be with you forever except on your honeymoon when married people need to be alone and private."

Even in the dark, Scott knew Vivian was blushing.

"Well, that is sort of a special time," she attempted to explain.

"Actually, you just don't have any idea how special and fine it will be," Scott whispered huskily in Vivian's ear.

Their hands managed to find ways to touch each other then, almost forgetting about Sarah bunched to the side of them.

"Scott says I get to help take care of your babies, Vivian," Sarah announced, reminding them both of her presence.

Vivian gasped, but Scott only chuckled.

"Better not be making any more plans to move off to California, Vivian," Scott said. "Sarah and I both need you right here."

"At our home," said Sarah on a sigh.

"Yeah, so welcome home, Vivian Delaney. It looks like I'm going to get two foster girls for the price of one."

Epilogue

*T*HE WEDDING THEME, SARAH'S IDEA of course, was an elaborate fairy kingdom. Keeping in the spirit of that fanciful notion, the celebration was held outdoors in the camp amphitheater at dusk, the local fireflies adding their light to the twinkling artificial lights of the caterers. From the stone amphitheater seats and the surrounding hillside, guests watched the wedding progress down a flower-draped bower.

Sarah, Chelsey, Scott's niece Abby, and Vivian's Delaney niece, Melanie, all served as flower girls. Decked out in tulle skirts of pale pink, yellow, green, and blue with matching diaphanous wings, the girls skipped down the arched aisle in front of the bride. Flower garlands with ribbon streamers adorned their hair.

The four bridesmaids who preceded them, Ellen, Nancy, Patti Delaney Hale, and Vivian's friend from California, Jan Paulson, wore similar pastel dresses with circlets of flowers in their hair. They formed a colorful parade as they marched down the aisle.

Vivian wore a simple, ankle-length white dress with a gauzy train and a garland of flowers over a filmy veil. Scott, and the four groomsmen - his three brothers and Quint Greene - wore traditional black tuxes, but each had pastel ribbon sashes draped over their shoulders and wore floral boutonnieres.

Everyone in the valley attended, along with a large contingent of Vivian's new family from Dandridge and many of her old friends and family from California –including the press. It was just the sort of wedding that the Hollywood journals and tabloids loved to document and photograph. And, as Scott told Quint after the wedding, "The publicity certainly didn't hurt the camp."

The McFee girls, Loreen and Betty Jo, were thrilled to be a part of what they called a 'real Hollywood wedding right in Wear's Valley, Tennessee'. Both of them hoped to catch Vivian's bridal bouquet and were real annoyed when it fell unexpectedly into the arms of a dark-haired young woman visiting from New York City. Shocked when the bouquet dropped into her hands, the girl, later identified by the press as Jenna Howell, quickly tossed it over into the arms of the woman standing next to her - who happened to be Alice Graham. The press had a heyday trying to follow it all with their cameras.

The McFee girls were miffed for the rest of the day that neither one of them caught the bouquet. Both vocally protested that it was unfair for an outsider to catch the bridal bouquet at a valley wedding and even more unfair for her to throw it off to a woman with six foster children in tow. "After all," Loreen complained, "who would marry someone like Alice with all those foster kids."

Sarah, listening in, put her hands on her hips primly. "Men can marry outsiders if they want to. Scott did," she told them. "And men can marry women with children, too, if they want to – even foster girls." This brought a laugh from all, and Sarah's words were even printed in one of the Hollywood journals.

.....Are you interested in meeting the New Yorker, Jenna Howell, who caught Vivian's bouquet? ... Then watch for the next book in the Smoky Mountain series, *Tell Me About Orchard Hollow*. ... And for more about Alice Graham and the six foster children ... keep an eye out for the third book in the series, *For Six Good Reasons*.

DR. LIN STEPP IS A NATIVE Tennessean, a businesswoman, and an educator. She is on faculty at Tusculum College where she teaches several Psychology courses, including Developmental and Educational Psychology, and a Research writing sequel. Her business background includes over 20 years in marketing, sales, production art, and regional publishing. She and her husband began their own sales and publications business, S & S Communications, in 1989. The company publishes two regional fishing and hunting guide magazines and has a sports sales subsidiary handling sports products and media sales in East Tennessee. She has editorial and writing experience in regional magazines and in the academic field. *The Foster Girls* is the first of twelve contemporary Southern romances in a series of linked novels set in the Smoky Mountains in East Tennessee.

AUTHOR'S WEBSITE

Special thanks go to my talented daughter, Katherine Stepp, who created my author's website. Visit me there to read more about my life and interests and to keep up with signings, events, and future publication dates for the continuing books in The Smoky Mountain series.

WEBSITE ADDRESS: http://www.linstepp.com

WGRL-HQ   FIC
31057100943490
FIC STEPP
Stepp, Lin.
The foster girls : a novel